Redline
the Stars

Tor books by Andre Norton

Caroline (with Enid Cushing)
The Crystal Gryphon
Dare To Go A-Hunting
Elvenbane (with Mercedes Lackey)
Flight in Yiktor
Forerunner
Forerunner: The Second Venture
Gryphon's Eyrie (with A. C. Crispin)
Grandmasters' Choice (editor)
Here Abide Monsters
House of Shadows (with Phyllis Miller)
Imperial Lady (with Susan Shwartz)
The Jekyll Legacy (with Robert Bloch)
Moon Called
Moon Mirror
The Prince Commands
Ralestone Luck
Sneeze on Sunday (with Grace Allen Hogarth)
Songsmith (with A. C. Crispin)
Stand and Deliver
Wheel of Stars
Wizards' Worlds
Wraiths of Time

***Tales of the Witch World* (editor)**
Tales of the Witch World 1
Tales of the Witch World 2
Four from the Witch World
Tales of the Witch World 3

Witch World: The Turning
Storms of Victory (with P.M. Griffin)
Flight of Vengeance (with P.M. Griffin and Mary H. Schaub)

***Magic in Ithkar* (editor, with Robert Adams)**
Magic in Ithkar 1
Magic in Ithkar 2
Magic in Ithkar 3
Magic in Ithkar 4

Redline
the Stars

Andre Norton &
P.M. Griffin

TOR®

WITHDRAWN

A Tom Doherty Associates Book
New York

For my dear uncle, Michael Murphy

REDLINE THE STARS

Copyright © 1993 by Andre Norton, Ltd.

A Tor Book
Published by Tom Doherty Associates, Inc.
175 Fifth Avenue
New York, N.Y. 10010

Tor® is a registered trademark of Tom Doherty Associates, Inc.

Library of Congress Cataloging-in-Publication Data

Norton, Andre.
        Redline the stars / Andre Norton, P.M. Griffin.
                p.   cm.
        "A Tom Doherty Associates book."
        ISBN 0-312-85314-9
        I. Griffin, P.M. (Pauline M.)   II. Title.
    PS3527.0632R44   1993
    813'.52—dc20
                                        92-43708
                                        CIP

Edited by James R. Frenkel

First Edition: April 1993

Printed in the United States of America

0   9   8   7   6   5   4   3   2   1

I would especially like to thank Andre Norton for permitting me to work in her Solar Queen universe and for her comments, suggestions, and encouragement while this book was in progress. Thanks are also due to Jim Frenkel for his work in editing the manuscript.

—P.M. Griffin

Foreword

In 1954 the Solar Queen series was conceived in answer to a request from one of the first Sf-Fantasy genre publishers in the field—Gnome Press. Since I was then reading manuscripts for this firm, I used for the books the pen name Andrew North. The publisher wished to develop space adventure stories which were not akin to the then steady flow of militaristic plots.

Because I had long been interested in the historical importance of the merchant adventurers of our own world in the past I plotted the ventures of the Free Traders—in my mind linking them to our earlier trader explorers and the tramp freighters of present day—having traveled on one such "tramp" myself.

I tried to create a crew of diverse backgrounds and character and plunged them into various perils which might naturally arise from their way of life. Which was done for four books—*Sargasso of Space, Plague Ship, Voodoo Planet,* and *Postmarked the Stars,*

Ms. Griffin, creator of the justly well-ranked adventure series of Star Commandos, agreed with me that the Solar Queen and her crew might well swing back into orbit—with certain new additions—namely a feminine member for the crew. Thus the Solar Queen lifts again for some more fateful voyages.

—Andre Norton

1

"*Space Wrack!* 'Space Wreck' would've been a more accurate name!"

Dane Thorson shifted his tall frame to better view the speaker, taking care not to jostle Rip Shannon, who was standing beside him. The *Solar Queen*'s mess had never been designed to hold the full complement of the starship's crew at one time, and when an assembly like this was called, the twelve of them had to scramble for space. "She's sound enough, Ali," he told the Engineer-apprentice quietly, "and she's paid us well up to this point."

"Precisely, my innocent, but now that the *Queen*'s free of her mail contract, what in space or beyond it are we going to do with the *Wrack?* We won't find many buyers out here eager to snap her up—that's how we were able to get her in the first place—we can't keep flying both ships with half crews indefinitely, not if we ever intend to get back into real Trade again, and we certainly can't afford to hire enough hands to fill out the duty roster on the pair of them."

Their Medic, Craig Tau, nodded. "Ali's right about our not being able to keep on short-handed much longer. The strain's beginning to tell even now, and we've had no trouble yet to push either ship. It's time to cut, at a profit, and not wait for something real bad to happen."

Mícéál Jellico, Captain of the *Solar Queen,* said nothing as he listened to his crew's discussion. His gray eyes swept the company. Seated with him at the table were the starship's senior officers: Jan Van Rycke, easily the best Cargo-Master in the ranks of the Free Traders and maybe in all Trade; the Mars-born Com-Tech Tang Ya; Steen Wilcox, the *Queen*'s Astrogator; Chief Engineer Johan Stotz; Tau; and Cook-Steward Frank Mura. Standing above and around them were the three apprentices—Dane, who reported to Van Rycke; Rip, who worked under Wilcox; and Ali Kamil. With them, rounding out the roster, were the huge Karl Kosti and his slight, almost bleached-pale associate, Jasper Weeks, both, like Ali, from Stotz's department. A good crew, the Captain thought somberly. He hoped he had not repaid their services by effectively ruining the lot of them on this one.

The gamble in buying the *Space Wrack* had paid off short-term. They had been able to grab the Trewsworld-Riginni run when it had opened up and had more than recouped their initial investment and expenses, but now it looked like they were not going to find disengaging from the commitment quite so simple.

Damn it to all the hells! The *Solar Queen* and her crew were Free Traders. They belonged in deep space, out ranging the starlanes, not perpetually hopping back and forth between two planets in the same solar system.

They did not belong on a simple mail run, either. They had been glad enough to take it in the need of the moment and had done better than might have been expected with it, but profits were small, and the work brought little satisfaction. It was time and past time for them to return to Trade as they knew it, with all its hardships and with the chimera of either fabulous fortune or sudden, maybe highly unpleasant death shimmering over every voyage. If they were forced to accept another long mail contract because they could not dispose of their sister ship, it could be the ruin of them as a crew, a team, but if the careful feelers he and Van Rycke were sending out failed to pull in a buyer, they would have no other option. Better that than be unable to meet their port fees and have to turn miners in order to keep body and soul together.

His spirits lightened abruptly when his attention shifted for a moment to the Cargo-Master. Van Rycke was not quite whistling, but there was a distinct air of triumph about him.

The big man felt his gaze and met it. His brows, white-blond like his thinning hair, lifted. "Something on your mind, Captain?"

"Just wondering about what's on yours. You look like you've just found a fistful of sunstones in a bag of salt."

The other chuckled. "Nothing quite that dramatic, but I

might be able to add a bright line or two to our catalog of prospects."

"Spill it, then," Jellico snapped. Far be it from him to begrudge his friend the pleasure of dazzling them all with yet another of his miracles, but when the welfare of his ship was concerned, he preferred to be kept informed . . .

Van Rycke's eyes sparkled. "In due time, Captain." He sobered immediately. "We have a potential buyer for the *Wrack.*"

"What! — Why in space . . ."

"She only contacted me a few minutes ago. I was on my way to tell you when you called assembly."

"What's the offer?" Míceál demanded. "And who's the buyer?" He could not recall any likely immediate prospects. Trewsworld's government was the most logical candidate, but the colony planet lacked the trained personnel to crew a starship, and hiring the needed people would be an expensive proposition. They were figuring on long and careful negotiations to convince the on-worlders of the eventual wisdom of such a move.

"None other than Rael Cofort, acting on behalf of her illustrious brother, of course."

If the Cargo-Master had been looking to provoke a reaction from his comrades, he succeeded admirably. Teague Cofort had made so many incredible strikes in what was not a terribly long career that he was a legend throughout Trade. When he moved on anything, it was inevitably with purpose.

Cofort enjoyed the luxury of choice in the charters he took on or even considered, and his interest in this was confirmation of the strong base the *Queen* had laid down here, coming in as she had at the very opening of regular commerce between the two planets of Trewsworld and Riginni, and, indeed, in initiating it. Whatever his reasons for wanting the freighter, the opportunity of picking up the local Trade operation was likely a good part of the draw. Ships like the *Space Wrack* were easily found on the star-lanes he usually traveled for those with the credits to pay for them. The Trader prince had no need to come this far out on the rim hunting one. Space, he could order one new from the shipyards!

Jellico's finger pensively rubbed the blaster scar that marred his right cheek. They would be going into the negotiations very much on the weaker side, but there would be no negotiations at all if Cofort did not need or seriously want the *Wrack.* He was no philanthropist and drove a good bargain for himself, but he had a reputation for dealing fairly. There was no reason to expect less of his sister. If the *Queen*'s representatives kept their wits about them, they could come out of this with something to show over and above the gains they had already made.

No one spoke again for several seconds. Dane broke the silence. He had seen the famed Trader once but could not place the woman with whom they would be dealing. "I don't recall seeing anyone with Cofort at the Survey auction. Was she there?"

Tang Ya smiled. "If she had been, put credits down that you'd remember her."

Ali stirred. "Beautiful?"

Thorson frowned but immediately felt ashamed of his reaction. The Engineer-apprentice himself was strikingly handsome, to the extent that he almost seemed a caricature, the video stereotype of the daring star-roving hero. Why shouldn't comeliness in others interest him? As for the rest, Kamil was not to blame that his appearance and the poise that accompanied it occasionally annoyed Dane, and no one could fault his competence or his courage when the need to display either arose.

The Com-Tech shrugged. "Beauty is common in the universe. She has that, but there's something unique about her, strange even. — No, she wasn't at the auction. Rael rarely accompanies her brother when he's conducting surplanetary business. That's why none of you children has seen her yet."

"She does attend gem markets now and then," Jellico informed them. His usually cold eyes laughed as they flickered to Van Rycke. The shot was deserved payment for the surprise he had been given.

The Cargo-Master growled and then sighed. "I had the misfortune of trying to do some business on a day when the pair of them were out buying," he informed the others. "I might as well have stayed home. Between Cofort's store of credits and her eye, nothing—and I mean absolutely nothing—of real value remained that was anywhere near being in a Free Trader's price range."

"Why so many jewels?" Rip inquired curiously.

Van Rycke glanced up at his apprentice. "Answer him."

"Teague Cofort trades with powerful people on some highly developed planets and with fairly sophisticated, complex societies even on those less technically advanced. He has to carry quality goods, not trinkets, or no one would bother coming to him."

"Precisely."

2

Míceál was too accustomed to his brown Trade uniform to be much bothered by it even with all fastenings in place and the high, stiff dress collar squeezing his neck, especially not with so important a meeting as this to claim his attention.

He studied the woman who had seated herself opposite him and Van Rycke as closely as he could without making his scrutiny too obvious. Tang had been right in calling Rael Cofort attractive, and equally correct in saying there was something unique in her appearance. It was not easy to place her in one of the major Terran subraces or assign a planet of origin for her line. She had been space-born herself.

She was of about average height, slender, with the lithe, tightly controlled body of a veteran spacer. There was no accompanying tan, however, although her pallor was very different from Jasper Weeks's. That skin might never darken, but it was alive with a soft warmth of its own.

Her features were delicately formed, fragile looking, making the thickly lashed eyes appear impossibly large. They were a subtle violet color that seemed to alter with every change of thought or mood.

The hair was tawny, golden like the coat of a Terran lion. She kept it long, braided and fastened in a coronet to her head in the fashion adopted by most female space hounds.

Her hands, he saw as they shuffled through the contents of the slender safe-lock portfolio she carried, were long-fingered and beautifully formed. They were also very small. One of them would not have spanned Van Rycke's palm, or his own, for that matter.

She chose a document and held it out to them. "My authorization to act as agent for Teague Cofort of the *Roving Star.*"

The Cargo-Master accepted the paper and read it, as was his right in a matter of Trade. "Dated this morning?"

She nodded. "He fasmitted it when I informed him of the possible sale."

"We hadn't broadcast any interest in parting with the *Space Wrack,*" he observed.

The young woman smiled and shrugged delicately. "When I planeted, I prowled around, asked a few questions, and came up with some deductions. Teague told me to go for it if the deal was reasonable."

Van Rycke leaned back in his chair. "Ms. Cofort, I confess that I'm finding it a bit difficult to believe you were sent all the way to Trewsworld on the chance of finding a small freighter coming up for sale. Trade here isn't all that spectacular, and similar chances to latch onto a ship aren't all that uncommon even out here on the rim, much less in the inner systems you often frequent, not when there's a good supply of credits on hand to pay for her."

"I was not sent here, of course. I came on the *Mermaid*."

"The *Mermaid* lifted yesterday morning."

Her eyes flashed with the anger she otherwise chained. "I didn't like the way Riff Slate ran his ship."

Van Rycke's brows raised. "He just let you go, or hadn't you formally signed on?"

"I'd signed. — He didn't dare try to hold me. He doesn't keep many hands for long." Her lips tightened in a hard, cold line. "Most Captains economize when business is lean, but not on the life-support and emergency systems. An apprentice died during the voyage in an inconceivable outcome of an accident that should never have occurred and would not have occurred on any other vessel. To my mind, that death was nothing short of murder."

"You can't prove that?" Jellico asked sharply.

"No, and I wasn't vacuum-brained enough to spread my opinion around, either. I just muttered things about jinxed voyages, and Slate let me out of my contract before I scared the rest of his crew away or into making some move that might start a formal inquiry into the number of hands the *Mermaid*'s shipped over the last few years. As it is, he has a lot of extremely unhappy people aboard."

"What did you think you'd do here once you were let loose?" Van Rycke inquired.

"Stay alive. That's a singularly appealing idea even if one has to work as a planet hugger for a time to keep eating. I knew something would eventually come along."

Rael squared her shoulders. "If you are satisfied, perhaps we could discuss the *Space Wrack* instead of delving into my uninspiring history."

The Cargo-Master made a formal bow with his head. "What are Cofort's terms?"

It would come down to that. Teague Cofort was merely willing to pick the ship up if he could conveniently do so. They would have to work with his terms or be prepared to reject them outright.

"We'll give what you initially paid for her."

"Plus ten percent for the work we put into her."

The woman shook her head. "Our price is fair. You've knocked at least that much out of her, and right now she's chaining you hands and feet. You won't do better, and if you wait, she'll wind up costing you besides in port expenses and maintenance."

"We've been carrying those costs. We have to get them back at the least, or we don't deal."

"I'd say you already have. This isn't a wildly rich charter, but it's solid and it's steady."

Van Rycke leaned back in his chair, as if closing the discussion. "I'm sorry, Ms. Cofort. We have to do better than break even. If it means we have to wait a bit and take on another mail run, so be it. The *Space Wrack*'s a good ship, a fine one for her class. Buyers will eventually come for her."

She eyed him thoughtfully. "I have my brother's permission to trade for myself as well."

Van Rycke bent forward again. "We'll be happy to accommodate you in any way consistent with the *Queen*'s welfare. What do you propose?"

"The expenses you mention in return for passage to Canuche of Halio, preferably a paid working passage. I could use a few extra credits, and I don't think you'll be sorry for my services. You'll be heading for there anyway," she added practically, "so I won't be putting you out."

"What makes you imagine that?"

"Canuche's the nearest planet where you'll have a reasonable chance of picking up a decent charter as well as be able to flesh out your stock of trade goods."

The Cargo-Master took the ID she withdrew from her portfolio. He looked sharply at her. "A Medic?"

Rael nodded. "Aye. Fully accredited."

Her fingers reached for the disk and closed over it. "I'm aware that you don't need an Assistant Medic aboard. No ship of the *Queen*'s class does, or believes she does, unless the incumbent plans to retire in the near future and wants to train in his replacement. I'm working my way as a jack-of-all-trades."

"The *Solar Queen* is fully staffed," Jellico interjected. "I'm not about to let go any of my permanent crew."

"Hardly," she agreed, "but tell me the department that can't use a bit of help now and then—Mr. Van Rycke's when cargo's being laded or shifted, the Engineering section during preventive maintenance, even the Steward and Medic once in a while depending on the press of their particular duties. About the only place I won't volunteer to serve is on the bridge. I'm as good as the next and probably better than most at basic astrogation, but that one is definitely best left to the experts."

The smile she turned on them was winning. Rael was sure of getting the passage, but she was out for more than that. "I want to be part of the *Solar Queen,*" she told them frankly, "if only for one voyage."

"Why?" Míceál asked bluntly. "She won't match a Cofort ship, especially not the *Roving Star,* for comfort, and you can put credits down that we won't be calling at the Federation's most fashionable spaceports."

The woman sighed. "You talk about our holdings as if we were a miniature Company. I assure you that is very much not the case. We have a few frills, aye, but we're Free Traders like the rest of our kind. We don't live soft.

"My interest in your *Queen* stems from two sources. First, your former Cargo-apprentice, Mara Ingram, is the best Cargo-Master we've ever had. She obviously had superb training, and, happy as she is on the *Star,* she speaks with nothing but pride and affection of her time as part of your crew. Second is the response of your apprentices and Mr. Weeks to the crisis of being framed as a plague ship. They proved they could think quickly and clearly and then make and carry through the desperate plan needed to clear you. Furthermore, at the end, the *Queen* not only came out of it all solvent with a relatively good contract but managed to avenge herself on her enemies as well. I think I could learn more serving with you for a voyage or two than I could in ten years bumming around the rim."

The violet eyes studied him somberly. "I have no ulterior motive for this. You don't compete directly with my brother, and even if you did, Teague doesn't deal in back-alley work."

"No one ever said that he did, Doctor Cofort," he responded quietly.

She carefully closed her portfolio. "You have our offer. Take your time to talk it over, but please consider it well. It's generous since we are seriously interested in acquiring the ship, and you're not likely to better it, or equal it, either, in the foreseeable future."

Van Rycke was silent for a moment. "That won't be necessary. We accept your brother's bid. — You'll want to inspect the *Wrack?*"

"Of course, as will our Engineer when the crew gets here, as a formality in this case. You've been flying her, and none of you appears to be suicidal. — My request?"

"The *Queen* will carry you, but if you want to work, it'll have to be as an unskilled temporary hand with no share in the ship's profits." They would have to check the rates. Only the huge transgalactics, most of those passenger liners, plying the inner-system starlanes, used unspecialized labor. Out here on the rim, no Captain could indulge in that luxury. Every crew member had his or her specific place and could usually back up at least one other shipmate as well.

"That's all I had in mind, Mr. Van Rycke." She glanced at Jellico. "If it is agreeable to the Captain. Hiring a crew member goes beyond a Trade agreement. I'll have to honor his will."

"It's agreeable, Doctor."

"Excellent! Thank you, Captain Jellico."

Rael came to her feet. "I won't be long. I'll pick up my things and have the formal contract drawn up. You can check it over, and we can seal it when I return."

3

Jan Van Rycke's head lowered. He had done all he could, the little he could. The senior members of the crew would appreciate that, but he knew the others had expected in their hearts that he would pull off some bit of magic for them. Damn it to all the hells, he had half expected that himself . . .

Jellico looked at him. "Not bad at all," he announced with satisfaction. "We'd already made our original cost and expenses back, so this is clear profit. As nice a pot as the *Queen*'s seen in many a long voyage."

The tension melted from their comrades, and they crowded around the Cargo-Master to offer their own congratulations.

"The only question now is what we're going to do with our new hand," Steen remarked.

"No one has to worry about that," Tau responded. "I can put her to very good use. I've been doing, or trying to do, a study of interspecies/interracial transmission of viral and bacterial infections on the planetary, interplanetary, and interstellar levels. The inputting alone is a galactic chore. If all Rael Cofort does is take over that, it'll be worth it to me to ship her, and with a medical background she should be able to manipulate and interpret some of the data as well."

"You do believe she's not setting us up for anything?" Rip pressed, voicing the nagging concern of most. They all had good reason to recall some of their recent passengers.

"As sure as we can be," Van Rycke answered. "As Doctor Cofort pointed out, we're not of a class to compete regularly with her brother, and we don't even have a charter at the moment, much less anything he'd want to fight to get away from us, which he'd do openly anyway. He's certainly not going to enter into a Trade war over an intrasystem mail run like this one. Míceál will have to confirm Rael's credentials with him, but if she checks out there, we should be safe enough taking her aboard. It shouldn't prove a loss to us, even apart from whatever she can do on Craig's project. She's at least proven she's able to trade."

"That she has." The Captain shook his head, as if in amazement. "Hard as titanone, though she looks as fragile as one of Loren's ghost lilies."

Craig Tau chuckled. "The habitual errors of our kind! — Slight build is not the equivalent of either a weak body or

reader. "Your period of service will be from the present until the *Queen* is ready to leave Canuche of Halio, with the option to negotiate another run or a more permanent contract should either course seem desirable to both of us."

Rael nodded. "Agreed." She smiled. "The gem market?"

"Mr. Van Rycke would like to test your skills there, aye."

"I'll be glad to put them to the *Queen*'s service, though a certain amount of luck is always a strong component when buying jewels."

"We recognize that fact as well, Doctor."

The man looked thoughtfully at the disk in his hand, then glanced back up at her. "Sit down for a moment, Doctor Cofort."

He remained silent until she had complied, then went on. "I've been in contact with your brother."

"A reference check was a logical move on your part, especially after I admitted to breaching my contract with the *Mermaid.*" She said no more, although his silence invited further comment.

It was the Captain who continued. "Cofort reports that you're as good a general hand as is to be found in the starlanes and that your medical qualifications are impressive."

"However?" she prompted, readily picking up the expected reservation in his tone. Teague would not have lied for her.

"Cofort tells me that you don't respond well to the sight of suffering or major injustice."

The woman's eyes brightened momentarily. "Neither does he." She was grave again in the next instant. "It is true that I've drawn him into a couple of confrontations he would as soon have avoided."

"I can't afford to have the same thing happen to me or my crew," Jellico told her bluntly. "A Free Trader Captain, the Captain of any starship, is responsible not only for his vessel and cargo but for every living thing she carries. He can't always act as he would if he were an unencumbered individual. There're always going to be times when he has no option but to look the other way. That's true of your brother and even more so of us; we don't pack the same payload."

"I am aware of that fact, Captain Jellico. Too aware of it. I had to satisfy myself with leaving the *Mermaid* and saving my own skin instead of properly challenging Slate's negligence."

Her eyes dropped, and she bit down on her lip. "I hope someone does." She looked up again, her hatred open and strong. "Soon."

"You can count on that if the crew's got as much reason to be dissatisfied as you said." He slid the ID into his recorder and pushed the button, officially sealing his new hand to the ship. That done, he returned it to her. "Welcome aboard, Doctor. Thorson should be waiting outside now to show you around. You'll have just enough time to see something of the *Queen* and stow your gear before we lift off."

4

Dane glanced at his timer. What was keeping the woman in there anyway? His own initial interview had taken only the few seconds necessary to process his ID. . .

He glared at the door, angry with her and with himself because he recognized that his present ill will stemmed from his own uncertainty.

Damn, he thought. He knew as well as the next that mixed crews were supposedly better on every count, but the *Queen* had managed just fine with only men since he had joined her company, and he was not anxious to see anything intrude that might cause trouble now. They faced enough of that from the outside without introducing it into their own company.

It was no question of Rael Cofort's probable skill or lack of it that was bothering him. Certainly, it was not her gender. There had been an abnormally low percentage of women in his class at the Pool, but they had still comprised more than a third of the total. To a one, they had proven equal to the work and had pulled their part both individually and in the group projects assigned to them.

He sighed to himself. The newcomer's capabilities hardly interested him at the moment. He was simply afraid of what she might do. He liked the *Solar Queen* the way she was. He was settled, comfortable, and he did not relish the thought of any changes this potentially disruptive recruit might bring about.

Recruit! Cofort had not even been invited to join the crew. She had bludgeoned her way in with that blasted charter.

Memory rose to Thorson's mind, and his irritation ebbed. He had not been with the *Queen* so long that he could not remember his fears and feelings during his own first days aboard. This woman might be older and fully accredited in her specialty, but he did not believe she would be entirely immune to at least some of the same emotions that had made his initiation such a misery for him. He would be a proper bastard if he added to her trials with a show of causeless hostility.

No, he told himself decisively, in all fairness and all humanity she would have to be given her chance, maybe several of them, but let her prove a source of trouble, let her even begin to try to destroy what they had here . . .

The panel slid open, and Rael Cofort stepped into the

corridor. She gave him a quick smile. "All set," she told him. "I'm now an official—"

A shriek as loud and teeth-jarring as a civilian attack alert silenced her. Even out here they could hear Jellico slamming the bottom of the cage, setting it bouncing violently, but for once this usually sovereign remedy had no effect. The siren wail continued undiminished.

Thorson winced. "I wonder how much of that the old man can take. Or Queex, for that matter. It's a wonder that jostling doesn't scramble his brains."

The woman laughed. "Hardly! He loves it."

"He'd have to be even odder than he looks to enjoy taking a beating."

She looked at him strangely. "You haven't read up on hoobats?"

"I'm afraid not. I've been too busy studying the finer points of cargo management," he responded, manfully keeping out of his voice the defensive note threatening to sharpen it. Ali used to make him feel like this, sometimes still did, with his superior air. He wondered if that was a characteristic of all extraordinarily fine-looking people who were also uncommonly intelligent. "You have, I suppose?"

His companion failed to notice his discomfort. "Mara's description intrigued me, so I did a little research. They're rather fascinating little things. I can well understand why the Captain would want to adopt one, given his interest in X-Tee wildlife."

"That's more than the rest of us can say," he remarked, his curiosity aroused almost despite himself. "How about sharing your findings?"

She laughed. "Sure thing. — Hoobats come from Tabor and are quite rare even there, filling a very specific niche. They live only in certain canyons that are little less than wind tunnels and spend their entire lives clinging to stone projections or ledges or to wildly swaying branches, waiting for something falling within the appropriate size range to come within striking or luring distance. They don't have to eat often, and they hunt, of course, the way Queex did when he rounded up those poisonous pests for you.

"The young are nurtured in free-hanging nests depending on slender branches to safeguard them from predators. Both parents feed them during their short period of dependency, but otherwise, hoobats are completely solitary creatures. That's why Queex can exist happily in isolation from his kind the way he does. As for the jarring, that's actually soothing, a flashback to his old life and to his time in the nest. In fact, a hoobat appears to require a certain amount of sharp movement to remain healthy."

Dane grinned. The image of Captain Jellico tenderly rocking an overage hoobat infant to rest was one worth cherishing in the heart if not to be openly shared—at least not in the skipper's hearing.

"You didn't really believe he'd consciously abuse an animal or keep one in intolerable conditions, did you?"

"No," he replied seriously after a brief pause, "I guess I didn't, or I wouldn't if I'd thought about it. I have read some of Jellico's papers, and all of them show too much liking and respect for his subjects to allow any mistreating of them."

The man glanced at his timer. "Let's have a quick run-through of the *Queen* and drop off your gear. We'll soon have to be strapping down."

"Good idea." She hefted her kit bag, which she had eased to the floor while they had been talking.

Thorson eyed it sourly. It was the standard size and obviously of manageable weight but was easily three times as full as his had been when he had boarded the *Solar Queen.*

Reason quelled his resentment. What else could he have expected? Rael Cofort was not some raw recruit out of Training Pool. She was a veteran of the starlanes who had literally been born in Trade and had hitherto lived and worked under conditions of considerable prosperity. She should have accumulated a few possessions. He, on the other hand, with no kin to back him, had come to his post with only his bare issue gear and the pathetically few extras he had been able to buy for himself to augment that.

The Cargo-apprentice first led the way through the bridge area and pointed out the personal cabins of those working there. Then they descended the core ladder to the next deck, which housed the engine and drive controls, where Johan Stotz commanded and lived with his staff.

The public cabins in which the hands and any passengers gathered during off-duty time were located below that. Here was the mess and galley, Frank Mura's chief domain, plus the small crew's cabin with its media readers and other equipment designed to help dispel the boredom of interstellar travel.

Farther down, close to the holds that, with the fuel coils and drive tubes, comprised the greatest part of the *Solar Queen*'s interior, were the Cargo-Master's and Thorson's own cabins plus those of Frank Mura and Doctor Tau and the two minute chambers kept for passengers, one of which would be assigned to Cofort for the duration of her service aboard the *Queen*. The final cabin there was, of course, the combination sanunit/fresher that was a mandatory part of every deck containing permanent sleeping quarters.

The newcomer briefly surveyed the cabin to which her guide showed her, then dropped her pack on the foot of the bunk. The room was small even by spacer standards since it had never been intended to serve anyone as a permanent home, but it was adequate. The bunk at least was full size, and there were sufficient lockers for both clothing and bulkier belongings. A large metal panel could be unfastened and swung down and outward from the wall to provide a desk or workspace with the bunk taking the place of a chair. The lighting, she saw, was well placed and more than bright enough for reading or close work.

She did not linger to unpack but quickly went outside again to follow Thorson down to the final deck that they would be visiting. There would be no time to see much more, and she doubted that she would be invited to examine the holds for a while, although they were unsealed, empty for the most part save for a small store of trade goods. A Free Trader was usually cautious about whom he let into that treasury of his business, the storehouse of the magic he hoped to wield among the denizens of the planets he visited.

The level to which they now came was the most interesting of all to Cofort. Here was the sick bay, Doctor Tau's surgery and laboratory, and the hydro, the large chamber housing the plants that replenished a starship's oxygen, scrubbed the waste products of respiration from the continuously recirculated air, and supplied as a by-product fruits and vegetables to vary the otherwise monotonous diet of concentrates that was the nearly perpetual lot of space hounds who ranged the vast reaches between the stars.

The portal giving entrance to it was partly transparent, and they paused for a moment to admire the lush greenery within.

"So much!" she exclaimed. "And such variety! — I thought you were forced to flush it all out when you picked up those Sargol pests."

"We did. Mr. Mura's worked hard to bring it back."

Dane took a deep breath as he opened the door, savoring as always the crisp freshness of growing things. Everywhere else, the ship's air was stale, processed stuff. Here, it was alive.

Feeling something brush against his leg, he glanced down. A large, orange-striped tomcat had slipped in behind them and was rubbing him in the traditional greeting of his kind before turning his attention to the newcomer.

Cofort lightly lowered herself to her knees. "Hello, big boy," she said softly as she offered him her hand to sniff. "You're the Chief of Pest Control, I presume?"

"He is," Thorson confirmed. "This is Sinbad, an honored member of the crew."

"Rightly so." She shuddered. "I shouldn't care to voyage far on any ship lacking a good cat."

"You won't find too many who'd give you an argument on that," he agreed.

She scooped Sinbad into her arms. "He's enormous! Ours are kittens by comparison."

"The *Roving Star* has more than one cat?"

She nodded. "A senior citizen and two former foundlings who now sort of run the place under her supervision."

Rael rubbed the big cat under the chin with the tips of fingers obviously well accustomed to that delicate work and received a rumbling purr as a reward.

Reluctantly, she put him down once more and came to her feet. She sniffed the scent-rich air appreciatively. "I'd know you had a master chef aboard even if Mara hadn't apprised me of that fact. — Thyme, sage, basil, honey seed, sharp grass—all the old faithfuls, and I detect some real delicacies as well."

"Detect? We're not near the spices at all . . ."

"I've got sensitive senses, smell included." Her nose wrinkled. "That's not always an advantage on some of the holes we visit. Besides, I've worked in the *Star*'s hydro quite a bit and more or less know what to expect in a good one."

One familiar aroma was missing. "You should have some lavender," she told him. "There's nothing like it for freshening the air, and it's not overpowering even in the smallest cabin."

Three whistles sounded over the intercom. "Lift-off coming," Dane remarked, unnecessarily since the signal was universal to the starlanes.

They carefully sealed the hydro door after seeing Sinbad out, then scrambled up the ladder with the ease of long custom to strap down in their cabins. Very soon now, the *Solar Queen* would be space-borne, and shortly after that would come the jump into hyperspace and the long voyage to Canuche of Halio.

5

Boredom was the great plague of interstellar travel, but Rael Cofort suffered very little from that in the days that followed. Chiefly, she worked with Craig Tau, but she spent some time with every department, more or less depending upon current need and her expertise in the work at hand.

It was well after mess time but she was still at Tau's terminal, obviously deeply involved in the task before her and quite oblivious to their presence, when the chief Medic and Jellico came into the surgery. She seemed equally unaware of the discomfort of the position she had for some unexplained reason chosen to adopt, sitting so far back that her arms had to stretch to their full length for her fingers to reach the keyboard.

The change in perspective won by another step provided the answer. A furry head and paw rested on the woman's upper right arm. The remainder of the big cat extended down her trunk and filled her lap.

Sinbad's eyes opened at the men's approach. He gave a wide yawn, then leapt gracefully to the floor, where he stretched to his considerable supple length. Still purring in feline contentment, he strode off, tail high, to resume his patrol of the starship that was his universe and domain.

Cofort smiled tenderly even as she flexed her stiff arms. "I love those little fellows so much that sometimes I think I must have been one."

"Reincarnation?" Tau asked, curious as always about the magic and beliefs of others.

"Aye," she responded, still smiling, "but the reference was poetic. I think we humans are granted only one voyage in which to prove ourselves. — I like to imagine that Sinbad's kind might return more often, though, at least when and where they choose. Their life spans are so much shorter than ours that it's nice to feel we might be reunited with a friend of our youth at a later point in our lives."

She eyed them for a moment, as if waiting for some challenge, then flexed her shoulders again and glanced at the screen. "The fifth section's almost in. It's slow going, but complex enough to make the inputting fairly interesting work."

"Exhausting work," Jellico snapped. "You look burned down."

The Medic studied her. "You have some Soft-Tear, I presume?"

"Of course." The soothing drops were a widely used remedy for eyestrain throughout the Federation.

"Break off here and use it, then. This is a long-term project and won't be finished before we reach Canuche whether we kill ourselves on it or not."

"I know, Doctor," she agreed ruefully. "I just find it hard to stop sometimes once my navputer's programmed for a job like this, especially when things're moving well."

She came to her feet. "Mind if I see Queex first, Sir?" she asked Míceál. "I missed dropping in on him today, and . . ."

"I know. I haven't enjoyed a moment's quiet since noon. — See him by all means, and from now on you are to spend at least thirty minutes every day entertaining him. I need some peace, at least in my own quarters."

"Thank you, Captain!"

"That was not meant as some sort of reward, Doctor Cofort," he told her severely.

"I know, Sir, but it is all the same."

The woman took her leave of them after that with a wave of her hand.

Jellico watched her disappear through the door. If she was tired there was no sign of it in her step, but he still fixed his comrade with a stern look. "I want to knock full value out of her, Craig, not kill her. This isn't a slave ship."

Tau turned to the locker where he kept his implements and more common medications. "I can't see that one meekly submitting to abuse. — Roll up your sleeve, Captain. This won't hurt a bit."

"You say that every time."

"True, when I'm giving an immunization shot. It's medical tradition."

He stopped talking while he prepared the laser needle, then continued. "It also seems to be tradition that no ship's crew is ever on a nice, convenient, easily remembered schedule to receive them."

"You could drop this one for all the good it does," his commander grumbled. "No matter how many shots you get against Quandon Fever, a new mutation inevitably crops up, and if you're exposed you get sick despite them all."

"Not as sick. We hope. Besides, why make a home for the old versions? None of them're good tenants."

By the time Jellico felt the spark of heat from the needle, Tau had already deactivated it. He glanced briefly at the tiny red spot it had left then rolled his sleeve back into place. "How's your assistant doing?"

"Cofort? If I'd placed an order directly with the Spirit ruling space, I couldn't have gotten better, at least not for this study of mine."

"It's more or less in her line, isn't it? She's an epidemiologist."

"That title scarcely describes it. Rael Cofort knows just about every detail of every plague since premechanical Terra, and she's very nearly as knowledgeable about mostly every other major disaster as well. She's been even more help correlating data and interpreting it than she has been with the inputting."

"What about practical medicine?"

The other shrugged. "Luck's been with us, and we haven't had to put her skills to the test."

Craig lowered himself into the chair Rael had vacated. "What do the others report?"

"According to Johan, she's competent. No genius, maybe, but he can use her. Tang would put her on the screens or transceivers any time. Steen says she's got the theory, some of it pretty obscure, but real-life calculations're another matter. She probably could bring a ship through if pressed. He just wouldn't care to be aboard when she tried."

"Astrogation's a specialized art," the Medic observed.

"So's surgery. None of us flyboys'd want to take a crack at that."

"Frank's opinion?"

"He wouldn't need to have a blaster put to his head to make him eat her cooking, but he'd rather keep her chained to the hydro. Claims she could pull fruiting plants out of deep space."

Tau nodded. "She seems to like dealing with living things, which is natural enough for a Medic, I suppose. At any rate, it can get results. — Trade's people work on a grand scale. What has Van to say?"

Jellico spread his hands wide. "That she knows goods, especially luxury items, but whether she can do anything with them is anyone's guess. Her dealings with us are no indication. We're her own kind, and she was holding the blaster."

That was about what Tau had expected to hear. "Strong in biotic areas, adequate with machines and math." The common pattern. Most people leaned to one or the other. "It's the degree of achievement she's attained in the areas where she's good that sets her apart. I'd say Teague Cofort was none too pleased when she lifted off the *Roving Star.*"

"Credits down he wasn't," Mícéal agreed. Even if he had been more than a little relieved to see her go.

"What about you? Have you been able to learn anything yourself?" He knew Rael had been spending a good part of what she would allow herself of free time in the Captain's company, although there was little help she could give him on the bridge.

"Not much. She's got a layman's knowledge of animals, but it's broad and detailed. She likes them, so I guess she retains whatever she reads about them. It works that way for me. At any rate, I haven't had to talk down to her yet."

He glowered. "Queex'll never be the same after she goes. He looks for her to show up now. To be more precise, he demands her presence."

"Maybe she should continue showing up," the Medic suggested seriously.

His companion looked at him incredulously. "We know hardly anything more about that damn woman than her name!"

"Be reasonable, Mícéal," Craig said smoothly. "We could establish a precedent, a whole new rank. Hoobat-Sitter First Class . . ."

Too late, Jellico saw the sparkle in his dark eyes and knew he had been taken over the jets proper. He informed the other, graphically, just where and how he should file that particular suggestion.

Both were grave again in the next moment. "She isn't terribly communicative," Tau agreed. "Plenty of detail on a lot of different subjects, but nothing about one Rael Co-

the rim. Once she logs in some practical experience she could then rejoin her brother's organization on her own terms or link up with some other inner-system ship. She can't be blamed for not going for a Psycho placement. Its decision's binding and long-term. If she's hoping to go back to her own people in anything like the near future, she wouldn't want to lock herself up elsewhere.

"The rim's a reasonable place for her to come, too," Tau went on. "She can find work here without having to worry about having her knowledge used in a Trade war against Teague since none of us deals with the same markets on any regular basis, or at least not regularly enough to form a threat."

"So you've been considering some of the problems as well, I see, for all your enthusiasm about our new hand."

"Naturally. I'm not completely space-addled yet, I hope and pray. I'm just willing to make use of her talents while I'm wondering."

"So am I, assuming she's after what she claims she is. We can't confirm that, not with almost everything we've got to go on coming straight from Rael Cofort herself."

Jellico said nothing more for a moment, then he sighed. "She's so damned good, Craig. Why did Cofort let her go? — I know. She claims she wants to try herself on her own, but Teague owns several freighters outright and has a strong interest in a number of others. Just about all his apprentices find places in his organization when they qualify. It doesn't make sense that he couldn't manage to come up with anything at all for his own sister."

Míceál gave a sharp shake of his head. "What's the matter with her? I can't find it, but Cofort actively wanted to be rid of that woman or was at least more than willing to see the end of her.

"Even the way she fits in here's against her. She's trying too hard. No one not working at it full time could have the right answers, the precisely correct phrases, all the time." The Captain frowned. "How much of Rael Cofort are we actually seeing and how much a skillfully constructed facade?"

Míceál's face hardened. "Right now, I wish we had turned Cofort's damn offer down. I may well have shipped a potential nova aboard the *Solar Queen*—that or something half a universe worse."

6

Jellico had little time to dwell on the puzzle of his unwelcome temporary hand the following day. The *Queen* was scheduled to set down on Canuche of Halio by late evening, and all the myriad tasks that accompanied planetfall kept him and the rest of her hands fully occupied.

Excitement ran high. The direction their immediate future would take would be decided on the rapidly nearing world.

Would they be lucky enough to pick up a charter, paying passengers or cargo that would enable them to write off the expense of their next voyage, albeit at the cost of dictating what the destination would be?

What sort of goods would they find to restock the *Solar*

Queen's nearly empty Trade holds? Jewels, textiles, luxury products, a vast array of manufactured items, raw materials, native produce—the planet's markets offered them all, along with a smattering of other, more exotic goods brought in by Traders calling at the busy spaceport, but they could not predict what the exact mix or quality would be during their own stay on-world.

Soon now, they would be able to start answering those questions. In the meantime, they could only speculate and do what they could to prepare for whatever opportunities might arise—or be induced to arise—on Canuche of Halio.

A yowl and snarl like something issuing from the throat of a werebeast out of legend shocked Dane Thorson full awake.

The chill of the air told him the *Queen* was still on night schedule, but he did no more than note that as he cautiously made for the door panel of his cabin, feeling his way in the near-dark. He was not about to activate the lights, not until he ascertained what was wrong. Something most assuredly was. Anything out of the ordinary on a starship was to be viewed with suspicion, and a commotion in the middle of the night was the equivalent of a formal alarm, especially when she was on-world, as the *Solar Queen* now was.

Cautiously, he slid the panel back a crack. There was no noise now, but he froze at what he saw outside.

They had taken on a passenger, then, short a time as the hatch had been open yesterday evening. Sinbad had detected and tracked down the invader, but the challenge it presented was a real one. The beast was large, a good foot long excluding the whip-thin, hairless tail, and its low, slender body was solidly muscled. The claws on the digits of its four feet were inconsequential, obviously never intended to serve as a defense against a foe of the cat's size. The teeth in its long, bewhiskered muzzle were another matter. They were sharp, and the creature was fast enough to wield them efficiently. Both Sinbad's ears were torn, and there was a deep gash on the side of his jaw.

However scored, the cat was the stronger fighter. The intruder's brown fur was matted with blood, and it was obviously nearing the end of its strength. Sinbad recognized that. He crouched low, watching intently. Occasionally, his tail lashed with incredible, utterly controlled violence, but otherwise he was motionless, seemingly more statue than living animal.

Suddenly, with no forewarning detectable by either his prey or the watching man, Sinbad sprang. The powerful leap carried him high, then down with spine-shattering force onto the back of his opponent. Strong, needle-sharp teeth closed on the neck. Fraction-seconds later, he shook the thing and cast it on the deck, where it kicked twice in a final, nerve-fired spasm and lay still.

Dane's eyes flicked to it, then away again. Moving quickly, he caught up Sinbad in his arms. They were no mere scratches that the cat had taken. The bleeding had to be stopped and medical care instituted at once. Immunization shots or no, the bite of an alien creature was one of the most potentially perilous accidents threatening an offworlder. No prophylactic series could defend against every one of the myriad microorganisms that might be introduced into the body by such means, many of which could overwhelm with terrifying speed and deadly result the defenses of beings not prepared by nature to confront them.

His lips compressed into a hard line. Holding the injured cat, working to stanch the bleeding that might soon dangerously weaken him, he realized that he no longer saw Sinbad simply as an animal kept aboard to perform a useful service for his human masters. This was a friend, a full member of the *Solar Queen*'s crew, the Chief of Pest Control in fact, as Rael Cofort had named him. Aye, there were grave limitations to the degree of communication attainable between members of his species and the feline, but Cargo-Masters and their apprentices working with precious little more on occasion when making contact with newly encountered or rarely visited races could manage to achieve lucrative trade relations beneficial to both parties . . .

When the crisis of the active bleeding was under control, Thorson hit the intercom button with a force born of anxiety. Be the victim four-footed or biped, the situation remained a medical emergency. It was his responsibility to summon expert help to deal with it.

Rael was out of her bunk and drawing on her trousers before Dane had half begun his terse description of the situation. In the next moment, she had rammed her bare feet into deck boots and thrust her arms into the sleeves of her tunic, then, grabbing the medical kit that never lay far from her hand when she slept, she dashed from her cabin.

She reached Thorson's quarters at a full run, seconds before the senior Medic.

Her eyes sought and in the same moment found her patient. "Oh, Sinbad!" she exclaimed softly. "What's happened to you, my brave little warrior?"

The woman set her bag down on the bottom of the bed, snapping it open as she did so. Her movements, though quick, were smooth and quiet, designed not to further startle the injured animal. "Hold him steady, Dane," she instructed. "I want to take a quick look at those bites and then get to work on them."

"I've got him," he assured her.

Rael worked fast, with her full attention fixed on her small patient.

Dane watched in something akin to awe as her fingers seemed to fly of their own accord, at once gentle and sure in their mission. Medicine was sometimes described as an art, and he realized he was witnessing a manifestation of that aspect of it here, a healing of body that encompassed mind and heart as well. Sinbad lay quiet in his arms, without fear, despite the excitement of the fight, his physical pain, the shock of his wounds, and the strangeness of the procedures being performed on him.

Dane glanced at Tau and caught his slow nod of approval. The Medic recognized excellence in his own profession, excellence that surpassed mere skill.

At last it was over. Cofort ran her hands several times along Sinbad's back and sides, drawing a rumbling purr from him. She touched her lips to the top of his head, then looked up at the Cargo-apprentice. "You did well to stop the bleeding as quickly as you did. Otherwise, we might have had to transfuse him, never a pleasant experience for an animal."

"He'll be all right now?" Thorson inquired anxiously.

"He should be. Doctor Tau will want to look him over tomorrow . . ."

"It's rarely beneficial to the patient to change good Medics mid-treatment," Craig interjected. "I'm available for consultation, naturally, but Sinbad's getting excellent care from his present physician."

"Thank you, Doctor." Tau's comment was as much an assurance to the *Queen*'s crew, a public affirmation of her skill, as an acknowledgment of her right to treat as the first Medic on the scene.

Rael took the cat from Thorson. "What this poor little lad needs right now is a nice, comfortable, warm bed for the night. You won't mind him sharing yours, will you, Dane?"

"No. Sinbad often bunks with me." He liked the company and the feel of life-warmed fur beside him, but he sighed inwardly when the tom, as if on cue, jumped from her arms onto the bunk and settled himself, head on pillow, right in its center with almost mathematical precision. He would not have the heart to shift his guest tonight, and if Sinbad did not move of his own accord, he would have to spend the remainder of the sleep period pretzeled around their wounded defender.

That probability was equally apparent to those of his shipmates who had pushed into his small cabin, although given the circumstances they refrained from ribbing him openly.

Rael's eyes were still dancing with the laughter she had

not yet screened when they met the Captain's and found the same merriment mirrored there.

It lasted but an instant, then the cold solar steel returned to them. Jellico strode out into the corridor. "Let's have a look at what's left of his opponent."

"A port rat," Rip Shannon informed him, "and, space, the size of it! Sinbad got off lightly."

The whole crew was gathered there, as was inevitable on a ship as small as the *Solar Queen* when an event of note occurred.

Jellico knelt beside the invader's corpse, not touching it but studying it with an interest that overrode his innate Terran distaste for the creatures. "The beast can't be blamed for fighting well for its life."

Cofort smiled her approval, but her eyes were dark when they rested on the animal. "No," she agreed. "There was no real contest, though, not once Sinbad got it cornered."

"He was lucky all the same. It was big enough to have done even more damage than it inflicted."

"Canuche grows them big," she told him, "and they're all over this town, what with the space- and seaports, the warehouse complexes serving them, and Happy City. We'll have to put up mesh nets whenever the hatch is open if we've got a metal set, and even then, we'll be fortunate not to ship a few. The *Roving Star* lifted with a pair the last time we were on-world. — Aggressive little beggars, too, and smart enough to duck most traps. It was the cats who finally took them for us, at the cost of some skin."

No one received that piece of information with any sense of pleasure. If humankind had intentionally carried Terra's felines into space, other, less desirable denizens of the

mother planet had followed of their own accord. Few
worlds indeed among those first settled, before the advent
of the Federation's stringent pest control regulations, had
been fortunate enough to escape a visit from the tough,
incredibly adaptable rat, and where that colonizing species
came it generally stayed.

Oddly enough, rats had rarely wrought the ecological
havoc that had marked their spread on Terra. Rather, they
had concentrated their activities in and around the dwell-
ings and other establishments of their ancient hosts and
adversaries. Sometimes they grew larger than prototype,
more often smaller under the pressures and differences of
their new environments, but invariably they were a problem. Mostly, they were readily manageable; in a few unfortunate cases, where the rodents had either not been
detected quickly enough or had myopically been ignored,
they had developed into a scourge threatening the very
existence of the colony itself.

"We'll do what we can to keep them out, if only to save
Sinbad another battering," the Captain promised. "Now,
dispose of this thing, Thorson, and let's get back to our
bunks for what's left of the night. We'll have plenty to do
tomorrow besides sleeping the morning away."

7

Rael wrinkled her nose in distaste as she stepped through the *Queen*'s hatch out onto the boarding ramp. Canuche of Halio was a highly industrialized world with a great deal of heavy manufacturing and chemical processing. Every time she came here, she found the stink of the atmosphere harder to take. Fortunately, it was only unpleasant and not actually detrimental to one's health, however much it offended her sensibilities. Also fortunately, she had never been forced to remain very long on-world. Teague had always just stopped off to pick up a few supplies and lifted off again as quickly as he could.

"Where do we go first?" she inquired of her companions. She and the three apprentices had been given the day to take care of personal business and also to get a feel for the planet. Their officers would be expecting a report from each of them on various topics relating to their respective specialties when they returned that evening.

"The supply depot," Ali told her. "This is the first time since we took on that mail run that we've been near one, and we all have gear that needs replacing."

Dane fervently seconded that statement in his own mind. When he had joined the *Solar Queen,* he had been fresh out of Training Pool, physically still somewhat a boy. Since then, he had added muscle, gaining breadth of shoulder and chest. At this point, all his clothing was stretched tightly over his body and would not have gone on him at all had it not been for Frank Mura's efforts with a needle. He would be glad to be rid of the lot even though replacing everything would put a nasty hole in his already small store of credits.

A couple of hours later, the four left the Trade depot in good spirits. The men were wearing some of their purchases and carrying the rest. Only Rael was unburdened. She had come on board well supplied, and she informed her companions that she was holding her spare credits for the market.

"Let's drop off the loot," Shannon suggested, "and see about some real, honest-to-goodness food. — You're the expert, Rael, since none of the rest of us has been on Canuche before. Any suggestions? Someplace good in Happy City maybe?"

"Not there," she declared flatly. "They've got marvelous

restaurants in the northern section, right enough, but we wouldn't want to try paying for a meal in one of those.

"This is a working person's planet. Let's just take a transport to any of the factory areas, preferably near the big plants down by the waterfront. We'll find plenty of eateries around there, not fancy and the food's plain, but it's real, it's good, there's a lot of it, and it's reasonably priced."

"Lead on, good Doctor," Ali told her with an exaggerated flourish of his hand. "We can always escort the children through Happy City later on and show them something of Canuche's seamier side."

She frowned. "That's the locals' playground. We've got no guarantee that any of its delights are safe. Trade has blacklisted the gambling altogether. Space hounds have been made the mark too often in there."

"Do we look like total innocents?" Kamil demanded archly. "Besides, no one's suggesting that we venture there at night. Apart from the big restaurants, most of the place'll be shut down. It won't hurt to have a quick look around as long as we stick together." He said that last seriously. There were many areas in the galaxy where strangers were better advised not to wander alone, Canuche's pleasure districts, with Happy City at the top of the list, among them. At least, rumor had it that an occasional tramp spacer had gone there for a night's enjoyment and had not returned to ship or comrades again.

Dane soon tired of Happy City. It might sparkle with excitement at night when all its lights were ablaze and its streets and buildings were alive with people bent on finding their particular definition of fun, but now, as Ali had predicted, most of the area was closed tightly while the greater part of its denizens slept away the hours of Halio's light. It looked dingy and tawdry and also a little sad, like a hope just beginning to fade.

Canuche permitted bawdry, gaming, and the sale for use outside the home of the many legal intoxicants, but strictly limited the areas in which such commerce could be conducted. The result was a series of pleasure districts, one for each of the provinces into which the big planet was divided.

There was no need to conceal the nature of Happy City's major industries, and no attempt was made to do so. Every block had one, and usually several, scarlet-fronted erotic houses with their posters of provocative symbols describing the company and substances to be found within. Interspersed among these were a bewildering number of drinking and smoking establishments, all featuring both live entertainment and gambling. Some offered facilities for dancing and food as well, the latter limited to light dishes geared to the desires of people whose main interest was in consuming products of another sort or to those wanting something to nibble while watching a show or taking a brief break from their exploration of the various haunts of the region. A few would also provide chambers where darker products could be purchased and used away from the prying eyes of the local police and the Stellar Patrol.

The remaining buildings housed straight dining places, the more pretentious of which called themselves restaurants. Those, too, were closed, and from the look of them, he was glad their guide had steered them to that eatery down by the waterfront. He doubted they would have found much of a spacer's definition of either quantity or quality in any of these.

That would not be true once they reached the northern section, of course, with its legitimate theaters and fine restaurants, but none of those were priced to attract the patronage of apprentices from small rim Free Traders.

Thorson shook his head. The existence of the facilities around them was hardly cause for amazement. Every spaceport of any significance provided similar services, all carefully supervised for the protection of reasonably cautious spacers. The concentration of them and the sheer size of the district was something else for one accustomed from his youth to the almost ascetic standards of the Pool. Gut level, he found this wholesale dedication to raw physical amusement a little disconcerting and more so the realization that Happy City was not unique in the universe. Many planets shared the same legal attitude toward the activities pursued here, and just about every one of them sported similar areas, all more or less notorious. Where excess was expected, and encouraged, it usually occurred.

All at once, his mind snapped back from the contemplation of the cultural phenomenon of the pleasure district to fix on their immediate surroundings. He stiffened as he did so. There were few locals on the streets, but his party was drawing an uncommon amount of interest from those who were about.

To be more precise, Rael Cofort was attracting it. The time they had spent living and working together on the *Solar Queen* had bred a familiarity that had blunted his awareness of the Medic's beauty. Canucheans were not so blinded, and to their way of thinking, there was but one reason why so pretty a woman should be wandering around a region like this.

The same held true for a particularly handsome man. Ali, too, was receiving some close scrutiny.

Thorson could feel his temper rising and also his concern. Sure, the four of them could defend themselves against the single or couple of individuals they encountered, but those one or two had friends, doubtless within easy call. There was precious little anyone could do against a mob except hope to outrun it.

His fear eased in the next moment. It was inevitable that they should attract attention. The fact that they were obvious strangers would in itself ensure that they were noticed. Ali and Rael merely increased their conspicuousness. They were a singularly handsome pair by any standard that appreciated even marginally the Terran prototype, and in a place where beauty was routinely bartered, they had to expect close scrutiny.

There would be no trouble, not as long as they conducted themselves circumspectly, at least not at this hour, while Happy City was quiet and its patrons unfired by chemicals and the nighttime excitement of the place. They were, after all, off-worlders, not merely outsiders. They would not be expected to understand the nuances of appropriate behavior, much less to abide by them.

Space hounds were no more immune to that error than were their surplanetary kindred, he had to admit in all fairness. Almost to a one, they tended to regard the planet bound with precisely the same overblown, parochial tolerance. It was an odd prejudice when one considered it, and it applied almost exclusively to the various branches of humanity originating on Terra—races and species with other roots usually demanded more exacting compliance with local custom, with far heavier penalties for failure— but spacers, at least, had reason to be grateful that it existed. The attitude might in theory be a bit demeaning, but it did allow one to get on with the work at hand and conduct business effectively on planets with restrictive societies and moral or social codes strongly at variance with those ruling the starlanes.

Relaxing again, Dane turned his attention back to the silent, waiting city. They were passing one of the narrow alleys separating two outward-facing rows of buildings, and he paused a moment to study it.

The long, deeply shadowed passage was like any one of the countless others they had seen on their informal tour. It was set exactly one step below the buildings lining it on both sides and was paved or tarred with a smooth, dark substance resistant to staining and capable of withstanding the heavy morning traffic engaged in the removal of garbage and other refuse and in the delivery of various supplies.

He noted again that each establishment seemed to possess the ability to close off its own share of the alley by means of high, retractable chain link fences, all of which were now drawn back in whole or part into their sheaths to allow the various service vehicles ready access to the entire passage. "Why the fences?" he wondered aloud. He could see no ready explanation for this apparently universal proprietary interest in these small, ugly patches of real estate.

Ali gave him one of his superior looks that still had the power to irritate the starlight out of Dane. "Well, my boy," he pontificated, "consider the number of people, many of them total strangers, frequenting these worthy palaces of entertainment. Quite a few of those individuals would probably like to enjoy the delights of the house and then quietly depart with their store of wealth intact. The proprietors are doubtless unsympathetic to such initiative and most likely reason that a forest of high fences will render a quick dash out the back door ineffectual."

"Why all the chain, then?" Thorson inquired, refusing to let the other annoy him. "A solid metal barrier of this height'd be harder to scale, especially by someone who'd had a few."

"Spare us, Ali!" Rael pleaded, laughing. "A straight reply really will do just nicely."

The Engineer-apprentice started to scowl but then merely shrugged. "Actually, I don't know the answer to that one," he confessed.

"It's so the Canuchean police and the Patrol can see at a glance what's happening when they go by, which they do frequently and on an irregular schedule," she informed them. "That's why a minimum amount of lighting's required as well. Drunks still get rolled, I'm sure, and troublesome or slow-paying patrons worked over, but this does help to keep a reasonable hatch on such practices."

As she was speaking, Dane moved closer to the wall to study the mechanism of the fence. His companions started to join him, but Rael quickly stepped back again. "Space, what a stink!"

Ali cleared his throat. "With the volume of drinking and

mixing of substances," he said delicately, "a certain efflu-
vium is to be expected around the back door."

"All right, Ali," Rip Shannon interjected. "We get the
picture."

Kamil grinned at his companion's squeamishness but
followed the others readily as they hastened to move away
from the shabby yard. He had not been aware of any particularly unpleasant smell until Cofort had mentioned it, but
once she did, he caught it as well, a muskiness tinged with
ammonia.

The four paused when they reached the front of the
establishment, a drinking bar called the Red Garnet. It was
open, not merely undergoing a cleaning and set-up for the
night ahead but apparently inviting trade.

"How about having a look?" Dane surprised himself
with the question. The whole pleasure district repulsed
him, more strongly the longer he remained in it, but he was
curious, too. Damn it, he wanted to see the inside of that
place or of some other like it.

The Engineer-apprentice hesitated. They were at liberty,
but he had a feeling that did not include permission to
patronize anything in Happy City beyond a straight restaurant. "If we go in, we'll be expected to buy . . ."

"Not all of us," Rael cut in sharply.

Kamil's brows raised. "Give me time, Doctor. I was about
to say that only two of us should order. The others won't.
Does that meet your approval?"

She nodded curtly. "Aye. It's probably unnecessary,
but . . ."

"Precisely, Doctor. Where Trade blacklists part of an
operation, let the wise space hound beware the rest. —

Now that we've settled on our strategy, we need only choose our two drinkers. I'll pass. Thorson's one since this excursion is his idea. What about you to keep him company, Cofort?"

"No thank you," the Medic responded coolly.

"You don't drink, Doctor?" he asked smoothly.

"Not in dives like this!"

"Shannon, then, since you don't feel adventurous."

Ali smiled to himself, pleased to have been able to penetrate Cofort's armor sufficiently to get a rise out of her. No one appreciated a person's right to create defenses more than he did, or the right to keep quiet about the reasons for doing so, but Rael Cofort's were so good that finding a few chinks in them was a sort of a relief, as if it confirmed her basic humanity.

8

Dane felt sorry he had suggested coming inside as soon as he stepped through the door. The Red Garnet was just another bar where people came to do serious drinking. It was not particularly attractive, and it presented no features of special interest. Even the bustle of life and talk that would enliven the single big room later were absent now.

The set-up process was well under way, and tables were being maneuvered back into place on the freshly scrubbed floor by a half-dozen burly men. The chairs were still stacked along the walls one atop the other in groups of six.

At that point, the bartender looked up from arranging his glasses and spotted the Free Traders. "We're open, space hounds. What'll it be?"

"A couple of beers for the children, here," Ali responded lightly, seeing the man's close-set eyes begin to narrow at their apparent hesitation, "then we'll really have to stop playing and get back to the ship, or we'll be spending the rest of our time on-world scrubbing tubes."

That last had been addressed to his two male comrades. Rip recognized his move to ease potential tension and answered him appropriately, then he and Thorson stepped up to the bar to confirm the order.

They were served quickly. Shannon sipped the golden liquid. "This is good," he averred.

The Canuchean made a sarcastic bow to acknowledge the surprised compliment. "A local brew," he informed them. "We export a lot of it. You might mention the fact to some of your pals around the spaceport. We'd all like to see a few more off-world faces in Happy City."

He collected their credits and went back to his previous occupation with the glasses, but the spacers could see that he did not take his small, sharp eyes off them.

Neither did any of the roustabouts, or whatever their real occupation might be. "If this were an adventure tape," Rip whispered to the Cargo-apprentice, "we'd all be shanghaied before this scene was played out."

"I know," Dane responded glumly. "This wasn't one of my better ideas."

Shanghaied. The term had come with Terrans into space and was recognized throughout the starlanes although it was so old that its origin had long since been forgotten. Except possibly by Van Rycke. The Cargo-Master was a storehouse of odd lore.

That might not be so far from their hosts' minds, either,

he thought darkly, even if they did not quite dare to act on it. Both Cofort and Kamil were coming in for more of the same kind of study they had received on the street but far more openly and more intently. No legitimate erotic house would touch such captives with a long-range tractor, but doubtless there were a number of less scrupulous operations in the district. Maybe the wide staircase to his right led not only to the gambling rooms but to an unlicensed facility of that nature as well.

If so, and the on-worlders moved successfully, he and Rip would wind up on the bottom of the bay . . .

He glanced at Kamil. If the black-haired apprentice was worried, he gave no sign of it. Thorson did his best to imitate the engineer's air of ease. He knew he was probably just building trouble out of nothing but his nerves, but it would be best not to reveal any unease or weakness. That in itself could provoke an incident. They were outnumbered, and it might not be easy to fight their way out of here.

Rael Cofort remained standing close beside Ali. She had quickly lost interest in the scene at the bar. She did not like the Red Garnet and wanted nothing better in that moment than to get out of the big room as quickly as possible. — Would those two never swallow their beers?

Her hand closed convulsively around her throat. She felt as if she were choking.

Her medical training kicked in when she felt the race of her pulse through the arteries. Spirit of Space, what was wrong? Her body, driven by some subconscious warning, was terrified. What was triggering this panic?

She fought to master herself but could not drive off the

horrible eagerness filling her, a hunger, as if the room itself were a great maw seeking to devour them all.

Her left hand gripped her companion's arm. "Ali, let's get out of here. Now. Please!"

Cofort's nerve broke with that, and she bolted for the door.

Her flight galvanized the Canucheans. They straightened and began to move in on the off-worlders.

Thorson instinctively drew closer to his remaining comrades and braced himself. Two to one. Bad odds in themselves, and a couple of their opponents had drawn knives, long, thin assassin's blades that could readily slip between a victim's ribs or thrust into his back to sever the spinal cord. All three Traders were unarmed . . .

Not quite, he saw suddenly. Kamil had unhooked a length of chain from his belt. Attached to one end of it was a broad double ring padded to provide a secure grip and act as a shield for the wielder's own hand. The other ended in three wickedly curved claws.

Ali smiled coldly as he swung the chain before him with practiced ease. The on-worlders gave ground. That devilish weapon was as readily recognized in the back alleys of the ultrasystem as were their own knives, and it was a light year more feared.

Dane swallowed hard. The Engineer-apprentice had survived the Crater War and its aftermath. He never discussed those dark years, but he had just shown them one of the means by which he had managed to do it.

With Kamil acting as rear guard, the off-worlders quickly made their retreat to the street and fell back in the direction from which they had come until they reached the alley once more. Rael Cofort was waiting for them there, and the three glared furiously at her.

"Hold up," Ali ordered. "They won't follow us now that we're on the street."

"What's to stop them?" Shannon inquired in a tight whisper.

"They'll stay put," he assured him. "As it stands, it's our word against theirs. They never verbally threatened us, and both sides pulled equally illegal weapons. To cap it off, there's a Canuchean police station halfway up the block. We raise a ruckus, and the law will swarm all over the lot of us."

"They could call ahead, arrange to have us back-alleyed someplace."

"Precisely why we don't want them to see which way we went. They'll never imagine we'd be so stupid as to linger around their own back door." He believed and fervently hoped.

As he spoke, Kamil casually, or seemingly casually, re-hooked the deadly chain to his belt. Dane shivered in his heart. The older apprentice had worn the thing so naturally that neither of his shipmates had even noticed it, though he supposed any of the senior officers probably would have done so and confiscated it. Traders, Free or Company, went armed only in situations of open peril and only at the command of their officers, and Canuche of Halio was sup-posed to be a highly respectable planet.

He turned his attention to other matters, to one specific matter. His eyes fixed on the Medic.

Ali beat his comrades to challenging her. "What in all

the hells did you think you were doing?" he demanded. "Do you know what you caused in there?"

"I'm sorry," she said in a voice so low as to be scarcely audible.

"That doesn't quite pull it," he told her bluntly.

Cofort's mouth tightened. He was entitled to an explanation. All three of them were. "Something was really wrong in there. I don't know what the danger was or how immediate it was to us, but it was all around us." Her eyes closed. "By all I revere, it was there . . ."

Dane spat out Van Rycke's favorite expletive, but the Engineer-apprentice silenced him with a sharp wave of his hand. Kamil gave the woman a strange look. "If you'd told me that, Doctor," he said, "I'd have lit my burners and gotten us out a lot sooner with a lot less trouble."

Rip looked at him in surprise but kept out of the discussion. Whatever had sparked Cofort's flight, she had not lied about her fear. That was still with her, or some part of it was. She appeared normal at first glance, but the pupils of her eyes were fully dilated, huge and round like those of a cat in mortal terror. Almost despite himself, he felt sorry for her.

He looked about the alley for some distraction to draw his shipmates' attention away from her for a few moments. "They actually do take pains to wash the place down occasionally," he ventured in the end since he could find nothing better to say. "At least, that step nearest us and part of the surface around it have been scrubbed."

The Medic's hand flew to her mouth. "Spirit of Space!" she whispered. "Sweet Spirit ruling space!"

The others stared at her as if she had suddenly started a conversation with the Whisperers.

"What's the matter now?" Thorson demanded testily. Something definitely was. Rael's eyes, already too large, looked enormous, and her face had drained completely of color.

"No one washes a step and three feet to one side of it. You do the whole thing, or you don't start the job at all."

She was trembling slightly, but she made herself peer even more closely at the place where her eyes were already riveted.

Something white seemed to be jammed into the crack where the single step met the pavement. "Look! They must've missed that." Her back straightened. "We'll need it if I'm in the right starlane."

Dane's eyes narrowed. Despite her terror of a moment before and her distaste for the place, Cofort obviously intended to fetch the little scrap. "Stay put. I'll get it." He felt like a damned fool trying to play the hero out of some ridiculous adventure tape, but Rael had been scared and probably still was, even if she was hiding it now. It would not be right to force her to go in there when he had no qualms at all about doing so.

Her fingers closed on his arm with vise-tight urgency. "Dane, no! We're not even armed!"

She forced the panic out of her voice. "I'm probably just being Whisperers' bait, but it's my idea . . ."

"What's going on here?"

The four spacers whirled about. Absorbed as they had been, they had failed to notice the nearly silent approach of the flier now parked on the walkway behind them. Two men wearing the black and silver of the Stellar Patrol were standing beside it.

"The Patrol!" Rael exclaimed in patent relief. "Praise whatever gods rule Canuche! I'd rather have you lads take this than the locals. There's no knowing how they stand with the owners of this place."

The pair were unimpressed. "Just what are you four doing back here?" the agent who had challenged them, a Sergeant, demanded even more sharply.

"I believe that white object over there's a pretty damning piece of evidence. We were going to collect it and bring it to you people before it disappeared. It'll be gone for sure by this time tomorrow, if not a whole lot sooner."

"Right," he said unsympathetically. "How about telling us what sort of crime it's supposed to betray?"

"Murder. Brutal, particularly horrible, multiple murder."

9

All five men stared at the Medic. "Murder?" There was a new sharpness in the Patrol-Sergeant's voice.

Rael shook her head. She had herself well in hand now. With the responsibility that rested on her, she could not afford a show of panic that would weaken and in all probability annihilate her hope of convincing the necessary authorities to take her bizarre and very repugnant theory seriously. "I want to talk to your commander. This could be a big operation with some fairly important people involved."

The agent nodded. "We'll play it your way, space hound, but if this is some sort of joke, trust that you won't be laughing when our old lady gets through with you."

"Do I look particularly amused, Sergeant?"

"No," he admitted. "That you do not. — Keil, collect our 'evidence,' and let's light our burners back to headquarters."

Dane saw Cofort stiffen and felt his own stomach tighten, but the Yeoman was back again in a matter of seconds without mishap. Once more, he felt foolish, and he shot the woman a quick, sharp look. What in space or beyond it was she thinking, and, more to the point, in what kind of stellar mess had she involved them all?

"**R**ats!" Patrol-Colonel Ursula Cohn's blue-gray eyes fixed the younger woman in no friendly fashion. "That's some tale you expect us to believe, Doctor Cofort."

"I hope I'm wrong, Colonel, for the sake of the unknown number of men and maybe women who I think died in that wretched place," Rael replied evenly, "but I don't think I am. The evidence is circumstantial, but it's there."

"And you're the only one who happened to spot it, just picked right up on it, a stranger to Canuche of Halio and her ways?"

"My comrades can attest to the fact that my sense of smell is very acute. I'd been near heavy concentrations of port rats before and knew the odor, but I'd never come across anything so perceptible as that at a distance in the open air. There simply wasn't a mundane explanation to account for it. If the beasts were present in sufficient number to create a pack nest of the necessary size, they'd be all over the city, to the point that they'd represent a severe and immediate threat to human survival. Commercial starships would certainly be warned off until they could be exterminated. Since none of that was the case, I could only deduce that a vast number of rodents were being purposely kept confined close by under anything but the cleanest conditions. There're no industries or legitimate laboratories in Happy City as far as I knew to require the creatures, nor could I imagine any experimenting on that scale. I was completely baffled." Her mouth hardened. "Until Rip mentioned the clean-up."

"Clean-up?"

"Your agents saw it. Nobody washes a step and a ragged patch beside it."

"You or I wouldn't," the other corrected. "Navy-standard cleanliness is not a characteristic of those alleys. Mostly, the worst mess is just scraped away to satisfy the basic sanitary code."

"There would be more than one nasty patch, wouldn't there, after any normal night? There weren't any more scrubbed spots and no untouched messes that I saw, or any older residue, either. To judge by that absence and the pattern of traffic stains, it looked like that whole section of the alley had been cleaned, really gone over, in odd patches at one time or another over a considerable stretch of time."

"So you came up with a scenario to explain all the anomalies?"

The tawny-haired spacer nodded. "The motive I don't know, but I can picture the events all too clearly. Some poor bastard meeting the criteria for a victim is gotten very drunk and maybe drugged to render him, or her, helpless or sick and is pushed or flung out back the moment the police or Patrol have made a swing by the alley. The rats are either waiting or are immediately released. They've obviously been accustomed to their work, and they're great enough in number not to need much time to complete it. After a few minutes, they're recalled, maybe fed again as a reward to ensure their speedy return, and the few remaining scraps are swept up. There isn't even much blood left, and the pavement doesn't absorb the stain, at least not if it's mopped up quickly enough."

"Yeoman Roberts went into the place and returned without trouble," Cohn pointed out.

"Naturally, though I was terrified for him at the time. The things couldn't be always on the loose. Besides, they have to be well fed to be kept under control and at the necessary concentration. They wouldn't feel the need to be out foraging in the daylight."

"It's a bit odd that none of the neighbors has noticed anything amiss if this has been going on for some time as you suggest, isn't it?"

Rael fixed her gaze on her tightly clasped hands. "A single incident wouldn't take long. The thud of the victim falling probably triggers the rodents. — It can't be the opening of the door itself since that happens all the time. — There might be a muffled scream if the poor wretch was conscious, some thrashing, maybe, but little more than that. They'd work fast."

Her eyes glittered with a hard anger as cold as the depths of interstellar space. "However, I do agree that total long-term concealment would be impossible. Those running the swill joint across from it have to be involved and probably the staffs of the next one in from each of them as well. The third and fourth buildings on either side could be clean. They're erotic houses. There wouldn't be much activity out back from them, and the windows're either painted over or shuttered. As for passersby or patrons inside, with the general clamor, a bit more just wouldn't be noticed, or questioned if it were. It wouldn't be loud enough or last long enough to make that much of an impression."

"You've got all the answers, don't you?" The Colonel's face was a mask, her eyes hard, almost unblinking as they bore into the Free Trader.

"No, unfortunately. As I said before, I can't supply the motive, though I suppose it has to be greed. The involvement of several establishments rules out psychosis or vengeance unless they're all owned by one person. Even then, he couldn't do it without the knowledge and active assistance of a good number of others."

"Who are you proposing for the victims?"

Rael shook her head. "No one definite, not without knowing the why. They're probably more or less alone, people whose presence wouldn't really be noticed in a busy pleasure house and without friends, or powerful friends, to cause a stir about their disappearance, but the very opposite might be true, at least in one or two instances. — I just don't know!"

The emotion she had been holding in check had momentarily gotten away from her, but the woman gripped herself again in the next instant. "That's about it, Colonel. I've told you everything I can visualize that might be useful."

A knock caused her to glance back over her shoulder. The Patrol-Sergeant took a note from the Yeoman manning the desk outside and brought it to his commander. She glanced at it, then called out permission to enter.

Two men strode into the already crowded room. Rael's spirit lightened at the sight of them. Míceál Jellico and Jan Van Rycke! She had no idea how they came to be here, but she felt a galaxy easier in her mind now that they were. A really good Trade Captain/Cargo-Master team was a force to be reckoned with on any level, even by the ranking officers of the rightly famed Stellar Patrol. Short as her term of service aboard the *Solar Queen* had been, it was long enough for her to recognize that these two were among the best in the starlanes. Their support would go a long way in bolstering her cause . . . if they believed her story.

The Captain came to a stop before the Patrol commander's desk. "Jellico of the *Solar Queen*," he told her. "This is Van Rycke, my Cargo-Master."

"Patrol-Colonel Ursula Cohn."

Míceál gazed coolly at his junior staff. "What have these four shooting stars managed to stir up this time? Your agent informed us that you're holding them here but that they're not in trouble themselves."

"They're not unless they've dreamed up what they conceive to be an elaborate joke, which," she added hastily, forestalling an outburst of the anger she saw flash in Rael's tired eyes, "I don't believe is the case. They may, on the other hand, be mistaken. — Doctor Cofort, please repeat what you've just told me. I have it all recorded, but I'd prefer to hear it live again myself."

The Medic complied. Although she felt drained and her nerves seemed stretched beyond the snapping point, she was encouraged by that request. It meant Cohn was giving serious consideration to her theory.

She did not take nearly so long this time. There were no interruptions, and her thoughts were fully organized and consolidated.

No one spoke for a few moments after she had finished, then the Patrol-Colonel pressed her hands on her desk as if trying to shove the whole matter away from her. "It doesn't sound any less wild on the second hearing."

Jellico walked over to the chair where Rael was sitting and lay his hands on her shoulders. Strength seemed to flow from him, bracing her so that her shoulders straightened a little. "Whether she's right or navigating clear off the charts," he declared flatly, "given their nature and the logic backing them, Doctor Cofort had no moral or legal option but to report her suspicions."

The older woman sighed. "No more than I have any option except to investigate her allegations." The spacer's suggestion was mad, vile, and an on-world police officer might have dismissed it outright as sheer insanity, but the Patrol had its file of atrocities; this would not even make the list of its stellar entries. Considering what misnamed humans had done to their fellows in the past—and not the terribly distant past—it had to be viewed as well within the realm of possibility.

"Then why are you holding us?" Ali demanded. He had picked that up from the Captain's introductory comments, and he recalled too clearly the treatment they had received while under suspicion of being part of a plague ship. It did not sound at all good to him.

"You four are staying out of sight until I've made some

preliminary arrangements. I don't want any evidence destroyed before we can get our hands on it. If someone noticed my lads picking you up by that alley, I'd as soon let them imagine it had to do with a cargo or starship question, smuggling perhaps, and forget all about you. Slight though the chance might be, I can't risk having a member of a conspiracy spot you on the loose, make some sort of connection, and start protecting his fins."

"Why bother calling the Captain if that's the case?"

"Because the Stellar Patrol doesn't make a practice of detaining innocent citizens incommunicado indefinitely!"

The surplanetary transceiver on her desk buzzed for her attention. The Colonel listened for a couple of minutes, then thanked the caller on the other end.

She carefully deactivated it again and turned to those crowding her office. "That was the lab," she reported somberly. "Your evidence seems to be the real thing, Doctor Cofort."

"Bone?"

She nodded. "Human, not long dead, and every part of it is scratched and scored, as if by the action of numerous small, very sharp teeth."

10

"Not to tell you your business, Colonel," Van Rycke said after an instant of grim silence, "but it might be advisable to pay that alley a visit real soon."

"This very night, Mr. Van Rycke. All of us." She nodded when his brows rose. "I'm deputizing you six. My command's limited in number, and I'll need the others elsewhere. — Keil, get us a leg of rambeef, a fine big one with a long length of exposed bone."

Thorson frowned. "Will it work, Colonel Cohn? They've killed recently, apparently. No matter how nameless their victims, they'd still give themselves away if they did it too frequently. If the rodents are caged . . ."

"We'll give it a try. I'm putting credits down that the fall of a relatively heavy object on or near that step is the signal that calls them. If they respond in sufficient number, we've got a good part of our case. If they don't, all we've lost is a nice piece of meat. We're raiding those swill joints anyway, and the erotic houses as well. If the port rats are there, we'll find them. If we're extremely lucky, we may pick up some documentation as well, but I'm not counting on that."

"You'll be able to get warrants so quickly?" Rael asked in surprise. "With so little evidence of any sort?"

"We don't need any. Such niceties don't apply to Happy City and its sister pleasure districts."

She saw the spacers' frowns and shrugged. "The Canuchean government doesn't approve of what goes on there. The lawmakers were wise enough to realize that an attempt to bar such activities outright would only result in driving them underground and open the way for a lot more besides. By confining the questionable industries to fixed areas, they can keep control over what does occur.

"Those who work in a pleasure district can, and often do, reap large profits, but they all must sign waivers accepting unannounced and possibly frequent searches of their businesses and residences, which also must be located within the district.

"Actually, not many complain. Most stay only a few years, make their pile, and run, and the legitimate concerns do recognize that the policy helps keep some less scrupulous folk relatively honest. The sale of raklick, crax, and a half dozen other similar poisons, the abuse of minors, grossly rigged gaming, plus all the violence that goes with them would be rampant without strong, unremitting control, to the point that a large part of the current clientele would be frightened off. Needless to say, there's always some of that going on, but it's at least kept in check, especially with the stiff penalties handed out for engaging in any of it."

"None of that's really Patrol work," Van Rycke pointed out. The interstellar force was on Canuche of Halio, one of this part of the Sector's better-developed planets, as a check against smuggling and to provide assistance to any ships coming into difficulty in the nearby starlanes. They should not have a great deal to do with basically surplanetary affairs.

"No," she agreed, "apart from watching for attempts to import controlled substances. The local police normally take care of Happy City, though we're legally empowered to do so as well. We'll prowl around in a slack period to see that visiting space hounds don't get into or cause trouble, but that's about the usual extent of our on-world activities. We step in when we're asked, of course, or if we happen to spot something that looks amiss. Otherwise, we leave Canuchean business to the Canucheans."

Halio was well set by the time the flier left headquarters. Rael Cofort was in the backseat, jammed between Jellico and Thorson. Colonel Cohn and Yeoman Keil Roberts were in the front, the latter at the controls. Their comrades had left some minutes earlier under the Sergeant's command, also in a civilian-type machine, to approach from a different direction. Those who would move in on the swill joints and erotic houses themselves were either already in place or would be so shortly. The spacers had seen none of them.

The others were waiting for them, concealed by the deep shadows, when the flier reached its destination a few minutes later. Their vehicle had merely dropped them off a couple of blocks back and returned to headquarters.

Keil frowned. The alley behind all four of the suspect drinking establishments was in total darkness. "We have them on lighting violations anyway," he said in an almost soundless whisper to his commander.

Cohn nodded absently as she and her companions in the rear slipped from the flier. She could see a little, thanks to the weak illumination provided by the erotic houses farther in. The fences were extended along the whole of the passageway, all save those that should divide the space of each of the suspect buildings from that of the others. So. Whatever was going on here, and she could not doubt that something fairly extraordinary was, the swill joints were indeed in partnership, or at least actively cooperating with one another.

Music filled the air, blaring from every establishment, drowning out the more readily confined babble of voices.

Nothing moved out here. It was too early yet for the first loads of refuse to be dragged outside for morning pickup and far too soon for drunks to be seeking air or to unload the contents of their abused stomachs. Certainly, she could see no small, moving, furry things . . .

"All right, Mr. Thorson," she whispered, handing him the twenty-two-pound rambeef leg she had been guarding. "You look like you've got the strongest arm among our junior members, not to mention the greatest height by an inch or two. Hop up that fence and give this a good toss inside."

"No!"

She glanced sharply at the Cargo-Master. "Mr. Van Rycke?"

"Look at that fence!"

The Patrol officer's mouth hardened as she realized what he meant. "Thank you, Mr. Van Rycke," she said quietly. "I'm sorry, Mr. Thorson. I don't know how much of a charge that thing carries, but if you had been injured or worse, the guilt would've been mine. — Whatever about Doctor Cofort's theory, these sons of Scythian apes are involved in some strange business, and it's neither clean nor small."

She glanced at their vehicle. "Keil, bring the flier over here. He can throw it from the hood."

"I could just fly over and drop it," the Yeoman suggested.

"No. We'd be begging to be seen. Keep outside the fence. We're taking enough of a chance as it is. Nothing vanishes faster than solid evidence."

The machine's body might be that of any civilian craft of the same general type, but its innards were all service standard. It started and moved with barely a whisper, hardly sufficient sound for them to catch although they were instinctively straining to detect the slightest noise. It would not give them away unless someone actually came or looked outside, and if that happened, they were betrayed anyway.

Jellico tensed as if for battle as Dane scrambled onto the rounded hood. The vehicle rose smoothly until it was level with the top of the wall, then hovered there. Thorson cautiously rose to his knees, his spacer's balance holding him in place as he prepared to make his cast.

Míceál glanced at the woman beside him. Rael Cofort was standing straight and perfectly still. She seemed utterly alone in this moment of testing, and as he had done in the Patrol-Colonel's office, he placed his hand on her shoulder, this time only one hand. The other grasped the hilt of his blaster.

He could feel the tension in her. In the next few seconds, her story might or might not be verified. That in itself was enough to draw the nerves taut, and if it did prove out, they could conceivably find themselves facing the same dire peril that had claimed the owner of that pitiful scrap of gnawed bone and an uncounted number of others before him. She had to be afraid, she who had the power to envision all this. The rest of them were.

No, he thought, he wronged the Medic in that, or wronged her in good part. He had learned something of her by that time. Rael was certain in her own mind of the accuracy of her deductions and had the imagination to appreciate very clearly the potential consequences of forcing this confrontation, but she was also thinking of the victims who had been taken in the trap they were trying to break and of those who would follow if she failed to prove her case tonight.

Dane made his throw. There was a sharp crack as the big bone protruding from the meat struck the pavement beside the step.

Jellico slowly drew his weapon. Like those of the others, it was set at broad beam to slay to provide the greatest possible defense. He glanced once more at Rael and nodded in satisfaction. She, too, had her weapon at ready in her hand.

Determination hardened in him. If the worst happened, if they found themselves facing the horde they had come to detect and could then not fight their way free, he would see to it that this woman met a clean death and then give that same grace to as many more of his companions as he could before being brought down himself. That responsibility, too, lay upon a starship Captain . . .

For several interminable seconds, there was no response, then an irregular stain of deeper darkness flowed, flooded, out from the base of the building. A chittering squeal, as if issuing simultaneously from a hundred thousand small throats, accompanied the charge. In the next moment, the bait was covered.

"Let's have the beams," Ursula commanded in a tone hushed as much by horror as by the need to conceal their presence.

The flier's lights might have penetrated the Federation's worst hell. There before them was a mouse-brown sea of writhing, struggling bodies, all snarling and fighting to reach the impossibly inadequate bounty that had summoned them.

A myriad on the outer fringes turned to face the intruders, fixing them with baleful, red-reflecting eyes, cruel fangs exposed in a desire that needed no common tongue to translate.

The outermost rodents came for the humans but stopped again as if at a wall a couple of inches from the fence. There they remained, stymied, access to the rambeef denied by the mass of their fellows, frustrated in their hunger to claim the greater feast beyond by the well-known power of the fence.

"That explains why it's electrified," Cohn muttered.

She brought the transceiver clutched in her left hand to her lips. "The rats are here," she said tersely to the raiders awaiting her order. "Go on, but in the name of all we revere, be careful when you hit the cellars. These things came out of there. They may go back in, and there might be still more of them waiting down there."

11

The crew of the *Solar Queen* crowded into the mess the following morning to hear their Captain's summary of the report he had just received from Ursula Cohn.

"... The Patrol got everything they needed—records and live rats, four-legged and plenty of the biped variety just begging to sing in order to save their own hides, if only to spend the remainder of their days in the galactic pen.

"It was as nasty an operation as I've ever heard described. There's a lot of gem mining on Canuche, apparently, mostly mid-quality amethysts and garnets with an occasional small sunstone thrown in to keep the prospectors dreaming. Everything's minor scale, one or two guys roaming around the mineral country and leasing claims for a couple of years, then coming in with the take. No one ever gets enough to make a larger or more complex operation economically feasible, but the total is a welcome addition to the stocks of the local gem merchants, even without the odd sunstone. The stones facet nicely and can be priced low enough to be readily affordable by the bulk of the laboring people, who form a steady market for them."

"Maybe we should keep that in mind and bring a small stock of semiprecious material back with us if we plan a return visit," Van Rycke said half to himself. "But go on, Míceál. What do a few not particularly exciting gemstones have to do with murder by rat?"

"They can't be eaten," he responded grimly. The Captain marshaled his thoughts. "The prospectors fall into two general types. The most common are those who work at it for a few years, then take the money and use it to complete their education, stake a business start, or finance a trading venture or some personal dream. The rest are the perpetual drifters, not much different from their counterparts throughout the Federation, marginal folk, many of them in their middle years or older, forever talking of striking a big pocket of sunstones and retiring in luxury but lacking any real purpose or concrete ambition. Some eventually do save a good bit, enough for them to finally leave the work comfortably fixed, but most're content to mine their claims until their leases expire, sell off the rights, and use most of the credits to pick up another, then blow the better part of whatever remains on a week-long fling in Happy City or one of the other pleasure districts."

"The prospectors were the targets?" Jasper Weeks inquired.

The Captain nodded. "The drifters, chiefly. The others have plans for their gains and aren't about to spend or lose much on a binge. If they show up in Happy City at all, it's with a very small squandering purse.

"Most of the others aren't vacuum-brains, either. They don't want to get back-alleyed for flashing a big roll after they've been sampling the local wares for a while. They make sure they've secured a new lease and have whatever stones or credits they want to keep banked somewhere safe before they start to party.

"There are always the few, though, who insist on a couple of drinks or a smoke at once, as soon as they get their hands on some credits, much to the joy of the unscrupulous. It goes without saying that they usually wind up voluntarily tossing away or being relieved of everything they have on them, whatever their original intentions.

"About twelve years ago, the proprietor of the Red Garnet began to cast about for ways to capitalize on that particular source of income. First off, he assigned employees to try to sniff out vulnerable prospectors at the leasing office or, failing to carry them off there, to trail them to another establishment and lure them back to the Garnet.

"The next problem was to keep them there long enough for them to hand over whatever credits they had. According to Colonel Cohn, most Canucheans want to sample the full spectrum of a pleasure district when they visit one, move from one place to another, stretch out their fun as much as possible. To counter that tendency, he brought his neighbors in on his plan. He knew he would have to do so anyway if he was going to carry it to fruition. They were already in partnership for importing and distributing controlled substances and rigging gambling, so he knew he'd have no trouble convincing or working with them. He kept full control of the operation from the start and gradually introduced its grosser aspects.

"He realized from the outset, of course, that even with gaming he had few legitimate or semilegitimate means of getting at the stones his victims might be carrying, which in most cases form the principal part of a prospector's hoard. It's not permitted to accept them as payment for any goods or services in Happy City, and the police keep the district crawling with spotters to catch any violations of that rule."

"Drunks can be back-alleyed," Shannon pointed out.

"Only so many before the authorities begin to establish a pattern. However, if the victims can be made to vanish quickly, quietly, and completely, the operation could conceivably go on indefinitely as long as the conspirators don't get too greedy or overconfident and move too often or without proper care."

"Twelve years?" Dane whispered.

"Very nearly."

"The rats?"

"They were in it almost from the start," he averred. "The whole cellar of the Red Garnet was given over to them. They were closely caged but had free access via ramps to the alley, having been trained early to avoid the barrier of the fences. Similar guards defended the rest of the building and the other conspirators' places. They were always well enough fed to keep them willing to remain and accept the confinement. The only times feeding was cut back were the two periods each year when leases came due and prospectors were in town in number."

Craig was frowning. "That's still an awful lot of people in on a very black secret. The bosses I accept, but all those underlings? For that span of time?"

"Control was no problem," Jellico told him grimly, "not with raklick and a couple of the old opiates to tighten the leash, and if anyone seemed likely to rebel after learning a bit too much, well, the rats would have full bellies that night.

"It looks like only the four swill joints were involved, by the way. The erotic houses both appear to be clean."

He eyed Rael somberly. "You'll get a Patrol commendation for your part in this and maybe one from Trade as well. Those rumors of spacers vanishing now and then in Happy City have taken on a new significance in the last several hours." Particularly for Jan Van Rycke, he thought grimly. An old Pool comrade of his, a loner, never very successful, had been among those thought to have disappeared in that wretched hole.

She shuddered. "I'll be content if it's just all over."

"Everything but the trials and executions," he assured her.

"One question, Rael," Rip Shannon put in. "Would you have been so quick to go to the Patrol if those two agents hadn't cornered us?"

The Medic looked surprised. "Naturally. I had to report my suspicions to someone. Surplanetary police are usually all right, but an off-worlder can never be sure in a situation like this. On the other hand, corruption's almost nonexistent in the Stellar Patrol, and some of its agents know how

97

to think. Besides," she concluded practically, "Teague says it doesn't hurt any ship to gain the reputation of cooperating with them, as long as she doesn't play the fool about it, that is."

"I wonder if you'd be speaking in such glowing terms about the folks in black and silver if you'd shared our recent experience with them," Ali observed lazily.

"They were only doing their job! Those Company sons who framed you should've been sent to the Lunar mines for attempted murder, but to the Patrol, you were suspected pestilence carriers. They had no choice but to act strongly against you."

"Very magnanimous of you," Kamil commented with the same sleepy sarcasm, "especially when you can do your judging after the fact from a nice, safe distance."

Rael placed her hands palm down on the table. She fixed her attention on them. "It's true that I've never had to go through what you did, but I was part of the real thing."

Her eyes rose once more to briefly meet his before dropping again. Their expression was as somber as the memories she was recalling. "I was still a child at the time. Father had planeted on a pre-mech world and was treating with the inhabitants of one of her chief trading centers when we discovered that some sort of sickness had broken out in the community, in the very section where we were operating, and was slowly but steadily gaining ominous force. We'd been on-world for several days at that point, in daily contact with the inhabitants of the infected region, and our Medic could make no more headway against the disease than could his primitive counterparts. Only one course of action was possible for us, and we took it, even as other spacers trapped in similar situations have in the past. We couldn't risk carrying an unidentified and as yet incurable, highly contagious, deadly illness back with us into space, so we chose to stay where we were. We couldn't even remove ourselves from the stricken city for fear of bringing the infection to uncontaminated areas of the planet."

Her fingers whitened where they met the table. "Whatever our fears at that stage, they paled before the reality that followed. About three hundred thousand people lived and worked in that community when we arrived. Ten months later, one hundred thousand of them were dead, more than eight thousand in a single, awful week. Seven of our crew, including my father, were among them.

"So was our Medic, but he had identified the causative organism, and before he died he gave those people both a cure and a vaccine that stopped the plague as if it had hit a high security wall. The on-worlders realized what we had done for them and recognized that we had chosen both to remain and to work among them despite the proven danger to ourselves. They were grateful, and when Teague took our survivors off-world, it was with the means to buy a fine new ship outright, re-crew with top-rate hands, and fill the holds with prime trade stock."

Her eyes suddenly locked with Kamil's, then moved to fix each of her shipmates sitting or standing opposite her. "That fact neither softened the horror of those ten months nor clouded the memory of it, no more than any on-worlder living through that time is likely to forget it. The dying and the sickness itself were only part of it. The misery and want were everywhere, the fear, the ever-growing, crushing despair, and with all that, too much, far too much human-nastiness. I was young and a stranger, but even I was aware of rampant filth and evil.

"Never, ever, can a similar scourge be permitted to strike any planet, not while the power or the possibility of preventing it exists. That need holds true and must hold despite the danger of occasionally serving individuals or starships with the gravest injustice."

"I don't think any of us will argue that, Doctor," Míceál Jellico said quietly after several seconds of grim silence. "If our lads had believed us to be plague-stricken in fact, the *Solar Queen* would've met her end in a star's heart. Spirit of Space! Had I imagined them capable of any other course, that's where I would've sent the *Queen* myself before I passed out."

Rael smiled. "I know. If I'd doubted that, I'd never have come on board at all."

Jellico shook his head as he watched the woman leave the cabin several minutes later. She would have been young, he thought, probably not much more than eleven, when she had gone through that plague. It would have been a hard experience at any age and explained both her basic gravity and her fascination with mass illness and other disaster situations.

That was no condemnation of her. Every human being reaching adulthood had his defenses and his own way of viewing the universe around him. Those who experienced massive trauma, physical or mental, and who were not shattered by it had made some pretty powerful adaptations to accommodate it, especially when it had been suffered in their vulnerable formative years. The awesome slaughter of the Crater War had shredded Ali's childhood. Somehow, he had lived through that carnage, but it had left him one of life's observers. He would allow nothing to penetrate the armor he had carefully constructed around himself. Rael Cofort had been somewhat older and the deadly situation in which she found herself had been of considerably shorter duration, but even so, she, too, had her facade and her scars . . .

He saw the Cargo-Master start to push out into the corridor. "Van, hold up."

The other waited for him and fell into step beside him. "Quite a story," he remarked.

"Aye."

"You believe it?" Van Rycke asked. "She never mentioned a ship's name or a planet's."

"That can all be checked. The timing'd be right. Cofort appeared as a force on the scene suddenly and very young out of a spacer clan who should never under normal circumstances have been able to finance the setup he created for himself." The rest of his history, of course, was the result of a lot of luck and even more hard work and shrewd dealing, but that early start had often been a source of speculation among the ranks of the Free Traders.

Jellico shrugged, dismissing the question for the time being. "It's Rael herself who interests me at the moment. You and Thorson'll be checking out the market soon. Take her with you and give her as free a hand as seems prudent. I want to see what she can do."

"Her brother never or only rarely used her in that capacity," Van Rycke reminded him doubtfully. "From what I

saw, she'd choose the goods, but Cofort would trade for
them."

"Put it to the test anyway."

Van gave him a curious look. "Why bother?"

He shrugged. "A xenobiologist looking for more data,
maybe. Cofort's a puzzle however you try to look at her."
His eyes narrowed. "You and I're both old foxes, but given
all the information she had, would you have reached the
same conclusion or come to it as quickly as she did?"

"Not in a star's life span," he admitted.

"That kind of deductive power might prove very handy
to a Free Trader—if she can use it for more mundane
purposes than uncovering bizarre murder plots."

"It wouldn't do to make a career of that," his companion
agreed dryly.

"Not unless one was straight Whisperer bait or planning
to ally himself permanently with the Patrol, which would
amount to the same thing."

"You don't believe Rael Cofort's thinking along those
lines?" the Cargo-Master asked.

"Who knows what that woman's thinking?" he responded wearily.

Van Rycke eyed him closely. "Craig mentioned that you
had some serious reservations about her."

Jellico smiled. "I still do, but at least I think I know now
why Cofort dumped her."

Jan's pale brows rose. "That's more than I can claim."

"Some perfectly capable people draw trouble. I believe
Doctor Cofort is a prime example."

"A jinx?"

Míceál gave a short laugh. "Does the Cofort operation

show much sign of any such influence? — No, but Rael appears to have an overdeveloped sense of what's right, or maybe the sight of the downtrodden just sparks a powerful protective response in her. Whatever the cause, the result can be pure headache for her Captain and shipmates, if not outright disaster.

"Look at her behavior in that alley, Van. The starlight was scared out of her, but she was all set to march in for that scrap of bone and then blast off to the Stellar Patrol at warp speed. She never gave a thought to our strained relations with that organization or a Trader's natural instinct to navigate clear of all brass as much as possible. Add to that the fact that she's admitted to dragging her brother into more than one scrape he'd have preferred to duck and you have the makings of a problem of no mean magnitude."

"Why court trouble ourselves? We'll be rid of her soon."

"Curiosity mostly," the other responded. "Besides, she's tied to us until we're ready to lift anyway. I'd like to see if she's any good in real Trade. The *Queen* might as well reap some benefit if she is."

"All right, I'll give her a shot at the market," the Cargo-Master promised willingly enough. "Come with us yourself. She'll know she's under observation anyway, and it'll be late enough now by the time we're ready to go that some of the big industrialists might be scouting around there. I understand they usually do when a new ship comes into port, and several have this past week. We could possibly pick up a charter."

Jellico nodded. "I'll do that," he said. "I'd intended waiting a bit longer before giving it a walk-through, but it won't hurt and might help to look the place over at once."

12

Ali Kamil quickened his pace until he came up beside Rael. "I'm sorry," he told her quietly. "I was navigating right off the charts in there."

"So was I," she replied bitterly. "Firing off my mouth like that was inexcusable. I knew what you all had been through."

"It was no more than you had."

He frowned and stepped aside to allow Dane and Rip to pass. Sometimes, he thought sourly, finding a place to have a private conversation aboard a starship was about as easy as netting an asteroid made of pure platinum, at least for lowly apprentices lacking the luxury of a private office or work cabin.

The Medic sensed that something more was weighing on him, but Kamil was the last person to broach it in the busy corridor. "I want to check on some seedlings," she said. "You could lift out the germination trays for me if you've got the time and don't mind."

"I'm happy to assist, Doctor Cofort."

Rael breathed deeply of the rich air in the hydro. It was her favorite place here, even as the one on the *Roving Star* had been when she had been serving under her brother's command. All it needed was some lavender . . .

The Engineer-apprentice walked over to the tall bank of germination trays. "Which one?" he inquired.

"The top two. You've got enough inches on me that we won't have to get out the ladder."

It took only a few seconds to carefully remove the trays and set them on the nearby work bench.

He peered at the closely spaced, neat rows of minute plants, each of which bore two leaves. "What are they?" he asked curiously. "There are a couple of different kinds, I think, though it's hard to be sure. They're so small."

"Most just put their heads up this morning, the others yesterday afternoon. They won't be readily identifiable for a while yet. — One box contains tarragon, the other gray pepper. Mr. Mura wants them for the galley. He'll be trying some new spices as well for more variety."

"That's always welcome."

Both fell silent while Rael checked the moisture and nutrient content of the growth medium and examined the seedlings themselves. The time to catch trouble was early, at the first sign, before it could develop into a full-blown problem that might sweep the whole little crop.

At last she stood up. "All our infants are doing well," she announced. "You may return them to their cradles, Mr. Kamil."

The man complied. When he was finished, he leaned back against the bank and studied her speculatively. "How is it that you're so good at everything, Doctor. Or so many things?" he amended. His own chief did not sing her praises the way Tau and Mura did, but then Johan Stotz rarely praised anyone. Just keeping one's position without having one's head verbally removed on a daily basis was compliment enough coming from him.

"I just sort of picked things up along the way. I was interested, of course, and I wanted to be of real use and not just so much inert cargo until I finally managed to officially qualify for something."

"Ah, yes. You were raised and trained in the comforting bosom of your clan."

"I was lucky," she agreed seriously, "especially since I love Trade." Her face clouded suddenly. "But, Ali, I've never been on my own, never once had the chance to see if I could pull it by myself. I was never even physically at Training Pool. All my classes, even my medical courses, were taped, with clinical experience gained at accredited hospitals wherever we planeted."

The apprentice gave her a sharp look. "That's allowed?"

"Aye, of course. The ongoing testing is stringent, with a ten percent higher grade required for passing."

"Which I presume was never a problem."

"No, not really. Don't forget, I had a shipload of captive tutors all eager to help out."

"What about the Psycho?"

"I never asked for a ship assignment since I was staying with my own clan, but classification was compulsory, of course. — Free Trader all the way."

"Not even a shot at the Companies?" he teased.

Rael laughed. "I wouldn't last twenty-four hours on a Company ship!"

Her expression darkened again, not pleasantly. "I didn't manage so marvelously on the *Mermaid*, did I?"

"You cut your losses and ran, which was as much as anyone could have done under the circumstances." His voice softened. She had not concealed that her failure to secure the berth cut her. "You'll make out. You know Trade work and don't mind doing it."

It was a new role for Kamil, offering comfort and support. He stopped speaking for a moment, not quite knowing where else to go with it.

Unless . . . Cofort had picked up on that incredible murder plot.

"Doctor," he said suddenly, before he could give himself a chance to back down, "can you keep your mouth shut?"

"I'm a Medic. That comes with the job. — I don't expect you to fasmit our recent conversation to the universe at large, either, you know."

"I won't." He eyed her gravely. "What do you think of Canuche of Halio?"

"I detest her," the woman replied in complete surprise. "I like gloriously wild planets or else beautifully civilized ones with powerful conservation and anticruelty laws, all full of furry, feathered, and scaled creatures, not malodorous chemical stews."

"Maybe there's a galaxy more wrong with Canuche than that."

Rael Cofort's eyes narrowed. "What do you mean, Ali?" she asked quietly. She had never seen him deadly serious before, but he was now with that softly voiced suggestion.

The Engineer-apprentice did not respond for almost a full minute. "Maybe I don't know," he said at the end of that time. "I just don't want to wind up in the clutches of the psychomedics as straight Whisperer bait or worse."

"I'm no psychomedic, and I have been around the starlanes long enough to be aware of some pretty odd things, odd enough not to dismiss an unlikely-sounding theory outright."

Kamil turned away from her. "A number of people have wondered how I managed to survive the Crater War given the fact that I'd only just started school when our community got hit."

When she made no answer, he steeled himself and went on. "I woke up that night, a bit after midnight, terrified, in a cold-sweat panic. If I'd been older, better able to think, I'd have awakened my parents, but that would've ended me. I'd have been soothed, put back to bed, and been blown to bits with the rest. As it was, I simply ran. The fire ladder was outside my window. I went down it, took to my heels, and so great was my fear that I kept going until I was outside the town limits before it eased up enough to let exhaustion take over. By that time, the bombs were already falling. I was the sole survivor out of thirty thousand and some odd people.

"No one discovered that for some time to come. I was usually hungry and always cold, but I scrounged enough to get by and spent most of my time in hiding for the next couple of years. Something inside me told me to keep away from people. They'd try to help, maybe, but they'd stop me from running if I had to get out fast again.

"I did, too, twice more from air raids and twice from those butchering . . . When they advanced through our area and when they were being whipped back at last.

"After that, things got quieter. There were still dangers to be faced, but they weren't on the same scale, and I'd learned to look out for those on my own. I didn't get the same kind of warning against them."

Ali began pacing, as if the act of movement helped him to clarify his thoughts. "When I reached puberty, something else started, and that's continued. Whenever I come onto a site where something really bad or some enormous tragedy occurred, no matter how far back, I feel this great weight, this sorrow, settle, not on my shoulders, my body, but on my spirit, my soul as it were. I didn't feel it in that alley—it's got to have a bigger scope than that, I think—but I felt it where the *Heaven's Hope* crashed, killing all those people. I felt it in the ruins on Limbo and in the Big Burn on Terra, though I made damn sure I kept quiet about it. Besides, we were in too much trouble of our own at the time to be worrying about the problems of the past."

He risked a look at the Medic. She was standing spear straight, her attention fixed on him as if by compulsion.

The woman drew a deep breath. "You sense the same about Canuche?"

Kamil gave her a grim, bleak smile. "Doctor, I have to

13

It took time to shake the chill Ali's dark prediction had put on her, but Canuche Town's huge outdoor market proved to be an effective antidote. Rael Cofort's eyes were bright as she surveyed the long aisles of booths and less permanent stands and open tables filled with items being offered for sale or exchange. The capital boasted enclosed facilities as well, of course, but those were not designed to draw small Free Traders seeking to supply themselves for a venture among the primitive planets and struggling colonies of the rim.

There was more than enough out here to meet their needs and give delight. She loved prowling around a big market, and this time she was going to be allowed to do some buying for stock, albeit under discreet but definite supervision.

She would look over the gems, certainly, she decided at once, but so much else was available that she resolved to do a quick inspection to see precisely just what was being shown. The mix of goods here had never been the same on any visit she had made to Canuche of Halio. She smiled again. Besides, it was fun to look.

Canuche was a thoroughly civilized industrial planet, and so the din, the intriguing, not always entirely pleasant odors, the basic strangeness of an alien or primitive mart were missing here, but it was an interesting place for all that.

Findings and setters were settled beside the long rows of loose gems, and next to them stood the stands of those selling finished jewelry. Fabrics and the trimmings, tools, and machines required to turn them into completed products were in another area along with clothing. Food supplies and the equipment to prepare them formed yet another section, and large industrial products, chiefly represented by salespeople supplied with illustrative samples, tapes, and literature, formed a major portion of the complex. Only the prepared food stalls broke the pattern of grouping like with like. They were scattered throughout the huge field so that patrons would not be forced to leave their areas of interest to find refreshment.

Rael drew in and held a deep breath. The aroma of cooking was everywhere, wonderfully tempting although she had eaten only half an hour before. She wondered how Dane Thorson was responding to those beckoning fingers of scent. He could stow food as if he had cargo holds in both of his legs, and this stuff was real. That alone made even the worst of it infinitely desirable to a space hound.

"Let's cut past the cloth booths," she suggested since the lead had been given to her. She had no interest in the finished clothing; Van Rycke already had a full stock of such goods. The fabrics were another matter. Brocades and faux gold and silver cloth rarely failed to interest the wealthier classes and individuals among primitive buyers, and good quality, attractive material could be counted upon to attract attention and customers on most Federation planets, especially when it was blessed with the added allure of being an import. The *Queen* already had a good supply, but Canuche's market had been particularly good for textiles on each of her previous visits, and they might well run across something. There were other freighters in port, and some of them might be trying to sell off part of such a cargo.

"Rael! Rael Cofort!"

The woman turned quickly. "Deke!" Her voice dropped. "Deke Tatarcoff of the *Black Hole*," she explained to her companions. "He's been a rival and a damn good friend of Teague's for years. Do you mind . . ."

"Space, no!" Jellico told her. "A Free Trader does not ignore his friends or fail to make the acquaintance of a potential ally." He also did not neglect an opportunity to size up potential competition.

The *Solar Queen* party walked over to the covered stand the other spacer had rented to display his wares.

Míceál studied the other Trader. Tatarcoff was short and stocky with a breadth of chest that bespoke some Martian ancestry. His eyes were brown, sharp and steady in their expression. His features were pleasant but well schooled; they would betray little he did not want to have read.

He was doing well, the *Solar Queen*'s Captain judged by the quality of his uniform and accoutrements and by the thick, three-inch-wide gold luck band circling his left wrist. Just the fact that he had rented an enclosed stall, and a large one at that, was evidence of prosperity.

"What's Trade's brightest star doing on Canuche?" Tatarcoff asked when they were in comfortable speaking range.

She laughed. "Put it on freeze, Deke," she told him. "I'm on my own. The *Roving Star*'s not here. I'm serving with the *Solar Queen*. — This is Jellico, Van Rycke, and Thorson, Captain, Cargo-Master, and Cargo-apprentice respectively."

Even as the introductions were being made, Rael was studying the Trader's stock. It was mostly amotton, she observed, nicely woven in a variety of pastel solids and stripes well suited to the extremely light fabric.

"You folks interested?" Deke inquired. "I'll make you a good deal."

She shook her head. "Sorry, Deke. We've got all we need. This is lovely, though. It'll move well here."

Well and quickly, she judged. The fabric, a natural fiber from Amon, breathed like a second skin and felt as if it had no weight at all. Those were highly desirable characteristics on a world with summers as blisteringly hot as most of Canuche of Halio had to endure. These bolts were sure to catch the eye of the big garment manufacturers. In point of fact, she was more than certain that a few of their reps were even now evaluating Deke's store from a discreet distance.

Her eyes drifted over the carefully stacked bolts at the rear of the stand. She fixed suddenly on a patch of intense blue. "Oh," she breathed unconsciously in pure delight.

Tatarcoff looked at what had caught her attention and smiled. "Leave it to you to spot that. It's worthy of you, too," he added as he fetched down the examination length for her party to see. "It suits you considerably better than it probably will whoever finally takes it."

She nodded her thanks. That was a compliment and a statement of the fabric's value, not a sales lure. Tatarcoff knew that no Free Trader could afford the likes of this, not for personal use. Even her brother could not have justified that expense.

Rael found herself gazing down at an incredible, seemingly infinite mingling of blues and blue-violets in a shimmering field as soft as a cloud might seem to be in a dream of wonder. "Thornen silk?"

"Aye. One of my tubes gave out, and I had to planet there. I managed to pick this up in exchange for the finest sunstone I've ever seen come honestly on a rim market." There was no regret in his tone. He would make that expense good twice over when he did sell the bolt. It was breathtakingly beautiful, and it was rare.

Thorne of Brandine had given rise to a highly advanced human population independently of Terran seeding. Their planet-wide society had been pre-space when discovered and was still basically anti-mech, but it was complex, well developed, and heavily oriented toward their version of Trade. As befitted such a populace, they were ruled by a network of hereditary merchant princes owing ultimate allegiance to an official they called the Doge.

They also had very little liking for the presence of off-worlders and less still for alien ways. They permitted the existence of a full spaceport to serve as a refuge for ships coming into trouble in the nearby starlanes, but they had only minimal intercourse with spacers, visitors or those running the complex. The planet was completely self-sufficient and preferred to remain so.

The rulers had a good eye for business, that notwithstanding, and they fully appreciated the value of their luxury goods, particularly their textiles. They would permit no steady trade that might grow too important, too essential to their economy, but they made occasional sales to keep Federation markets aware of their products and hungry for them. Always, they worked with individual Free Traders rather than Company ships and absolutely refused to accept any off-world agreements that would limit their choice of markets. Because their decision whether to trade among the stars or sell to their own kind was completely free and because their products were so eminently desirable, they had the power to dictate their will in the matter.

Neither Deke nor any other independent freighter Captain complained about that even if it did mean that the surplanetary merchants held a fully charged blaster in their dealings with off-worlders. Without that liberty of action, no Free Trader would ever get a crack at any of those prize cargoes. The Companies would have Thorne of Brandine locked in tighter than any space seal.

The woman sighed with regret as Tatarcoff started to fold the length again. She stole a glance at Van Rycke and saw the same hunger on him. He, too, longed to have the beautiful cloth and had no love for the reason that decreed that the *Queen* could not afford to sink that much capital into what was in actuality a single item, one that, given their current plans, would be singularly hard for them to place if they did acquire it.

"Good fortune with it, Deke," she said sincerely, "though I think you'll be sorry to see it go. I know I would be."

"So I shall," he admitted. "It won't be for a while, at least. This won't move until I planet on Hedon again. I'm not letting it go for less than it's worth."

Van Rycke's brow raised. "There're credits enough right here. Any of the major industrialists could take that bolt."

"They could, but they won't, not that lot. — You've never been on Canuche before?"

"No. The *Queen*'s pretty much new to this Sector apart from the Trewsworld-Riginni mail run."

"Well, the veeps here aren't old money or flying on school prestige and secondhand knowledge. Nearly every one of them came up through the ranks in his particular industry or via the prospector's route. They're capable, tough, and, since they've earned them the hard way, they appreciate the value of their credits. They may like luxury and its brag value as much as the next one, but reason rules, and it'd just about take a supernova on their office desks to get them to step beyond its bounds for an extravagant toy like this."

Rael's fingers caressed the silk. She glanced over her shoulder. The market had grown more crowded in the short time they had been at the stand, but many of the same people she had noticed earlier were still studying it. Most were laborers or the owners or representatives of small businesses looking for a length of material or a few lengths at most, but several had that air of importance every Trader comes to recognize, be it in a tribal chieftain, government official, military officer, or industrial tycoon or manager. Those individuals had the power and means to buy and buy big. "Deke," she asked softly, "will you trust me with this?"

"Aye," he responded, surprised.

"Let me play with it a while."

"Have at it."

"How long is it?"

"Three yards."

"Perfect." The size of a major veil. Her plan would work if she knew anything at all of human nature.

The Medic straightened. Her rib cage arched slowly, with infinite precision, as each muscle of her body obeyed the command of her will. The motion was subtle, seemingly almost nonexistent and certainly indefinable to anyone trying to classify or describe its individual components, but the close-fitting uniform shimmered sensuously even as her bones appeared to dissolve in a rippling swaying, as if in response to the light motion of the air.

As her body followed the strange rhythm directing its movements, her fingers closed on either end of the silk panel, and in that instant, it swept, wafted, into the air.

Up it swirled, glistening in the glory of Halio's light, held a breath's space on high, and swooped down again to envelop the woman as she slowly turned with it.

Again, the Thornen veil swept out. It seemed no independent thing but rather part of she who controlled it, even as together they appeared to be an exquisite extension of the light and air in which they flowed.

Míceál Jellico tore his eyes away from the apparition to study those around them. Van Rycke, too, had recalled himself to the world of the market, but the others were fully ensorcelled. Rael's performance was so unexpected in a place like this and so perfectly executed, the material so marvelous in itself, that nearly every eye in the vicinity was riveted on her as if by the command of some irresistible compulsion.

Three times and again a fourth, the veil rose to fill the air, then with a sigh and a lowering of the head as precise and perfect as the vision preceding them, Rael closed it in upon itself and returned it to its owner.

In so doing, she released her captives. Tatarcoff recovered nearly as quickly as the *Queen*'s senior officers and claimed it from her with a proprietary pride. His eyes were on the several individuals making purposefully for his stand.

"I knew you'd approve, Rael," he remarked for his potential customers' benefit.

"It's wonderful. I envy the one with the spirit and credits to buy it," she responded, her voice seemingly low but in actuality pitched to reach those who were approaching. "Fly well, Deke. I hope we'll run into each other again before we lift."

The *Solar Queen* party went some distance before Jellico gave a sharp glance at his temporary hand.

She was laughing softly but stopped and looked up at

him when she felt his gaze. "I love doing that," she explained, "and I so rarely get the chance. Teague doesn't approve."

"Of Ibis dancing?"

She was not surprised the Trader Captain had recognized what she had done. "Of using it or similar techniques to enhance one's goods. He doesn't think it's quite the most respectable way of doing business."

"It was effective," he said, "and you made no false claims. Thornen silk is beautiful. You merely . . ." He paused a moment. "You merely spun it into a dream."

"It's up to Tatarcoff to sell that dream," the Cargo-Master interjected, "though he'd have to have a crater instead of a brain not to do it now. Everyone back there wants it."

"Deke's good," she assured them. "He'll move the silk and probably most or all the rest with it."

"You moved it for him," Dane said, forcing himself to speak naturally. He was embarrassed by the spell Cofort's performance had cast on him. A Trader, particularly part of the Cargo department, had to be able to keep his wits on his surroundings and business.

If the others said anything, now or later, so be it, he thought. He deserved no more after that lapse. In the meantime, walking around as dumb as a lump of inert matter would do no one, especially himself, any good. He was curious about the magic Rael Cofort had wrought—and magic it had been, Trader magic rather than the kind that so intrigued Tau. Van Rycke was one of the best, and he had not seen even him use anything the like of this . . .

"No," the Medic responded slowly. "Thornen silk itself requires no selling. Better simply doesn't exist. That bolt is such a patent extravagance here, though, quintessential luxury beyond anything required for any conceivable occasion on a planet like Canuche of Halio, no matter how formal. It was bound to be admired, but to lift the idea of actually purchasing it out of the realm of insanity, I had to waken the hunger for beauty, the ideal of beauty, that lies buried in every normal human soul."

"You succeeded," Jellico said, an obvious understatement in the face of the number of determined people who had pushed in around Tatarcoff's stand even as his party had left it.

She gave him a sharp look. "There are no objections, I hope?"

"None. We're not competing, not on this run anyway, and if the locals buy from one Free Trader, they'll be more inclined to patronize the rest of us as well." His eyes rested pensively on her. "You were selling more than Deke Tatarcoff's silk back there."

"That's part of the purpose of this excursion, isn't it?" she countered evenly. "I'm supposed to be displaying my skill in handling the various aspects of Trade, am I not?"

"You are. You've shown some strange talents, Rael Cofort. I'm curious to test the extent of them."

"Test away, Captain Jellico," she responded lightly. "I think you won't find me wanting, nor, perhaps, the scope of my abilities so readily fathomed as you seem to imagine, either."

14

The off-worlders paused to examine several more displays but were not tempted to make a purchase until they were nearly ready to quit that part of the market. A metallic glitter on the foremost table of one of the large booths caught Van Rycke's eye. Even from a distance of several feet, he could see that it was a synthetic cloth of silver netting, exquisitely complex and extraordinarily fine.

He touched Dane's arm. "Give that a look over. If it seems worth it, make an offer."

The Cargo-apprentice nodded and stepped briskly toward the booth, taking care to conceal from both the Canuchean merchant and his own companions the considerable trepidation with which he viewed the assignment. True, his chief had been giving him an ever-increasing amount of responsibility, but the transactions he had thus far initiated had been small and straightforward, all of them concerned with minor outfitting of the starship. This was much larger in scope and was for Trade itself. It would also involve real bargaining, or it would if he did not blow it the first time he opened his mouth.

The Canuchean displayed the examination length of the silver netting with a grand flourish, all the while extolling its beauty and virtues as enthusiastically as if it were the genuine article straight out of Siren's far-famed mills.

Once his litany of praise ended, however, he eyed Thorson's brown uniform as if in askance. "We deal chiefly in credits on Canuche," he said doubtfully.

Dane declared that the *Solar Queen* intended to pay by that means. He saw the flash of greed glint in the other's eyes and set himself for battle. Specie or specie credit was always the preferred method of payment on any Federation planet, and the merchant was going to attempt to secure as much as he could.

It was the apprentice's job, on the other hand, to minimize what the *Queen* had to lay out. Straight credits, being more desirable than an exchange of goods or services, were also more valuable. They generally bought more as a result, and Thorson was determined that those entrusted to him should do so. He held to his role as a prospective purchaser interested but by no means overwhelmed by the proffered goods and most assuredly in no desperate need of them. In the end, after much discussion, he succeeded in shaving off an 8 percent discount for the *Queen* and then heaped another 2 percent on top of it as a bulk order bonus for taking all twelve bolts available.

"Not bad at all," Van Rycke gloated when they were out of sight and earshot of the booth. "The youngster's beginning to show a little promise. I don't know if I'd have had the nuggets to demand a bulk discount for a dozen bolts of cloth."

"A nice move," the Captain agreed, "but do we need twelve bolts?"

"It'll sell," Jan assured him. "Some primitive society will go for it, and it's absolutely stellar quality. If that cloth was real silver, we could take it anywhere in the inner systems."

"We still can," Dane interjected. "Those planets tend to enjoy greater wealth and luxury than the outer and rim worlds, but there are plenty of very ordinary people working away on all of them. They can't afford clothes spun out of precious metals, but those conscious of fashion will grab a good synthetic. If we aren't planning a trip in there ourselves in the near future, we'll be encountering ships like the *Black Hole* that are. Any one of them'd be glad to pick up some of this in exchange for goods we'll find more immediately useful."

"I agree," Rael said, "but I don't think you'll have to trade any of it off. You'll sell, and you won't have to leave the outer systems to do it. A dozen bolts wouldn't be anything to a large manufacturer. It could go even faster in individual sales in a fairly big town, much less in a city. Aphrodite comes to mind at once. So does Sultana, which might actually be your best bet if you can swing in that far. The teachers there'd jump at this for use in training, although, of course, they won't bring anything fake into the temples."

"Hera's even closer," Dane suggested. "According to Mara's notes, the priestesses there love glitter. They sew and paste mirrors and all sorts of beads and pieces of metal and strips of lace on their robes. They should go for this like a drowning man for oxygen."

"True enough, and as you so sagely point out, Hera's close by."

Thorson's head lifted in gratification at his chief's ready acceptance of the viability of his suggestion. He did not see the look of pride that accompanied it. That was an extremely obscure bit of information, a one-line margin note jotted down as a reminder on an old reorder list. Van Rycke had not recalled it himself, although he doubtless would have done so before long, and he was pleased that his fledgling, who had obviously been studying the files, had beaten him to it.

With the business of the cloth's potential saleability settled, the Cargo-Master felt at liberty to address another matter whetting his curiosity. His blue eyes flickered in Cofort's direction. "Speaking of Sultana, Doctor, I'm wondering how you've managed to pick up her most cherished art form."

She smiled. "I first saw her Ibis dancers when I was eight years old. It was love at first sight. I'd always detested sports, and even then I thought formal exercise a galactic-class bore, necessary to maintain health and muscle tone, perhaps, but a waste of time, plentiful as that is in space. This beautiful, complex dance was different. I wanted it, and I was determined to learn how to perform it.

"I bought every tape and book my credits would allow and pestered my father for more, then I secretly worked with them, deciphering and copying the moves as best I could. I'd made such progress by the time he finally caught me at it that he sought to arrange for lessons for me the next time we planeted on Sultana, which was a regular port on our trade route. I was good enough that his request was granted."

"He was damned lucky you didn't disappear," Míceál told her bluntly. "Those people worship beauty. You must have had that even then, and you were a dancer, besides."

She shook her head. "To them, I was the ultimate tragedy. I had the talent to dance, but it was stillborn. I had come to it far too late. Sultanites literally begin preliminary training when they're six months old. Their parents start giving them coordination exercises at that age. They encouraged me to continue all the same because they, their teachers, recognized that my love for their art is genuine.

"I'm fully aware of my limitations. I'd never be allowed on any temple floor, much less on an altar, but I don't expect that. I dance for my own pleasure and well-being."

"You can perform for us some day," Van Rycke promised.

Rael flushed scarlet. "You're not a tamed audience! And I know you all . . ."

Jellico laughed, but he draped a surprisingly comforting arm around her shoulders. "Power down, Doctor. Our good Cargo-Master's only running you over the jets. Ibis dancing's potentially too potent a force for disruption to be loosed in the confines of a starship. Rest assured that you'll be allowed to continue exercising to your heart's content in complete privacy."

The four spacers moved into that part of the huge market where the gems and jewelry were sold.

Here the difference between the *Solar Queen* and the *Roving Star,* the chasm between the credits each starship had at her disposal, between the routes they flew, were made clearly apparent. The really good pieces, finished or unset, coming for sale on Canuche of Halio were offered in the major enclosed facilities, not in this open field, yet they could not give the top line of even what was on display of the mounted stones more than a passing glance.

Míceál's expression darkened as he continued to watch the Medic. Inevitably, her eyes went to the best pieces, lingered on the really good ones. She knew they were beyond the means of her party and said nothing, but the way she looked at them was sufficient. It was not hard to imagine her disappointment. Teague Cofort would have gone for those choices. Space, Deke Tatarcoff probably could have picked up a couple or three of them. So could the *Queen,* he thought bitterly. Of course, then they would have nothing left with which to lay in a Trade store . . .

He stopped himself with a mental oath. What was he doing? Was this accursed woman driving him to feel ashamed of his own starship?

*　*　*

Jellico's mood improved again once they left the high-priced jewelry behind and found themselves surrounded by stalls stocking goods within their range.

He had no time for brooding then. The *Solar Queen* had almost no jewelry left, and these mid-line goods, particularly the numerous beads, were of intense interest to her Captain.

Now that she was free to act, Rael Cofort shone. She unerringly seized upon the beautifully marked agates, the oddly colored sodalite strand whose dark lavender shade might be a fault but was also strikingly attractive. She found the three unpitted strings in a bundle of otherwise poor garnets, and she spotted uniquely shaped beads and strange clasps to add distinction to the *Queen*'s growing collection of interesting if relatively uncostly trade material.

Van Rycke glowed with satisfaction. Cofort was performing exactly as he had seen her do in that other market but with the grand difference that on this occasion she was working for the *Solar Queen,* not against her.

He permitted her to do only the choosing. Although each individual piece cost little, the total of their gem and mineral purchases would be significant. This was *Queen* business, and he was not about to turn the crucial bargaining over to any temporary hand.

Dane watched him with the awe of a knowledgeable beginner for a superb master in his craft, and with pleasure. Someday, he would have a similar post and would perform, he hoped, with skill equal to that of his chief.

Jellico and Cofort's impressions might be less precisely tuned, but they were no less powerful. Both were veterans in Trade and recognized an ability so well honed that it transcended the professional to move into the realm of art.

Once the Cargo-Master was satisfied that they had secured everything they needed or wanted that the *Queen* could afford, he indicated that they should return to the freighter with their treasures. All four of them were burdened with a number of fairly substantial packages by that time. The cloth, of course, would be delivered to the ship, but when one purchased gems and minerals, he took care to carry them away with him.

"Could we at least go by the loose stones?" the Medic asked wistfully.

"If you like," Jellico replied. "I thought you agreed with Van that we wouldn't take any."

"Aye. This is for me. I just want to look."

"The *Roving Star* deals heavily in them," Van Rycke recalled.

She nodded. "We do our own setting, you see. Our Steward's a master jeweler. — He's taken prizes from some of the biggest guilds in the ultrasystem. — He mounts what we bring to him, both for Trade and for the rest of us personally. All we have to do is supply the materials, and he produces individual works of art. I've gotten in the habit of checking out anything that might conceivably be of interest as a result."

"It can't hurt," the Cargo-Master said. He touched one of the packages he carried. "This local stuff's nice. I wouldn't object to having a few loose stones on hand."

*   *   *

That part of the big market given over to unmounted gems and the metals used to complement them was not extensive, and there was almost no variety in the type of jewels offered. Canuchean amethysts and red garnets made up more than 90 percent of the stock. Most of the rest consisted of surplanetary fancy garnets, all of them flawed and none of good color, much to the woman's disappointment. The remainder were various small, imported semiprecious gems common throughout the ultrasystem. There were no sunstones at all that day.

The Free Traders bought a few stones, fewer than they might have if the quality had been better. All were single specimens. The sets, presorted packets containing from two gems to three dozen or more, they left alone. Most such lots were of very low grade, and they had plenty from which to choose at reasonable cost without having to settle for the patently inferior.

One stand featuring them did catch Cofort's eye. It was a small, uncovered operation specializing in both imported and on-world stones plus a smattering of the more interesting readily available minerals. The array of colors was wonderful and was rendered more striking still by the masterful arrangement the merchant had employed to display his wares.

She picked up several of the clear packets encasing his goods and held them high so that Halio's light might play over the contents before carefully replacing them again. When she seemed to linger over one lot labeled rose tourmalines, the Canuchean was quick to pick up on her apparent interest.

"Those have better than average color. They go for fifty a carat."

The spacer's arched brows lifted even higher. "Hedon's Gem Guild wouldn't get that for stellar-quality synthetics, which these are not."

The man drew himself to the full of his not inconsiderable height. "If they were stellar quality or anything approaching it, they wouldn't be selling in sets. As for the rest, these tourmalines are natural . . ."

"Save it for the locals," the Medic snapped. "Preferably the visually handicapped. It's painfully obvious that just about every stone on this table is manufactured. — If you wish to argue the point, Canuche has thoughtfully supplied appraisers to settle such disputes. Their booth's just over there. One of my comrades can fetch—"

"Power down, space hound. I'm only a salesman, not a gemologist. It's as easy to fool me as anyone else. This stuff looked good to me, and I took it on faith, that's all."

"Of course," she responded dryly. She had figured he would back down quickly under that threat. The official appraisers were noted for doing their job, and the penalties for fraud were severe. The merchant might have bluffed his way out of this, but he would then be under close observation for a very long time, which would seriously handicap the questionable enterprise he was running.

"Look, I'll sell at a loss to prove my good intentions. Take what you want for ten a carat."

"Ten? We do this for a living, too, remember? You got them for a quarter a carat, maybe half for a few of the best. You'll be making a good profit at one credit."

"One! I won't be able to meet my rent!"

"Stow that debris, my friend. By rights, I shouldn't go higher than three-quarters. Besides, we're only taking a couple of sets as curiosities, one for me, one for my comrades to split. Synthetics like these wouldn't move too well, and I really don't believe your style of doing business deserves the reward of a big order."

She looked over a number of the sets before selecting two, one containing all rose-colored stones, the other a mixture of rose and green. The gems in both were cut as cabochons rather than with light-firing facets.

After watching carefully while the discomfited merchant weighed her selection, she paid him based upon the scale he had named and, much to his relief, withdrew with her companions.

Cofort caught the way Dane was looking at her and laughed. "You didn't think I had it in me, Viking?"

He started. That was the nickname some of his more insufferable classmates back at the Pool had used to taunt him. There was no barb in it now, though. In fact, he rather liked the sound of it . . . "Well, you usually come across as a rather quieter individual."

Her eyes sparkled. "I wasn't loud back there, either," she teased.

"Neither are Patrol lasers," Jellico told her. "They make their point, too."

Her manner grew grave again. "I didn't think Mr. Van Rycke would mind my taking the helm. The sum involved was infinitesimal, and one set is for me. I'll keep the other as well if you really don't want it."

Andre Norton & P.M.Griffin

"Not at all," replied the Cargo-Master. "As you said, it's a curiosity."

"We'll see just how much of a curiosity when we get back to the *Queen.*"

There was such an air of mystery, of superiority, about her that his eyes narrowed. "That's where we're heading right now, Doctor Cofort. On all burners."

15

Van Rycke ushered his companions into his office. The panel had scarcely closed behind them before he turned to Rael. "All right. What treasure have you found for us amid the debris?"

"Maybe none," she replied, as she accepted the shears he held out to her and slit open each of the packets. She spilled their contents out in two carefully separated piles. "Which does the *Queen* want? The cost was the same."

"The bicolored one."

"Good choice," she said as she separated two pink stones from it. "These appear to be the only ones," she remarked after a few seconds' examination of the rest. A similar study of her own packet produced another prize, this one somewhat larger than the first two.

Rael peered closely at all three, holding them so that
they caught the full of the bright light from the desk lamp.
Her head rose in a gesture of triumph. "Star rubies," she
announced. "Very old and unquestionably the real thing.
They'll have to be tested for quality, but I suspect it's first
rate."

"So that's why you chose cabs rather than faceted
stones," Míceál said softly.

She nodded. "I'd spotted them right off. I couldn't be
entirely sure without examining them more carefully, but
I knew I did have something out of the ordinary. I just had
to be careful not to arouse his suspicion by paying too
much attention to those particular sets." She made a wry
face. "I'd probably have been vacuum-brained enough to
tell him if that son hadn't tried to give us such a doing. Fifty
credits a carat for those little mass-produced toys of his!"

"What if we had refused the packet you picked up for
us?" the Cargo-Master asked.

The Medic answered Van Rycke, but it was Jellico's eyes
that she met and held. "Temporary hand or permanent, I
am part of this ship, and I'm entitled to your trust. I'd
proven my knowledge of gems. If you couldn't go along
with me blindly, or at least indulge my whim if you suspected nothing more, when the outlay was so insignificant,
then you'd deserve to take your loss."

"You'd have just held onto both packets and kept mum
about the rubies?" Jan asked.

"Naturally. What else would you expect me to do?"

"Fair enough," the Captain said. "We were testing you.
You had the right to return the compliment."

Dane fingered the rubies, although he did not pick them

up. It would be too much like him to drop one of them—Cofort's probably—and send it skittering into some crevice from which it could not be extracted short of dismantling the ship. "What're they worth?"

"That I couldn't venture to say with certainty, not until they've been tested," she replied, "but if they're as good as they look, they're worth plenty. Mr. Van Rycke will be the better one to lay the proper valuation on them once he has the necessary information to do it."

"They're old to judge by the way they've been polished, probably Terran . . ." The Cargo-Master stopped speaking. His breath caught. "Spirit of Space!"

"What's the matter?" Míceál demanded.

"Most of Terra's good star ruby sources were played out long ago, the best of them centuries ago, and there's never been anything to equal their output since anywhere in the Federation. If these stones originated in one of those old mines, we're looking at the stuff of legend. They'll go for whatever the market'll bear."

"If we can locate that market," his Captain said gloomily.

"Hedon. We keep our mouths shut and fire all our tubes to get there. Our small constellation here, our double star," he corrected, recalling that one of the three did not belong to the *Queen*, "could well pay for that voyage and a number of others after it even if we moved nothing else at all on any of them."

"Do you really think that's what we've got?" Rael asked in awe.

"There's a very strong possibility of it, Doctor, judging by surface appearances at any rate. Neither this sheen nor this color has been around for a very long time."

"What if they aren't as old as we think or aren't from one of the famous Terran mines?" Thorson asked, trying to keep his head in the face of his superiors' enthusiasm. They had seen what seemed like real prizes turn sour before, and he did not want to work himself into the same pitch over what could be nothing more than an extremely costly shot at the next galaxy. A trip to Hedon of Eros was an expensive proposition, and they had nothing else whatsoever that they could hope to trade there. "They're not even very big."

"About a carat each for ours. The Doctor's is half that weight again. That's not bad for a major gemstone. They're also dead matches for one another both in color and cut, and the *Queen*'s two for size as well. That means we can bill them as a suite. No, provided they're natural, we have ourselves a treasure, whatever their age or source. — Assuming they're not hot, of course." Rael had been careful to secure documentation of the sale, but they would still get no profit in that event and would be out the cost of the voyage as well.

Dane nodded, inwardly hoping that their "treasure" would at least prove of sufficient resale value to match the efforts they would have to expend to establish its authenticity and then dispose of it.

The answer to that lay in the future, but there were other mysteries still to be resolved. He turned his attention to the woman. "How did you spot them, Rael? For that matter, how'd you know the rest were synthetics?"

"Oh, by the color. Manufactured stones are subtly different from their natural counterparts. Usually, they're more intense than real ones, and the shade or tone's at least a wee bit off." She forestalled his next question. "How these came to be in those sets, I couldn't begin to say. They've probably been knocking around for a long time, moving from place to place with no one suspecting their true nature. All the gems in these two lots look like they were previously mounted. They were probably part of a large, low-value shipment gathered from all over the ultrasystem and split up into sets for resale at marginal profit."

"That's more or less what I figure, too," the Cargo-Master agreed.

There was a strange note in his tone, and she looked up to find him studying her intently. "What's wrong?" she asked in surprise.

"I hesitate to use the word *preternatural,* Doctor. It's too melodramatic coming from anyone but Craig Tau. However, the stones on that stand were not the work of amateurs. The fact that they were synthetic would not have been instantly apparent to most of us, myself included, and I'm not precisely a novice at buying and selling such items. Add to that the fact that absolutely no one else I've ever known could possibly have smelled out that rats' nest and it rather makes me wonder about you."

"That's only because you're judging by purely Terran standards," she told him calmly. "When I introduced myself as Teague Cofort's sister, I should have been more specific. We're actually half-siblings. Our mothers were different. Very different. In point of fact, I'm a genetic impossibility."

Her chin lifted. "I don't know Mother's race or homeworld. My father just returned to the ship with her one day after a short absence on some planet neither they nor his crew would ever name. She definitely was not of Terran blood, not human at all, although she was very beautiful by human standards. There were some significant physiological and genetic differences, incompatibilities. Marriage was possible between them. Conception should not have been and certainly not a viable birth. That notwithstanding, I was conceived, born, and have managed to thrive.

"Like most intelligent beings, I have my own set of gifts and talents. Most seem to have come from my father, some from Mother, but none are of a nature to set me apart from the better part of the Federation's citizens. Whatever strengths I might have came by the time-honored means of determined effort and practice. If I hadn't been reared in an environment like space where the lack of other distractions does wonders for the ability to concentrate on a long course of study or training, I doubt I'd have achieved much with them at all, and even with that push, I'm a far voyage from being some sort of ultrawoman.

"Admittedly, my senses are pretty acute, but there's nothing super-anything about them.

"I do have a good feel for color and can differentiate between shades quite finely, but I learned that from our former Cargo-Master, Mara's predecessor. Other than that, my vision's not remarkable. — No pin spotting at ten miles or peering through titanone plates.

"It's much the same with hearing. My sense of smell is keen, which is usually more disadvantage than blessing. I have trained myself to separate and identify different odors even when they're components in a melody. That's a bit uncommon, I suppose, but don't imagine I can perform like a tracking or hunting animal, or you're in for a major disappointment.

"Sensitivity to aroma and refined sense of taste go together. You can be sure that I appreciate Mr. Mura's fine hand with his seasonings and that I don't let many chances for a good feed of real food pass me by when they crop up."

The expression of each of her companions brightened into a grin. That, at least, was typical of their kind. When a space hound hit the surface of a basically Terran-type planet and had some free time, it was almost inevitably to an eating place that he first hurried rather than to the local version of a Happy City.

Rael did not smile. "The last sense I have is touch, and that's not terribly extraordinary, though I'll admit to preferring the feel of that Thornen silk to that of our uniforms.

"There's nothing else," she continued firmly and a little wearily, "no sixth-plus powers. I don't read minds or see past or future or move solid objects by will alone."

"What about conversing with animals?" Míceál asked quickly.

"No," she said firmly. "I wish I could. They're often a galaxy nicer than our own kind. They like me because they know how much I like them. Maybe it's a little unusual," she conceded, "but it's nothing more than that. Plants, too, grow for me as they do for other gardeners who understand their ways and enjoy working with them. There's no particular magic in it."

The Captain gave a slight shake of his head. "No go, Cofort. A lot of people like animals, but none of them affects Queex the way you do."

Her eyes hardened, and a sharp edge turned her voice

into a whip. "A lot of people love animals and take tri-dees of them, too, but they don't often get results like you've got tacked up on your office wall. Do you use some sort of compulsion to force your subjects to appear and then pose and freeze in place for you?"

Jellico flushed so that the scar stood out white on his cheek, but he said nothing. The rebuke had been neatly delivered. It was not an overreaction, either. Had the Medic been a real member of the crew, it might have been different. There would have been strong bonds of trust and confidence between them then, though his right to pry would have been no greater. As it was, any admission of esper abilities could prove highly dangerous for Rael Cofort.

Van Rycke cleared his throat. "I suppose I can consider myself answered," he said to break the uncomfortable silence that followed. "Well, whatever the extent of your talents, Doctor, we've got reason to be grateful to them. They've done good work all along and have topped it off by locating a potentially very nice prize for us."

The Medic inclined her head in formal acknowledgment. "Thank you, Mr. Van Rycke."

"We seem to be finished here," he said. "The day's still young, and there's a good part of the market still left unexplored. — Thorson, you'd best stay here and classify our new acquisitions. Log it all in and stow everything."

"Aye," Dane responded cheerfully. He had been anticipating that.

"Doctor Cofort may be able to give you a hand later," Jellico suggested.

He glanced at the woman. "Write up a report about these

rubies now, while the details're fresh in your memory. Describe the purchase in full and put down all our surmises, clearly labeled as such. Just in case those stones should prove to be hot, I want as much documentation on hand as possible to attest to our innocence."

"Aye, Captain. — I'll just say we bought the sets by chance, though, if you don't mind. We're doing this to settle potential questions, not raise more."

"Handle it however you think best. If I want more or something different, I'll tell you when I see the report."

The four dispersed. Dane and Van Rycke hurried to be about their work.

Cofort moved quickly as well to get on with her assignment, but Míceál stopped her at the door. "How about some jakek?"

"Fine. I always enjoy a cup," the Medic responded, silently adding a mental reservation about quality. Jellico would never rival Mr. Mura in a galley.

Rael Cofort entered her commander's office first, automatically activating the cabin lights as she did so. Queex gave a delighted whistle at the sight of her but did not forget the duties of a hoobat for all his pleasure at this particular human's visit. He glared suspiciously at the door to see who else might be invading his territory.

Since only its rightful occupant followed, he satisfied himself with a single, decidedly unmusical call and grasped the bars with four of his legs, ready to leap out as soon as the door opened.

The woman did not disappoint him. She laughed softly

and slid into Jellico's chair so that she could comfortably reach the hoobat's cage, then slipped the latch and swung the barrier back. In that instant, Queex was airborne in a spring that carried him to her upper arm. From there, he scurried to her shoulder.

Cofort braced her hand against the edge of the desk. At that signal, Queex descended to her forearm and draped himself across it, three appendages dangling on each side. She began to rub the area between and around the protuberant eyes until he relaxed into a limp image of ecstasy.

The Captain watched them a moment and shook his head. "Are you sure you're not working some sort of spell on him?"

"Haven't you ever had a really good massage?" she countered. "Besides, he's such a sweetheart. It's easy to please him. — Isn't it, little pet?"

As if in answer, the odd creature started to emit a quiet, purring whistle.

Míceál said nothing. Any response he might have made—in any one of several languages—would have been appropriate only in very different company. He was fond of Queex himself, considerably more than he would publicly admit, but Rael Cofort was the only person he had ever met, human or xeno, who could call a hoobat a sweetheart and little pet.

He rolled the chair and its two occupants aside and opened the bottom drawer of the desk. Jellico took a big thermos from it. This he held to his ear and shook briskly. The resulting sloshing sound told him it was still about half full, so he stood it upright in the space he cleared for it between two stacks of papers and set the controls for reheat. That done, he retrieved two cups from the same drawer and put one before the Medic, the other beside himself as he casually dropped into the visitor's chair. "It'll be ready in a couple of minutes."

When a buzz announced that the jakek was hot, he filled his guest's cup and his own.

Rael sipped the dark liquid, concealing her grimace behind the thick rim. Jakek was making great headway all along the starlanes, threatening to supplant the caffeine-laden Terran coffee as the Federation's all-around beverage of choice. The crew of the *Solar Queen,* though, with the exception of herself and the Captain, remained staunchly loyal to the traditional brew despite the fact that it was available only in synthetic or concentrate form to space hounds plying the rim. Jellico appreciated too well how much the Steward had to do to demand special luxuries for himself. He usually prepared his own in the thermos, rather to the detriment of its flavor. For the four-hundredth time, she vowed to get up early some morning soon and wheedle or pummel Frank Mura into letting her loose in his precious galley. Jakek was heavily used on the *Roving Star,* and she could program a range . . .

She felt the man's eyes on her and looked up. His expression was somber. "Do you doubt my story?"

"I'm just sorry we put you through that inquisition in there."

"You had to ask, didn't you?"

"Aye, but we seem to make a habit of tearing your wounds. I don't enjoy tormenting you."

She looked into the steaming liquid. "There's no disgrace in my ancestry, and I don't mind speaking about my mother. She was respected and greatly liked as well as loved. All the crew who knew her told me that. Father was the only one who'd never talk about her."

"He blamed you?" Jellico asked gently.

"No, but he held himself responsible. I think it must have been with him all the time. He loved her, you see." She sighed. "None of us knew how much until he was dying. He never called for me or Teague or Teague's mother. Just for her. I believe he was glad to be joining her."

The man nodded slowly. His younger comrades would not have understood that, but he had lived long enough, experienced enough, that he could comprehend it somewhat.

Another thought struck him suddenly. "Your mother was a Medic, too?" he ventured.

"Among her own people, aye, or so we believed. She never actually admitted to it, or to much else about her past. She apparently had buried that completely when she came with my father. It is one of the reasons I was drawn to the profession, I suppose. She fought so hard for me, battled to remain alive long enough that I could live without her. I felt I owed it to her to do something positive with myself, to try to make some return for that struggle."

"Apart from being happy?"

Rael looked closely at him. "I don't knock that goal, friend, but medicine is in me, rising from several springs. This is undoubtedly one of them, and to my mind, it's as valid as any of the others."

"No doubt it is." He smiled. "You're a strong-willed woman, Rael Cofort, for all your quiet manner. I have trouble envisioning you being stampeded into any major course unsuited to you."

When they had finished the jakek, Jellico came to his feet and took the empty cups. He would drop them off in the galley on his way out. "You can keep Queex company and work in here if you want. Take your time, but if you do finish soon enough, see if you can't give Thorson a hand. Bear in mind, though, that he's boss with respect to Cargo when Van's away."

"I was born a Free Trader," the woman responded irritably. "I think I know the protocol."

"Aye, but you've also managed to establish yourself as something of an authority in the kinds of goods he'll be cataloging. — Dane's good. I don't want him overawed into surrendering either his authority or his duties."

"He won't be," she promised.

Míceál studied her somberly. He was not quite sure that he believed her, or, rather, that he should believe her. That mixed-blood story was an old standby for gaining sympathy, although in this case there was a considerable body of apparent evidence to support the Medic's assertions. He could not press her further, either, not yet. Her frankness— or seeming frankness—had tied him. He had no facts or so much as a solid suspicion to lay against her, and if he pushed Rael now, it would have to be in a serious challenge that could only result in the termination of her association with the *Solar Queen*. He was not ready to force that. He did not want to force it.

Morally, he could not do so without significant cause. Canuche Town was not Trewsworld, and it was most assuredly no place to abandon this particular woman. She had done extremely well for Deke Tatarcoff out there in the market, but the method by which she accomplished that service might well have bought her a passage straight into disaster.

Jellico hesitated. More than restraint from initiating a clash between them was required of him. As long as Cofort remained part of the *Queen*'s company, it was his duty to see to her safety, but apart from the two services, the Navy and Patrol, a starship's Captain could exert only so much control over the surplanetary off-duty activities of his crew.

Damn it, there was danger! It might be only potential, but it was quite real. "I don't know your plans for tonight, but I don't want you, or any of the others for that matter, wandering about Canuche Town alone or even in pairs. Go in at least fours or not at all, which is what I would prefer."

He braced himself. No independent-minded Free Trader, particularly one not even bound long-term to his ship, was likely to accept that remark or the imperious tone in which it had been uttered with any semblance of good grace.

Whatever her instinctive reaction, however, the woman's temper held. Her eyes narrowed, and she studied him sharply. "What's the matter, Míceál?" she asked quietly.

He sighed. "Beauty's a commodity in Happy City. If any of its creatures happened to witness your work with that piece of Thornen silk, they'll set the value of a small river tear, and a prime stone at that, on you and maybe more depending on their specific interests. The most spineless vermin in the ultrasystem would try to grab a prize like that if they thought they could get away with it." Anger shot through him, hot and sharp. "Whatever you do with your life, I won't see you slaving for those subbiotics!"

Rael's head lowered. "I'm aware of that possibility," she told him. "I wasn't planning on taking chances. As for wandering around, after that business with the port rats, I don't find the idea of exploring Canuche Town after dark particularly appealing. Once the markets and shops close, there isn't much here apart from the restaurants to draw me away from the *Queen* anyway. I'll be happier and better occupied working on Doctor Tau's study."

The Captain's anger deepened. Aye, he thought bitterly, she would have to have recognized that peril. Comeliness was as a rule an asset in Trade, particularly when dealing with humans, who tended to respond favorably to those they considered to be attractive. Anything greatly beyond that was another matter. Too striking an appearance could be a decided disadvantage under a great many circumstances, and Rael Cofort would have been a potential target even as a very young girl.

Sympathy swept over him. He wanted to take her in his arms, hold and shield her . . .

Jellico resisted that impulse, but he did not want to leave the Medic with the gloom he had aroused weighing her down. He made himself smile, as if at himself. "I've wasted a lot of breath with that warning," he said. "You know, or should know, all of it as well as I do. — Space, I may have some years on you, but given the fact that you were born on a freighter, there probably isn't all that much disparity in the amount of time we've spent wandering around the starlanes."

Her eyes sparkled. "You've certainly put it to better use,

then, making Captain while I'm still hopping from berth to berth."

She raised her arm so that Queex was forced to move back onto her shoulder, freeing her hands and arms for writing. "You'd best catch up with Mr. Van Rycke and see if the pair of you can't scare up a proper cargo. A few little stones and beads and some odd bolts of cloth won't get you very far."

"Doctor Cofort," he told her severely, "just because you are sitting behind that desk does not mean you've assumed command of this ship." So saying, he gave her a reasonable approximation of a Navy salute and quit the cabin with the welcome sound of her laughter ringing in his ears.

16

Dane set to pause the tape he had been studying, then switched it off altogether as he began reviewing in his own mind what he had read thus far.

A number of these synthetic stones were quite nice, and they were, in point of fact, real, chemically correct gems. The only difference between them and their naturally occurring counterparts was that they had been formed under human-controlled conditions.

They might form the basis of what could conceivably turn out to be a very lucrative business. Few Traders, even among the Companies, dealt in artificially created stones, none that he could name offhand on a regular basis, yet only a small percentage of the galaxy's population could afford to buy natural jewels. Synthetics could broaden the *Solar Queen*'s potential customer base enormously. In fact, given their greater intensity of color, the cheaper article might actually prove the preferred item in some markets. The credit outlay to get started would not be much, either, and the test stock would claim only a minute portion of their ever-precious cargo space.

The apprentice nodded to himself in satisfaction. He needed to do some more reading. Then he would put together the figures, outline probable good markets and a Trade strategy, and lay his proposal before his chief.

Van Rycke should go for it. Making a profit, not exposing obscure murder plots, was the *Queen*'s function in life, and this looked like a fine chance to open up a brand-new subfield and effectively monopolize it, at least in this Sector, for a couple or maybe three years until the other Traders caught wise and could move on their own accounts.

"Dane! I thought you were still in the hold."

He looked up. Rip Shannon had just come into the crew's cabin and was looking at him in mild surprise. "I finished up there twenty minutes ago," he responded.

The other's dark face clouded. "I saw Rael go down nearly that long ago, and the hatch was still unfastened when I glanced at it just now."

Thorson straightened. "That calls for some investigation."

"Easy, friend," Rip said hastily. "She probably has a good reason . . ."

"She's got no right to be there, not without the Cargo-Master's approval, or mine in Van Rycke's absence."

"You want some help?"

That gave him pause. "No," he replied slowly. "I'm not accusing her of anything." Once more, his expression hardened. "Just stick around. If I'm not back reasonably fast, come looking for me, and be real careful when you do."

Dane grimaced at the melodramatic cast of his whole reaction to his shipmate's announcement. Blast Rael Cofort anyway, he thought irritably. Why was it that she seemed to bring out that in him, or managed to get them all involved in situations that demanded an oversized response? On Ali Kamil, it might look good. He, on the other hand, made a ridiculous hero.

All the same, he did not stop. Cargo and Trade goods were his responsibility. He had no choice but to check out any interference with either. A sabotaged shipment had once given the *Queen* galaxy-class trouble, and he was not about to risk a replay of that. There was neither profit nor pleasure in the close proximity of extremely unpleasant death.

Cofort was still in the hold when the Cargo-apprentice reached it moments later. Everything looked to be in order, and there was nothing to indicate what she had been doing since her arrival, but she had the examination length of the silver fabric out and had unfolded a corner of it. This she was holding out from her so that she could view it against the gray background of the hold and against the warm, pale flesh of her other hand.

Thorson cleared his throat. The woman glanced at him,

then looked again at the silver net. "I didn't have a chance to examine our acquisitions closely before. This is really lovely. You did very well with it."

Rael sighed as she returned the length to its place. "When I was aboard the *Roving Star,*" she said bitterly, "I listened to Teague and didn't buy any such basically useless luxuries. Now, I can't afford them. I'll never be able to have them, either, not as long as I remain a virtuous, hardworking rim Free Trader."

The Medic stopped speaking, seeing the open suspicion in her companion. "Power down, boy," she snapped. "No Cofort's ever turned jack. I don't intend to start any new traditions in that line."

"You wouldn't admit it if you did," he replied, trying to make his response sound light but not quite succeeding.

Rael shrugged delicately. "We deal with some beautiful things. I'm not expected to be immune to the charms of all of them, I hope. — You certainly aren't."

The man started, and her lips curved into a smile that was not all good-humored sympathy. "I saw the way you looked at that leather utility belt before you settled for the one you bought. If you can want a lot of things you can't have, why deny me the same right?"

"But you can have some of this," he countered quickly, picking up on what he saw as the flaw in her argument. "There's nothing stopping a crew member from buying part of a cargo for personal use. This is faux cloth, not the real thing. A small length of it wouldn't run you that much."

She shook her head. "You don't have enough of it to split your stock. Twelve full bolts isn't much to offer as it is. Any less, and you can wave farewell to the hope of a quick bulk sale."

"You're so concerned about the *Solar Queen*'s profits?" Dane demanded sarcastically.

Rael's chin lifted. "One is always loyal to the ship to which one is bound, however long or short the term of service."

"So tradition goes," he said. "I haven't been out of Pool and in space long enough to see if it actually holds true or not."

"It holds. Usually. The ships where it doesn't have a tendency to disappear with all hands. Besides, Cargo-Master Van Rycke isn't likely to fragment the value of his stock by selling off part of it at this stage." Her response had been cold. Dane Thorson was too sensitive about his youth and lack of experience to call attention to them if he wasn't trying to be smart. "While I'm with the *Queen*, I'll serve her interests."

"And afterward?"

"Afterward, I'll compete with her if I have to. So will you, most likely, when you finally qualify."

Both were silent for some moments after that.

Rael's eyes fell first. "That was a low blow. I'm sorry, and sorry I was down here without your say. I came looking for you as per Jellico's instructions, but I should've left again when I didn't find you. I guess I just fell into old habits. I had free run of the *Star*'s holds."

"You were good with cargo, I suppose?" he asked sourly. Why not? She was good with everything any way important to him.

"Very good with a lot of it. Teague wanted me for Cargo-

Master. He was furious when I opted for Medic training instead." Her back seemed to straighten. "Maybe I was wrong. I liked cargo work and frontline Trade, and unquestionably, I'd have been more useful to him in that capacity, but medicine had the stronger call. I chose to answer it and stuck by that decision."

"That's why you left the *Star?*"

"No," she said wearily. Her mouth hardened. "I left, Thorson. I wasn't kicked off. I've given reasons why. If you don't choose to believe them, well, that's nothing much to either of us, is it?"

Dane decided to try one more tack, although he doubted he would accomplish anything. If the Medic was playing them false, she had thought her role through thoroughly. She had not lacked an answer yet for any question they had put to her. Even Van Rycke and Jellico had not been able to trap her or trip her up.

"By the sound of it, you had some real credits at your disposal on the *Roving Star.* Have you been on your own so long that you're completely wiped out?" He felt uncomfortable asking that. It was none of his business and crossed the border into discourtesy by a considerable margin. Cofort would be within her rights to tell him to go fire his burners someplace.

The woman frowned but kept rein on her temper. "No, I haven't been on the loose that long. The bulk of my former earnings as well as my inheritance from my father are hatching in the *Star*'s account. Teague wouldn't release them."

"What?"

For the first time, she gave him a genuine smile. "He's

not a villain of the starlanes. Everything's sitting quite properly in a trust. My brother's not using it. He can't. He's just holding it until I latch onto a permanent berth."

"You're out of your minority."

"I know, but those are the terms of the trust. Besides, there isn't that much involved. We Coforts pour most of our shares of everything back into our ships." Her head rose. "You don't think we got where we are without considerable dedication and sacrifice, do you?"

"No. Cofort and his crews are known for that, but . . ."

"But nothing. I wanted to make it on my own, and I'd be begging to be back-alleyed if I went wandering around the starlanes with too impressive a roll. It's worked out. I haven't starved even if I haven't managed to prove myself the greatest phenomenon to bless Trade in this century."

The woman laughed softly, ruefully. "I suppose I was sort of cherishing that hope, but you can probably imagine how fast I had to flush it down the disposal tubes."

Dane chuckled despite himself. "You may do it yet," he told her as he sighed inwardly. She had managed it again, he thought, turned the discussion completely away from questions uncomfortable to herself. He was not surprised, at least. Rael Cofort had proven remarkably adept at doing that since she had first brought herself to the attention of the crew of the *Solar Queen*. Only time would show whether or not she was using that skill to cover some sort of bad surprise she had planned for the lot of them.

17

The three apprentices, Jasper, and Rael were at the table when Jellico and Van Rycke strode into the mess the following morning. The Medic had Sinbad on her lap, cradled against her left arm. He was eating daintily from her other hand, which she held cupped before him.

"I thought he was beginning to look a little rotund," Míceál remarked.

Rael glanced up. "He's a hero again, fortunately an unwounded one this time. Someone," she added pointedly, "was careless about reattaching the nets properly when he returned to the ship last night."

"Ouch," muttered the Cargo-Master.

Weeks put down his fork. "Any good leads?" He had

been with the *Solar Queen* a long time, and he knew full well that these two would not have been abroad in the wee hours merely to sample the kind of delights Happy City had to offer.

Van Rycke's eyes danced like Terra's sky on a sunny day. "A charter, my friends, a nice, fat, easy charter that'll completely fill our bulk cargo holds."

"What're we carrying and to what port?" Dane asked eagerly.

"Equipment and chemicals to the dome mines on Riginni."

He held up his hands when the faces of the four men at the table fell. "I'm not overjoyed, either, at the thought of revisiting her again so soon, but it's a good run, and there could be at least a couple of others like it if we move fast enough."

He lowered his large frame into the chair nearest him. "We encountered one Adroo Macgregory, who is founder, president, chairman of the board, and just about High King of Caledonia, Inc. That's the biggest conglomerate on Canuche. He'd already realized there was a fine market for his products in those new mines and had personally ar-ranged via transceiver a large sale of everything from digging and crushing equipment to construction materials to chemicals of various sorts. He's eager to move fast, before some competitor can edge him out. There's no time to buy or license a freighter long-term, so he was planning to utilize several of those currently in port for his initial few runs. After witnessing the stampede Rael started in the market yesterday, though, Macgregory decided to give the *Queen* a shot at the whole charter, on condition that we're prepared to accept delivery and lift within the next couple of days. We carry through on that, and we'll get the work as long as we're willing to take it and he's still hiring independents, which he does warn won't go on forever."

He fixed the woman with a wicked grin. "Our agreement's only verbal as yet. He won't actually seal it until he has our Doctor Cofort present as well."

Seeing the mischief on the pair, Rael merely arched her brows. "Now that's a remarkable display of pure democracy!" she declared. "Imagine wanting not only the *Solar Queen*'s most exalted officers but also a lowly unskilled hand to officiate at so important a transaction!"

Jellico chuckled. "Actually, Macgregory wants to make a change in your employment status. He intends to offer you a place in his sales organization."

"He what?" she asked, simultaneously trying unsuccessfully to silence her companions' laughter with an impatient wave of her hand.

"That's absolutely correct," the Cargo-Master affirmed. "He claims that anyone capable of bringing two of his staid close competitors to the brink of fisticuffs—his word—by the mere act of waving a piece of cloth around in the air a few times could do good work in advancing the cause of Caledonia, Inc. — Seriously, Rael, he recognizes precisely what you did and promises that if you're willing and show both ability and industry, you've got an excellent future with his company."

"Why tell my superiors that he plans to bid for my services?" she inquired bluntly.

"He wants to avoid acquiring a reputation of being an underhanded dealer and scaring off potential interstellar customers. Besides," Jellico added, "he probably doesn't think he's got much real chance of luring you away from us. Space hounds just don't like quitting the starlanes, however good the offer."

"Not for a planet like Canuche of Halio, at any rate," she agreed firmly and with considerable feeling. "When're we meeting with him?"

"Noon. He's buying us lunch in one of Canuche Town's most exclusive restaurants, the Twenty-Two, down by the waterfront, so don't do too good a job on those syntheggs and sausage."

"No fear of that. I loaded up for Sinbad's sake, not mine."

Ali leaned against the padded backrest of the bench enclosing the table on three sides. "Now that that's settled," he drawled, "there remains a possibly intriguing tale to be told. No one made any mention of 'fisticuffs' yesterday."

"We'd left by then," the Captain told him. "We met Deke Tatarcoff on our way back to the *Queen,* and he confirmed that there was not one but several near battles before the Thornen silk found a home."

"He was one happy man," Van Rycke said as he picked up the story. "He got absolute top price for the bolt and then sold the little examination length for very nearly the same sum. Everything else went as well, albeit at a more reasonable price. He claimed all he's got left are a couple of scraps of lint and declared that if he'd found them in time, he'd probably have moved those as well."

Jellico placed the small delicate-cargo box he had been carrying on the table and reverently lifted two bottles out of it. "From Tatarcoff's private stock. — You're the one who earned them, Rael. You decide their fate."

The woman eyed the labels. Wine. Hedon vintage, golden white, dry, and the vineyard was good enough that she recognized the name. They would have no trouble trading this if they chose.

She shook her head. No. Deke was a connoisseur of wine. His personal supply was legendary, and he maintained it strictly for his own pleasure, not for sale or barter. These bottles had been given in that spirit, and she felt they should be used accordingly. "We're worth an occasional luxury. We'll turn them over to Frank and see what he can produce to accompany them. He should enjoy that challenge, especially here on-world where he can get his hands on fresh produce."

18

Rael smoothed a nonexistent wrinkle out of her tunic. Dress uniforms did that to one, she thought. With their high collars and stark, dramatic styling, they tended to render the victim wearing one acutely conscious of his potential for imperfection. Maybe that was even a subtle part of their purpose. A little uncertainty went far in keeping a person alert . . .

She glanced at her companion. Míceál Jellico, too, was encased in his formal uniform, but if he felt discomfort or a sense of confinement, he was far too practiced to give any sign of it.

Van Rycke, walking a few paces ahead, was, perhaps, the more striking figure with his greater height and bulk comprised of rippling muscle, but she found Jellico more impressive. Lean, wiry, with the feline grace a lifetime in space had bequeathed to him, bearing the aura of an authority that carried not merely the welfare but the very lives of others, he looked the part of the master of a starship plying the perilous lanes on the rim. The hard features, the blaster-burned cheek, the eyes like tempered titanone served only to emphasize that role.

Her eyes swept the constantly shifting lunchtime crowd. Their host had instructed the Free Traders to come to the lobby of this, the tallest building in Canuche Town, promising to meet them here and escort them to the exclusive restaurant at its summit.

The men with her raised their hands suddenly in recognition and greeting, and she studied closely the individual who returned the gesture.

Adroo Macgregory was like Míceál, she judged at once. He was older, with more white in his hair than dark. His eyes were a deep blue, his face rounder and fuller, but the two were of one breed. Space hound or planet hugger, she recognized that strength and independence of spirit. This one would not lightly bargain his soul or his season's profits away.

The Canuchean made his way through the throng to join their party. He immediately put out his hand in the ancient Terran greeting universally recognized wherever the mother world's seed had taken root. "Right on time. It's good to see you again, Captain Jellico, Mr. Van Rycke."

"We're pleased to see you as well, Mr. Macgregory," the former replied. He motioned the Medic to step forward. "This is Doctor Rael Cofort."

The man inclined his head in an old-fashioned bow. His eyes sparkled even as they seemed to penetrate her to her very soul. "You're lovely for a fact, Doctor Cofort, but mortal like the rest of us, I'm relieved to see. I'd be a bit uncomfortable trying to deal with a vision."

Her smile broadened. "You'd manage all the same if it was good for business."

Macgregory laughed. "I would indeed, Doctor."

Their host ushered the off-worlders toward a roped-off lift platform. As he passed the uniformed gatekeeper he said, "We have a reservation for four," unnecessarily, apparently, for the woman began to raise the barrier as soon as she saw him.

Other groups were boarding as well, chiefly pairs with a couple of threesomes thrown in. All fell silent as they stepped onto the platform, even as Adroo did. None were mere pleasure parties, and these close quarters lacked the privacy for the kind of top-level business discussions in which they intended to engage.

As soon as it was fully loaded, the lift started to rise. Rael leaned against the sturdy guardrail and peered over the edge to watch the teeming lobby recede as floor after floor flashed by. Soon, the crowd below appeared to be no more than a sea of animated miniature toys.

Because the lift was an express, free of any call to slow or pause in its ascent, it rose with a speed that almost crossed the threshold of comfort. Its motion was perfectly smooth, however, and it would take more than a peaceful rise like this to disturb the three spacers.

Only seconds after it had begun to move, the platform began to slow into a gentle stop that brought it flush with the floor of the Twenty-Two's reception area. The off-worlders stepped from it to find themselves on the stable hub of a broad, very slowly revolving disk on which were set a large number of tables, some near the core or in the center of the moving area, some right by the outer rim. They were not surprised by the arrangement; it was a very old one that remained popular for the simple reason that it was so effective. People loved to dine in such a setting wherever there was height and a view of sufficient interest and beauty to warrant the construction of such a facility.

This establishment made particularly good use of the design, Míceál had to admit. In place of the usual flat roof and tall, broad window panels, the entire restaurant was enclosed in a huge glassteel dome, inches thick in fact but so transparent as to seem not to be there at all. It must be truly spectacular here on a clear night, he thought, with the stars and Canuche's two tiny moons shining above, mirrored below by the lights of the populous town and the harbor. By day, much of that splendor was absent, for the high, steep slopes rising sharply on either side of the narrow bay restricted the view to the uninspiring community flowing up from the industrial belt at the water's edge to pour over the crests into the invisible regions beyond. The harbor itself saved the situation as far as he was concerned. The building was not so terribly high as to destroy the detail of the scene below, and the ever-busy port offered a wealth of activity to catch and hold an observer's attention.

A formally suited individual approached their party. "My usual table's on the outside," Adroo whispered, "but if that'll bother you, we'll change. You're here to enjoy a damn good meal, not to have your palates blunted by the peculiarities of the place."

Even as he spoke, his guests saw what he meant. The restaurant extended beyond the walls that confined the lower portions of the building, and the part of the floor that comprised the overhang was constructed of the same marvelously strong, clear material that fashioned the dome enclosing them. The tables placed there seemed to be standing on the air itself.

Jellico could bolt down food just about anywhere, but when a real feast was put before him he preferred to devote his attention to it and not be distracted by theatrics or dramatic surroundings, however attractive or interesting. Rael's delight, on the other hand, was open for once, and he offered no protest. "We're not likely to be eating in the Twenty-Two anytime soon again," he said. "Let's go for the full experience."

They were soon seated in comfortably upholstered chairs drawn up around a white-covered table. Water was immediately set before them, and they were given hot, moist towels for their hands.

The newcomers were conscious not so much of unease as of a sense of disorientation at first. The floor felt solid beneath their feet, but so clear was the glassteel that any downward glance seemed to make a lie of both touch and knowledge. For a time, all three off-worlders kept their eyes carefully fixed on their plates until the fascination of the scene revealed below outstripped the instinct to flight, and they began at last to enjoy the strange perspective and the array of activity it revealed.

It was just this experience that moved most people to

make their first visit to the Twenty-Two, and they were left in peace to savor it. Their waiter discreetly watched until the four began at last to look about for him. At that point, he approached their table.

"Will there be any change from our meat entrée? We also offer fowl, waterfood, or vegetables," he added for the benefit of the spacers, who were quick to declare that they would be delighted to have the house meal.

"What has Max put together for us today, Charles?" Adroo inquired after giving his own assent.

The man smiled expansively. "Just about heaven, Mr. Macgregory. Broiled round of rambeef, black and white pasta balls with gravy, and young sweet sil pods in white sauce. The after-sweet is a fourteen-layer cream torte." No pre-entrée courses were served on Canuche and no beverages save water during the meal itself so that nothing might dull or alter the taste of the main course. Dessert was always followed by either jakek or coffee.

"It sounds good, Charles. Thanks."

Once the waiter had gone, Macgregory drew an official-looking multicopy document from the portfolio he was carrying. "My lawyers drew this up for me last night. I've already signed and sealed it, so all that's needed to activate it are your signatures."

Van Rycke took it and read it over carefully. He nodded his agreement. "It covers everything we discussed," he said as he affixed his signature. He passed it to Jellico, who signed as well. He took the *Queen*'s copy, which he folded and slipped into the document pouch on his belt; the other he returned to the industrialist. "Thank you, Mr. Macgregory."

"My pleasure," Macgregory responded with satisfaction. He fixed his attention on Rael. "Now that I can't be accused of holding that contract over your head, I believe we have something to discuss, Doctor Cofort. — Your Captain did tell you of my offer, I presume?"

"He did," she replied, "or told me of its nature, rather. He gave me no details."

"Those are for us to work out if you're interested in pursuing the matter. It would entail no small change for you, and I expect you'll have to give it some pretty deep thought."

She smiled. "Deeper than you imagine, Mr. Macgregory. I didn't simply choose or fall into a career in space, you see. I was born on a Free Trader. The stars are in my blood. It'd go against everything I am to try to settle on any one world."

"Think about it all the same. I won't press you for an immediate decision—I wouldn't trust the judgment of anyone who'd give me one now under these circumstances— but a drastic change can work out well for a person. I had a bad case of wanderlust in my youth, and I've never been sorry for settling down and going into business."

The woman nodded slowly. "All right, Mr. Macgregory. I will give the possibility serious consideration, but I can't honestly see myself pursuing it. Even if I were willing to quit the starlanes, I'm still a Medic. I don't want to give that up to spend my life selling, whatever the product." Rael eyed him pensively. "Would you mind answering a question, Mr. Macgregory?"

"Probably not. If I do, I'll tell you when I hear it."

"You could've had the Thornen silk if you'd wanted it. Why didn't you take it?"

He chuckled. "Not for lack of interest, I assure you. — Every man should know himself and what suits him. I'm a worker ant and must content myself with the browns, blacks, and grays of my kind. Butterfly wings belong to other folk. That material would look ridiculous on my person or in my home, which is as plain as myself now that my wife's dead. I did toy with the idea of getting it for my sons and dividing it between them, but I've never spoiled them with extravagant presents and decided my best course was to stick to that policy." He laughed. "Besides, I was having too good a time watching my colleagues make noble fools of themselves. I didn't want to ruin the fun by entering the fray myself."

Jellico smiled at that, but his eyes were on the woman. Macgregory was right to try to lure her into his sales organization, he thought. Rael Cofort could move just about anything, herself not least of all, and she did not have to resort to conscious technique or flamboyant stunts to do it. Her talent for fixing her complete attention on a speaker, as if she found him genuinely valuable and infinitely interesting, saw to that. People were going to respond to that, and it would be a rare one who would not give her a favorable hearing in turn.

Their food was brought to them at that point, and the spacers quickly discovered that it was not the view that brought patrons back time after time to the Twenty-Two. Everything was absolutely fresh and superbly prepared. Canucheans did not go in heavily for strong spices, but the dishes they produced were not lessened because of their delicate, natural taste. The chef here had the best ingredients at his disposal, local and imported, and his hand, though restrained, was unquestionably a master's.

While they ate, their host filled them in on Canuche's history and present status both in response to queries by Van Rycke and in keeping with surplanetary courtesy, which prohibited the discussion of business while food was actually before one's guests.

". . . She's an old planet and an odd one. There's little or no life at all on any of the three continents in the northern hemisphere save a bit right along the coasts."

"Burn-off?" Jan asked.

"We don't know. If so, it happened so long ago that all direct evidence has disappeared. It wouldn't be the Forerunners who did it but rather *their* Forerunners. A lot of our scientists think a natural disaster, or series of them, might've been responsible, and a small minority says the north might never have supported more than we have now in the way of biotics."

"That's not very likely," Jellico said.

"No. It doesn't fit the pattern shown anywhere else in the galaxy where there's water and a reasonable atmosphere. Weathering makes soil, and something, evolutionarily speaking, eventually comes along to live in it."

"Besides, there is native life on Canuche."

"Yes. Very little and all low level in the north, as I said. The south has a reasonably rich flora. The fauna is species poor, but those creatures that are present often exist in vast numbers. Rambeeves are an example, as are the several kinds of fowl we've elected to farm."

"What about the sea?"

"The same general picture holds for all four oceans. Poor in variety but with large populations of the species that are present. Life of any sort is scarce or entirely absent from smaller bodies of water, north and south."

"Something happened here, right enough," the Captain declared. "Someday, maybe Federation scientists or Canuche's own will discover what it was."

"We keep hoping," Adroo replied.

Rael fixed her eyes on her plate. She did not have to hear more or read a library of documentation to be convinced gut level, in her own heart and mind, that Ali Kamil was right. The chill of that realization filled, all but overwhelmed, her. Canuche of Halio had been shattered in the past and maybe more than once, badly enough that most of the rich fauna and flora that should have graced such a planet had been eliminated, leaving the field open on each level of the food chain for the surviving species, plant and animal, to expand into great megapopulations.

She looked up again as the industrialist continued his account of his homeworld's history.

"Our First-Ship ancestors realized they had no natural paradise," he told them, "and decided to turn her peculiarities to their advantage and industrialize on a grand scale here in the north. The south, they devoted to farming. Canucheans knew from the start that we wanted to be self-sufficient and since this was a closed colony, claimed and settled by one group at one time, our ancestors enjoyed the luxury of being able to lay pretty definite and precise plans before ever taking ship for her surface. Canuche provides the resources to meet our basic needs on-world, and the colony's founders made that a prime part of our life charter. — No society can count itself secure, safe from the danger of being overwhelmed by alien influences, or from being annihilated or starved outright, if it has to depend on outsiders for the really essential goods and services. It hasn't always been easy, and there have been periods of strong temptation, but thus far we've managed to appreciate our founders' wisdom and stick with their ideals and instructions."

Macgregory was a native of the capital, and his pride in it was apparent when their conversation turned to Canuche Town itself a few minutes later.

"Canuche Town's actually a misnomer," he told them. "It may not be an inner-system megalopolis, but we have over two million residents and at least half that number again in the suburbs. That qualifies us as a city by anyone's lights.

"Like the other Canuchean towns, this is a community of individual neighborhoods. When our future First Shippers were developing their plans for the organization of our urban centers, it was decided to keep our workers near their jobs, ideally within walking distance or, at worst, a short commute away. Each of the neighborhoods thereby created is regarded and treated as a separate entity within the city and has its own schools, hospitals, shopping places, essential support services, and general entertainment and self-improvement facilities, which are often one and the same. Connecting and managing everything are an excellent public transport system and a civic government kept small enough and close enough to its constituents to remain responsive and effective. — The whole system's efficient, and everything's kept on a decent, human scale.

"You're actually seeing us just about at our worst from up here," Macgregory informed them. "Houses aren't packed in this tightly in most places, but between the plants down in the waterfront region and the docks themselves, there's a huge demand for workers. As I mentioned before, they live as close as possible to their jobs. It's a slum, in point of fact, or the Canuchean version of a slum. We don't have the poverty and the major problems associated with that in many other places."

"Why the docks at all?" Van Rycke inquired. "Air transport's efficient, cheap, and fast."

"So are our boats. Added to that, they don't take half a neighborhood out with them if one goes down. That happened with a big air transport during Canuche's early years. Once was enough. Besides, the boats provide work for a lot more people. As incomprehensible as that may seem to a lot of off-worlders, keeping our population fully employed has just about top priority on Canuche. You don't work, you emigrate."

"What about the spaceport, then?" the Medic asked hastily, hearing the defensive irritation in their host's voice. Handling the problem of a population a planet could not wholly support simply by kicking the excess off-world was not a policy favored by the Federation at large. "Granted it provides some good jobs, but starship crashes have been among the worst disasters in Federation history."

"It's not physically within the city," he replied a trifle grimly, "and we do insist that all ships make their approach and depart from the landward side."

"That's about as much as anyone can do," Jellico told

him, "and the general procedures at the port're as tight as I've encountered anywhere."

The Captain gazed a moment through the transparent wall. "What are we seeing down there? What, for instance, is that huge white building on the right?"

"That's Caledonia, Inc.'s, contribution to Canuche Town's prosperity." The industrialist scowled momentarily. "If I'd listened to my instincts instead of to my fools of financial advisers, there'd be two more stories on it, but even as it is, it's the biggest single facility in the city, employing some thirty thousand people on-site alone, not counting our cadre of longshoremen, the crews manning our ships and transports, and those maintaining our feeder lines."

"Factory?" Van Rycke asked.

He nodded. "Basically. It's what we call a hodgepodge plant. We do some light manufacturing from scratch and a lot of assembly of parts and products begun elsewhere as well as a great deal of research and development."

"Is that the usual procedure for the big manufacturers here?"

"Sometimes yes, sometimes no. Caledonia deals in construction and mining supplies, including very heavy major equipment, and in chemicals. Much of the preparation of both is done inland, either for safety's sake or on or near the mining sites for economic reasons. Some of the smaller items can go more completely through the manufacturing process here, but almost all the chemicals are piped to us in their component parts and blended or treated or whatever in the plant, then sent to their destinations as quickly as possible. We don't like holding them here. A good many

Andre Norton & P.M.Griffin

of them have properties that make it undesirable to store them in quantity in a populous region."

"What do the other factories make?"

"You name it. Every major company on Canuche has some sort of office in the city, and most of them do active work here. Few of us can resist the opportunity offered by the harbor. Anything produced in Canuche Town can be shipped directly from here with almost no intermediate transport costs, and the proximity of the spaceport is a plus beyond price for importers and exporters alike."

Van Rycke studied the body of water below, an inlet six miles long and approximately a mile wide, whose dark blue color proclaimed considerable depth. "You could have done worse than that," he remarked. "It's what decided your ancestors to build on this site, of course?"

"Naturally. It's one of the finest on a planet well supplied with good ports. — Just look at this setup! Twelve miles, six on each bank, of flat waterfront land perfect for industrial facilities of every sort. The slopes on either side are steep but not cliffs. People can readily live on them. The channel, which we call the Straight and Narrow, is sufficiently broad to permit the ready passage of any two vessels ever likely to travel our seas, and it's deep enough that in the old days, it would have been termed almost bottomless.

"We're truly blessed with respect to our defenses against the side effects of Canuche's bad weather, too. Both the current and the prevailing wind run parallel to this part of the coast, and only under the rarest combination of unfortunate circumstances does a storm pummel it head-on. Even in that event, we usually escape its worst fury. The heights on the seaward side break the force of the gales, and the Straight pushes in at a diagonal. It opens away from the flow of the current, and a lot of the sea's anger simply bypasses us. The harbor area has had real trouble from storms or the ocean on only four or five occasions since the area was first settled."

"There's still the potential for danger," the woman warned, "if not from nature, then as a result of your own efforts. A few products at least of all those made or shipped here must be inflammable or violently unstable. These slopes are high and steep enough to confine and reflect back a blast or a sudden fire acting like one. The rest of the town would be spared a lot of grief as a result, but this area would pay the passage for all."

Macgregory looked at her with new respect. "You've got an eye, Doctor, and a head to go with it. — The city planners are aware of that risk. It was brought home to us by the possibility scenarios we ran during the Crater War. Canuche went heavily into munitions production at the time. Quite literally every port of any size was handling the finished products or their components, and none of those in charge was stupid enough not to realize the enormous potential for disaster inherent in dealing with such matériel. We were determined to hold on to both our profits and our lives.

"Canuche Town responded by keeping the war goods as much as possible away from the city and inner harbor." He turned in his chair so he could gaze back over his shoulder. "See those red docks on the shoulders framing the mouth of the Straight?"

"Aye."

"They continue some distance beyond along the seaward side, as far as there's level land to hold the piers backing them. All combat matériel was loaded from them. Nothing ever did happen, praise the Lord of Light and Dark, but if a ship or dock had gone up, the worst of the blast would have broken on the heights or bypassed us, even as natural storms do. We'd have suffered some from the resultant sea surge, but that, too, would mostly have gone by.

"Munitions aren't the same industry now, I'm not sorry to say, and they're handled entirely on the west coast, where there are lower population levels. We use the red docks for fuel shipments, especially concoctions intended for the spaceport, the raw ingredients to make them, and other chemicals with chancy natures."

"Aren't those fuel tanks?" Jan inquired, pointing to a cluster of three tall cylinders just beneath their table. He could see approximately fifty similar structures scattered all along the waterfront. They were more heavily concentrated in some spots than others, but no section on either shore appeared to be completely devoid of them.

"Yes, they are that." The industrialist's voice was cold. "I've made myself an unpopular man trying to have them removed and that damned stuff stored underground where it belongs."

"One good fire'll educate everyone for you," Rael told him glumly.

"No doubt, but the poor people living and working around the thing'll be the ones who foot the tuition bill."

Jellico sighed to himself. They would wind up with a brace of disaster scholars in the party, he thought sourly. If the conversation turned to a detailed comparison of some of history's grimmer episodes, it would be to the decided detriment of a magnificent meal. He, for one, wanted to reap full enjoyment out of the incredibly rich torte the waiter Charles had just set before him.

The Cargo-Master was of the same opinion. "Canuche's citizens appear on the whole to be doing their part to ensure their safety. That and keeping on the alert are about all anyone can do." He was quiet while he ate an experimental forkful of the torte. "This is excellent! — What other cargoes do your ships handle? There's scarcely a dock vacant down there."

The older man smiled. "A graphic description of folks being blown halfway to the next galaxy is no aid to the digestion," he agreed. "To answer your question, almost anything grown or made on Canuche or imported from off-world finds its way to these docks at some point or other.

"Most of the bigger corporations own the port facilities fronting their establishments. — Caledonia has the four adjacent to our plant plus two red docks for the chemicals. — The rest are leased from the city by the smaller companies and the independent freight and passenger lines.

"The independents tend to group similar products together where practicable. Caledonia has its own longshoremen and equipment, but most draw on the city pool, and it's more economical to have any necessary specialists and specific gear more or less permanently nearby and on hand. For example, all sorts of southern-made goods and produce come in to the docks in the Cup area, right there below us where the Straight ends and the two banks meet, and the various products the north makes to meet their needs are sent off to them from there. Three large corporations pull in a big part of their profits on fertilizer alone at this time of year despite the fact that the farmers mainly use animal byproducts. Sil plants respond so well to a feeding of ammonium nitrate that a lightly treated field will produce three crops in a year in subtropical areas, two in temperate regions."

"Ammonium nitrate?" the Medic asked, frowning slightly.

"A common natural salt. Canuche has vast stores of it."

"It sounds familiar," she said, "though I don't recall the *Roving Star* ever carrying any. One of my brother's other ships or her predecessor may have done so at some time or other."

"I doubt it," Van Rycke told her. "There's no interstellar or even intrasystem Trade in it. The stuff's plentiful throughout the galaxy. Any planets we've found thus far who want it either have enough of their own or the means of readily making it or a reasonable substitute. As a matter of fact, I can't recall any other planet's making a real industry out of it, though my memory could be failing me on that. Synthetics and animal products have either overshadowed or entirely supplanted it in most places for centuries."

Adroo nodded. "True. It's the fact that we have so much of it so readily available that gives it its strength here, that and because sil plants respond so well to it."

He pointed to the scurrying workers and machines loading medium-sized crates on a squat-looking ship. "That freighter's kind of interesting. She bears the pretentious name of *Regina Maris* and is an independent that carries just about everything she can cram into her holds or on her decks. That's not the norm on Canuche. Most skippers don't care for a great deal of diversity. They'd rather not have to worry about more than one or two types of cargo at a time. Not this one, though. She took on coring drills and the stems supporting them from one of my competitors yesterday morning, then picked up an immense cargo of small items from another—screws, nuts, bolts, nails, and spikes of every conceivable description, some fashioned from metal and a lot from sundry synthetics. Passable stuff, too," he added grudgingly, "though none of it would win any contests against Caledonia's counterparts."

The industrialist smiled at that display of chauvinism. "Oh well, it's a sad man who can't or won't take pride in his own."

"What's she loading now?" Jellico asked, peering down at what seemed to be a scene of utter frenzy but which he knew was in fact a well-ordered operation. "Do you have any idea?"

"Considering where she's berthed, a good guess would be a consignment of rope of various types, including twine and string. A large shipment of it was brought to that dock yesterday evening."

"You know everything that comes and goes on these docks?" the Cargo-Master asked dryly.

Macgregory laughed. "Hardly, Mr. Van Rycke. It's just like I said before. A lot of the docks're either owned or permanently leased by fairly big organizations with well-known products and imports, and similar types of goods tend to move from fixed spots. I don't have a clue about the numerous small, independent lots that go in and out every day, and if someone wants to make a big secret of what he's doing, I wouldn't know what he's hiding." His eyes sparkled momentarily. "Unless I think it's worth the effort of finding out, that is." His guests would know full well that his position gave him the power if not the official authority to do that under most circumstances if he chose to exercise it. "Like most independents, the *Regina Maris* has her own band of regular customers. That makes for a similar cargo mix, just about what I described, often along with some ammonium nitrate or benzol thrown in. She'll spend three or four days in port loading up and refueling, make her run, and come back to repeat the cycle. — No mystery at all about her."

Seeing that the four had finished their torte, Charles returned to the table. "Would you like some jakek or coffee?"

"Jakek," Míceál responded quickly. Inwardly, he mourned that local etiquette forbade the requesting of a second helping of the torte to go with it. That had been one of the finest examples of the culinary art he had enjoyed in a stellar age.

"Jakek," Rael said somewhat absently.

Van Rycke eyed his shipmates with disapproval. "Coffee for me, please. Old is best after a fine meal like this."

"I'm old-fashioned as well," agreed Adroo. "That'll be two cups of jakek and two of coffee, Charles."

"Very good, sir." He deftly retrieved the used plates and cutlery and withdrew as unobtrusively as he had arrived.

Some minutes later, he returned with a tray bearing the four cups, which he set before their proper recipients.

Jellico sipped his. "As good as any I've tasted even on Hedon," he averred.

"So's the coffee," Jan remarked. "A special blend, Mr. Macgregory?"

He nodded. "Yes. Max's secret. We could easily enough find out the varieties he brings in, but not the proportions he uses."

"That would only spoil the mystery."

"Precisely."

Rael Cofort raised her cup to her lips but held it there while she gazed beyond it seemingly into the depths of space. Suddenly, she set it down again with enough force that the resulting click against the saucer caused her three companions to turn toward her. "Mr. Macgregory," she asked tensely, "you said ammonium nitrate is frequently loaded in the Cup area?"

"Yes," he answered, surprised. "Just about every week. Nearly daily at this time of year. Why?"

"Then Canuche Town is a death wish awaiting fulfillment."

19

A frown darkened the Cargo-Master's features, but Jellico silenced him with a sharp shake of his head. A cold dread chilled his own heart. It was not the Medic's words but the deadly, calm certainty with which she had spoken them that drove the spear through him. That tone compelled attention, the more powerfully from those who knew this woman at all.

Adroo Macgregory was not pleased, but he, too, was gripped by his guest's manner. Groundlessly or not, she was afraid for his city. "It's an old, stable compound, Doctor. You can jostle it, drop containers of it, run a transport over it without any effect whatsoever."

"Aye, but give it a sudden, extreme increase in temperature, and you've got an atmobomb on your hands. — I'm not exaggerating, Mr. Macgregory. Ammonium nitrate sounded familiar to me, not because I'd heard of it in connection with Trade but because of my own studies. History tells loud and clear what it can do. That stuff has caused galactic-class chaos before now, and given everything else stored and made around here, there's enough of it down there right now to literally annihilate everything and everyone between these slopes if absolutely everything went wrong, and maybe a good part of the city beyond as well."

"You're sure?" the *Solar Queen*'s Captain asked quietly.

"Aye. The incidents I'd studied took place in the far past. As Mr. Van Rycke says, ammonium nitrate hasn't been big business, or real business at all, for a very long time, but it has caused trouble before, and it'll do it again. Canuche Town's primed for it."

"She's right if that blasted stuff's as bad as she claims," the Canuchean cut in sharply. "The Cup's the worst conceivable place for an accident involving a volatile substance. — I'll look into this, Doctor Cofort. If your claims prove out, before you lift with your last charter from me, you'll find ammonium nitrate being handled on the red docks, with shipments so scheduled as not to bring it into contact with too much else that might exacerbate an accident."

"Will you be able to get the dock space for it?" Jan asked doubtfully. "Everything looks pretty locked up down there."

"Out at the very tip, yes, which is where it belongs anyway by the sound of it. Those piers're too far away from everything to be considered convenient, so there are always a number of them available. We don't ship that much sensitive material at a given moment nowadays to tie them all up. Or we didn't."

"You'll have to delve far back for confirmation," Rael warned, "to the first Martian settlement and pre-space Terra."

"I have the people to do the digging, Doctor. Don't you worry about that. I also have the means to collect evidence more directly. — I'll have to ask you to excuse me for a few minutes. They have sealed booths here. There are some calls I have to make."

Rael watched him go, then lowered her eyes to the table to avoid those of her companions. "I'm sorry," she said softly.

"He mentioned that two million people live in Canuche Town," Míceál said.

He took a sip out of his cup and scowled. "Space, woman, why couldn't you at least have waited until we'd finished our jakek?"

"The coffee's no less good," Van Rycke told him, although he glanced nervously below even as he spoke. The motion of the restaurant had already begun to put the Cup behind them. The effect would be strictly illusory in the event that the worst happened while they were up here, of course, but it was a definite psychological comfort to see it go.

He frowned again as an old memory stirred. "I think she's right, Míceál. Way back in my first year at the Pool, we had an old cracked-helmet retired Cargo-Master as an instructor. I recall his mentioning that ammonium nitrate used to be on the hazardous cargo list at one time before it was dropped for never being carried. I believe he also mentioned that it was actually used as an explosive in olden times. — Damn, I should have remembered that as soon—"

"Power down, Van," Jellico said calmly. "Even you're not a computer. — Here comes our host."

Macgregory did not reclaim his chair. "Come on, space hounds. We're about to witness an experiment."

One of the calls the Canuchean industrialist had made was to order a transport for his party, and a large four-wheel passenger vehicle was waiting for them at the entrance of the tower building when they emerged from it a few minutes later.

It made no delay in carrying them through the crowded streets and deposited them in short order before the main entrance of the giant Caledonia, Inc., plant.

Adroo nodded to the guard stationed there and led his guests inside. "Our research quarters are this way."

It was through the clerical portion of the huge facility that he conducted them rather than through those sections where Caledonia's numerous products were made or assembled. Here were no coverall-clad laborers driving their minitrucks, lifters, or manipulators or commanding their banks of robots but, rather, fashionably dressed men and women seated at desks or moving in an office worker's universal hurry along the seemingly endless hallways.

Once again, Rael was struck by the suitability of their Trade uniforms. They attracted no notice, or none beyond the inevitable interest aroused by the company in which they traveled.

She gave a wry smile. That held true only for their dress uniforms, she amended. They would not make such an appealing picture after a few hours shoving cargo around, particularly on some low-mech steam pit like Queex's Tabor or Amazoon of Indra.

"Here's the Research Center," Macgregory told them at last, echoing the sign on the big double swinging doors as he pushed his way through them.

Another maze of corridors awaited them on the other side, in general appearance much the same as those they had left behind save that the people they encountered now were wearing white. Most also had their hair confined in san-nets and their hands covered by the light, supple laboratory gloves that were standard equipment in such installations throughout the Federation.

A technician whom Rael judged to be about Dane Thorson's age approached them. "We're all set, Mr. Macgregory."

"Lead the way."

In response, she opened a door on their left, this one a panel that silently slid to a tight close behind them.

They found themselves in a hall or walkway about five feet wide that completely encircled a sealed chamber walled off from them by a barrier of some colorless, transparent material. The ceiling above the enclosed place was a mass of lights and odd instruments as complex in appearance as the bridge of the *Solar Queen*. The floor was a seamless sheet of dull-finished metal.

The whole place was empty save for a single metal

sphere approximately one foot in diameter resting in splen-
did isolation in what appeared to be its exact center.

"The control panel's over here," the technician told
them.

They followed her a quarter around the perimeter of the
room until they came to a two-foot-square board of dials
and gauges that made a fitting complement to the bewildering ceiling inside.

"That ball is a miniature laboratory," Adroo explained.
"We put the substance to be tested in the bottom half, seal
on the top, and introduce whatever forces or elements we
want while the sensors fixed on the interior monitor the
results. Despite being easily handled, it's a sturdy little
device and is equipped with escape valves to release gases
before they can build up dangerous pressure levels."

Jellico tapped the crystal wall separating them from the
ball. "Shatterproof?"

"Of course. We don't take chances when dealing with
potentially hazardous materials. Those balls are strong, but
they're not invincible, and neither are my staff members
who have to deal with them."

"What now?"

"We're more or less simulating the hold of a freighter.
We packed a proportionally equivalent volume of ammonium nitrate in the lab, and now we're going to subject it
to some abuse."

"Electricity first, sir?" the white-garbed woman asked.
"Or a spark?"

"I believe Doctor Cofort mentioned a sudden, sharp rise
in temperature. Try direct contact with fire."

"Very good, sir."

She bent over her console. Her fingers deftly touched one button, then moved to a finely calibrated dial. Immediately, a slender wire descended from the ceiling. It hovered over the sphere an instant before finding and entering a small hole at its top. "We'll start out with a relatively cool flame, like that of a normal fire," she said, "and increase the temperature every few milliseconds until there's a reaction . . ."

A sudden, searing flash lit the sealed chamber followed almost in the same instant by a sharp clap of sound clearly audible through the screening walls confining it. Rael stifled a scream as she threw her hands before her face in an instinctive effort to ward off the glowing objects hurtling toward them from the shattered ball.

It was over seemingly in the moment it began. When the observers collected themselves once more, they stared in awe at the place where the miniature laboratory had been. All that remained of it now was a blackened patch on the floor and some twisted fragments scattered throughout the chamber.

"Lord of Light and Dark," whispered the Canuchean woman. "The valves were operational . . ."

"They just couldn't handle this," Jellico responded briskly. His fingers followed the line of the scratch a piece of shrapnel had gouged in the shielding material in front of him. If the barrier had not held, it would have sliced through his throat. "Your little lab wasn't designed to endure old-fashioned brute force," he told her. "It was meant to conduct sane experiments, not contain a bomb blast."

"A what?" Macgregory demanded sharply.

Van Rycke shrugged. "What else would you call it? It

even fitted the stereotype image—a round, explosive-filled metal ball with a fuse sticking out of it, or sticking into it in this case."

"It behaved like one at any rate," Adroo agreed. He turned to his employee. "You recorded the whole thing, of course?"

"Naturally." There was no diffidence in that answer. This was her job; she knew how to do it. "There were some returns from the lab as well. I won't know how much we got until I go over the recordings."

"Get on it, then see if you can replicate the results under a variety of circumstances. Use less expensive bomb cases. We can recoup our costs later as part of a civic service claim, but we're not likely to collect in a hurry."

She smiled. "Yes, sir."

"And for the Lord of Light's sake, don't get yourself or anyone else killed. That may be a safe room, but it's not going to hold a baby planetbuster."

"I'll be careful. — What're we going to do, Mr. Macgregory? If a cargo goes up, the blast'll be almost literally infinitely worse than this little pop we just made. It won't be confined to a sterile, empty, shielded chamber, and more than one hold will almost certainly be involved even at the outset. Once the inevitable happens and the chain reaction starts, all the Federation's hells will be on us for a fact."

"We don't panic. — First, we've got to charge our blasters, get all our evidence together, then I hit the City Council with it. Luckily, everyone on it has some interest in the harbor. That should help jab a needle in their tails. —

Doctor Cofort, I'll need your historical information for a backup."

"I've just got a temporary berth on the *Queen* and have nothing with me. However, I can tell you where to set your researchers looking."

"Good enough. Fasmit the details to me as soon as you get back to your ship. Mr. Van Rycke has the code."

The industrialist gave his head a sharp shake. "I've been remiss. It's past time for another evacuation drill."

"Evacuation?" Jan inquired.

"Canuche was spared during the Crater War. A lot of other worlds weren't. I've seen the tapes, both of those struck by the combatants and those hit even more viciously by jacks taking advantage of the general chaos. I've also seen evidence of what can happen when people don't respond correctly or in time to natural upheavals—storms, earthquakes, and the like.

"All my employees are required to keep on hand a week's supply of concentrates, water, first aid supplies, any necessary specific medications, and blankets for every human and animal member of their household plus a tent or other portable shelter for them all and a surplanetary transceiver to keep abreast of news. Periodically, I order them to carefully shut down the plant and feeder lines, take their emergency gear, and leave the city for the hardpan beyond. The only concession I make is to exclude ailing or handicapped persons and a caregiver if one is needed. I'm out to save lives, not take or endanger them."

"They put up with that?" Rael asked.

Macgregory smiled. All spacers had to accept discipline, but such blind obedience would be an alien concept to the mind of a Free Trader. "There's always something extra to sweeten the paychecks of those who comply. The odd one who doesn't finds a dismissal notice. Besides, one of the very few times in its history that Canuche Town suffered real injury from the ocean occurred only a few years back. Our weather forecasters told us to expect trouble, and, because my people were concentrated in the most immediately threatened neighborhoods, I forced a full evacuation early. They spent one hell of a miserable night, but when the waters came, nobody was hurt, and those whose property was damaged received financial help to repair or replace it.

"The rest of the populace wasn't told to leave until much later. There was haste, some confusion, and a little panic at the end. A handful of injuries occurred as a result and a few deaths, all of those among the fools who refused to go at all.

"My policy proved itself in the time of testing, and since then, I haven't gotten much static when I've demanded a refresher course on the procedures."

His lips tightened. "Now I see how much more important it is than even I'd realized. Danger's a lot closer to us than a chance attack from the stars or a freak, fairly readily predicted combination of foul weather or geophysical events."

Adroo squared his shoulders. "That's my business and Canuche Town's. Thank you, all three of you, for your help thus far. I may also want a deposition from you, just a description of our conversation today and what you observed here plus any knowledge you have about ammonium nitrate."

"That shouldn't be a problem," Míceál answered for his party. "I can't help with background detail, unfortunately, but I'll apply to Trade records and see if we can't uncover more for you. Van and Rael will, of course, do what they can as well."

"Again, my thanks. — In the meantime, I have a living to make. To get back to our original reason for meeting, Captain, how soon can you begin to accept deliveries?"

"Right away."

"We'll start tomorrow morning, then." He turned to Rael. "Here's my card, Doctor. It lists my private code. I haven't forgotten my offer. Hell, after all this, you needn't take a sales job. Name what you want, and if it isn't on the books now, I'll create a post to your specifications."

She nodded gravely. "I'll keep that in mind, Mr. Macgregory, and if I turn it down, it won't be for want of gratitude."

20

Míceál Jellico watched the spaceport manipulator swing a huge, metal-banded crate to the *Solar Queen*'s wide-open hatch. There, Rael deftly guided the clamps of the starship's smaller version of the all-purpose large-cargo handler into place and signaled to Van Rycke, who was at the controls of their machine, to lock them. A second wave to the outer world caused the holds on the port manipulator to be released.

Once more, the crate rose. It disappeared through the hatch, where it would be delivered to Dane in the bulk cargo hold for final stowing.

Jellico walked over to the Cargo-Master. "That the last of the big stuff?"

"Aye," he said as he switched off the motor and swung down from the control seat. "Just those boxes now." He pointed to a tall stack of space-sealed containers of several different types and sizes. "We could handle those manually if need be, not that anyone's Whisperer bait enough to do it while better's available. We won't be getting the real small stuff until tomorrow morning."

"You and Thorson can manage without your assistant?"

"We had to manage before she came." He turned his head. "Cofort!" he shouted. "Come on down! Our Captain's pulling rank and commandeering your services."

Seconds later, the woman joined them. "What now?" she asked, smiling. As she spoke, she rubbed her hands against the legs of her trousers to dry them. Machine help or none, loading and sorting bulk cargo was still heavy work.

"As Van says, I want to borrow you for a few hours."

"Sure thing." She saw that he had rented a flier and glanced back at the ship. "It'll only take a few minutes to wash and change . . ."

"No need. Just grab your cap and silicates to screen out Halio's rays."

"Will do," she responded.

The Medic returned to the waiting men an edifyingly short time later. "All set," she informed them.

"Excellent." Jellico pointed to the flier's front passenger seat. "Hop in."

"Good luck with your lizards," Van Rycke called after him.

His commander scowled but then raised his hand in

farewell. "Just see that none of this valuable cargo's left out to face the rigors of the night air."

With that, he activated the controls, and the vehicle, a light-duty passenger four-seater, shot away from the *Queen.*

Míceál laughed softly. "He's right about the lizards. I am stealing you to help me on a personal project."

"So I gathered," Rael responded. "That's tri-dee gear I see on the rear seat unless I'm very much mistaken. — What's the story about the lizards?" she asked curiously. "I thought Canuche didn't have anything worth mentioning in the way of wildlife, especially here in the north."

"Nothing much in terms of variety, size, or high development on the intelligence scale," he corrected. "What's here is both interesting and important, simply because they are here, if for no other reason.

"The lizards we're seeking are a prime example. They're small—three inches long excluding that much again of tail—winged, and a beautiful deep green in color. They're relatively common in their natural range but can't be kept in captivity—Canuchean conservation and anticruelty laws forbid any further attempts to do so—and no one's ever been able to study or make any sort of pictorial record of them in the wild. As soon as a person gets even within long-lens range, every lizard present drops into the foliage. If they can be discovered at all, they're hunched up in tight little balls that won't release again until the intruder is gone, depending on camouflage and the poison in their skins to protect them.

"A number of theories have been proposed to account for the acuity of their senses, particularly since they're equally adept at avoiding time-set, unmanned equipment, and I've got one of my own that I wouldn't go about propounding before too many people for fear I'd be thought straight Whisperer bait."

"I'm flattered. — What's your explanation?"

"Some sort of telepathy would account for it." He raised his hand when he saw her look of incredulity. "I'm not talking about the fancy stuff beloved of novelists and video writers. This would be more basic, the ability to sense interest in them, perhaps. In the wild, that'd mean only a couple of things—either a potential mate or a potential predator. An excited xenobiologist would come across as the latter, I should imagine."

"You may well be right," she agreed slowly. "Biologically, they wouldn't have any reason to develop the power to differentiate more finely, and humans haven't been on the scene long enough to have had much effect on that aspect of their lives."

"That's about the way I've reasoned it out."

"What's my part in this?"

"I want to try an experiment, to see if your presence or your active efforts will calm them sufficiently for me to get some shots."

"But I have no power to draw them! I told you I didn't . . ."

"Not directly, maybe, but I've seen how Sinbad and Queex respond to you. Cats have been associated with humans a long time and are noted for the affection they sometimes bestow on those they favor. The same can't be said for hoobats. You've worked your own brand of magic on my six-legged comrade, and I'm hoping something similar might occur with Canuche of Halio's green lizards. At any rate, it'll do no harm to give it a try."

"No, I suppose not."

When the Medic remained silent for several seconds, he glanced at her. She was sitting quietly, her expression grave, her eyes lowered.

Míceál sighed. "This isn't meant to be a trial, Rael. If you really don't want to do it, you can just watch, or we can turn back altogether."

She looked up. "I know what a coup this would be for you if you could pull it off. I just don't want to disappoint you."

"No way. It's a chance worth taking, but if it doesn't work out, it doesn't."

The project was important to him, all right, but Jellico reined in his eagerness. Cofort's gift, assuming she had one in the first place, probably would not work if she was too upset. — Space, he did not want to upset her at all. "You never got a chance to eat," he said. "Reach back there and pull out the sandwiches Frank thoughtfully produced for us. I fear he innocently imagines we'll be stopping for a formal picnic someplace, but we'll be too busy if we succeed and back in good time for dinner if we don't. Either way, you won't have another crack at a meal for a while."

The woman was not slow to comply. She eagerly wolfed down the Steward's offering, both because she was hungry and because it was extremely good. "Treat Mr. Mura kindly," she advised. "He's an asset not to be underrated."

"I doubt any member of the *Queen*'s crew would be guilty of that particular error, my friend."

*   *   *

The flier had not left the spaceport and city very far behind before the nature of the country flowing by beneath them changed abruptly and to Rael's mind much for the worse. The yellowish ground was hard, compacted to the point that it could be classed as soft rock rather than soil, and dry save where streams and small rivers knifed their way through it. Vegetation was sparse and low even along the watercourses. It did not exist anywhere in sufficient quantity to significantly hold the particles worked loose from the miserly ground by the forces of weathering.

"Much of the interior's hardpan like this," Jellico informed her.

"It seems to go on forever," she replied with distaste.

"This patch runs about twenty miles wide and some three hundred long. Once we get across it, we'll see some more typical inner coastal land. That's not particularly pretty, either, but it's got some variety, at least."

The transition was sharp when they reached the end of the hardpan. The countryside now beneath them was wetter than the barren place they had left behind. Its soil was real, and a fairly continuous blanket of plants grew upon it, most of them ranging from ankle to knee high. The common color, varied by a number of lighter and darker exceptions, was a fine, deep green, and Míceál informed his companion that among these fronds, stems, and roots dwelled almost the total roster of the north's terrestrial wildlife, most of which was quite small and very low on the intelligence scale.

The Captain eased their vehicle to the ground. "Let's see

if we can't rouse some photogenic green lizards, Doctor."

Taking his tri-dee equipment and a pair of distance lenses, he started moving slowly away from the machine, walking carefully, as if he was trying to become part of the natural world around them. Catching up her share of the equipment, Rael did her best to emulate him.

They traveled several hundred yards, then he raised his hand to signal a halt. "This should be far enough. There ought to be a few around. Whether we'll be able to get a glimpse of them's another matter."

Jellico trained his lenses on a patch of vegetation and began to quarter it visually. It betrayed no sign of the little creatures he was seeking, and he moved on to the next clump.

A quarter of an hour passed before he straightened in satisfaction. "There! I can make out a couple of them. — See. They look like little balls of moss."

The woman spotted them as well. She could discern the lines where limbs and head were tucked in, but there was no sign that either creature was still alive.

They should be rather pretty little things, she thought, with that green color and equipped with wings. She would like to see them flying around, or even just relaxed enough to let her get a good look at them.

Green lizards must be harmless, peaceful, slow-flying beings if this was their typical response to interest from other life forms. It worked because their skins contained powerful poison glands; nothing biting into them once would repeat the experiment. Unfortunately, humans could not be repelled by that means, and she was glad

Canuchean authorities were taking steps to protect the small animals.

Rael recalled herself to her purpose for being with this expedition. She did not rightly know how to begin, but she decided after some reflection to start by thinking kindly thoughts about the lizards. If Míceál was right and they could pick up interest in them, they might also be able to read that.

It was not a major order, at least. She was gently disposed toward them and sympathized with their situation. It was probably wise to avoid most so-called intelligent beings, but she truly did wish they would make an exception in this case. She and Jellico meant them no hurt at all. They only wanted to watch a while and capture a few images for later study and enjoyment . . .

For several minutes, it looked as if the experiment was a failure; then a tiny, sharply pointed snout disengaged itself from the living ball and gazed tentatively about. Seconds later, the entire body uncoiled, followed in a breath's space by the second lizard.

Each animal climbed the stem nearest it and worked its way outward along the bottom of the lowest frond. When they had traveled so far along the big leaves that they started to bend, the creatures deftly released their front legs, retaining their grip with the rear pair and tails. Two membrane-thin, pale green wings unfurled and began to beat slowly to support the lizards' upper bodies.

Several times, she saw their heads dart in to touch the bottom of a leaf. Were they feeding, she wondered, picking up insects or spores or maybe some extrudate from the plant? Her lenses were not quite good enough to tell her that, but the Captain's tri-dees could be developed at very high magnification and should be able to give them the answer, to that question and to a number of others besides.

For over an hour, the two green lizards clambered and fluttered from leaf to leaf. At last, both scrambled to the ground and scurried away from the stand of plants. Within moments, the thick growth had completely screened them from the off-worlders' sight.

The Medic gave a long, lingering sigh. "They were so wonderful," she said softly.

Jellico looked at her, as he had more than once during the past hour. She had been completely absorbed in watching the little creatures, more so even than he had been himself, and she had been happy in her absorption. Happy and unguarded. He realized this was the first time he had seen her shields go down for any significant length of time.

Her eyes were bright when they turned to him, but it was no longer possible to read with any certainty what lay behind them.

"How do you think we did?" she asked.

He slid his camera back into its case. "If a small part of these come out, we'll have exceeded our goal by a stellar margin. — Thank you, Rael Cofort."

"My pleasure," she replied, happy in herself and for him, "though I can't rightly say that I did much. I didn't feel anything in particular happening."

"I'd say it's likely that you helped," he said dryly, "considering that no one has ever before been able to study those little creatures in action since the day they were first discovered."

The woman frowned. "Míceál, how're you going to explain what we did? We don't really understand it ourselves."

"I'm not going to attempt an explanation," he responded rather stiffly. "I'll probably forget to mention the telepathy theory altogether."

"You can't do that!" she told him sharply. "You're too much a scientist."

"No," he agreed slowly. "I couldn't. I'm only going to touch on it in passing, though, toss it in as a possibility, and suggest we may have succeeded because we were full of hope, not anticipation or excitement that might come across as hunting instinct. I can't say more since we don't know what actually happened or if anything did happen at all. — I imagine you're not eager to wind up as part of an esper research project?"

"Space, no! I'd hitch a ride on Sanford Jones's glowing comet first." She shuddered. "Apart from the likelihood of running into trouble about the mystery surrounding my mother's antecedents, I know too much medically. There isn't any such thing as esper training and won't be for another few decades—or centuries if the funding dries up. All they do now is take folks apart for weeks and sometimes years at a stretch, and they don't always remember to put them back together again."

"That's more or less the way I had it figured," he said. "We can't publish what we tried. If the wrong people read about it and got interested, I wouldn't be able to protect you and neither would Teague. Esper research is a government project, and if they really wanted you for it, they'd get you."

"They won't hear anything from me," she promised fervently. Rael gave him a sidelong glance. "You're an awful worrier, aren't you?" she remarked. "You can find the gloomy side of anything."

Jellico laughed softly. "That's a prerequisite for my job. A starship Captain lacking that trait doesn't usually last long enough to acquire it. Unfortunately, his ship and everyone else aboard normally go out along with him."

His fingers drummed on the controls. He glanced at her as determination firmed in him. "Rael, I'd like some answers. None of this will go beyond me, and I know I'm out of my lane, but . . ."

She sighed. "I'd like to be able to do more with animals. It seems that might actually be possible, and I'll work at it, but right now, I have to stand by what I said before. I don't know what happened here or if anything happened. I certainly can't supply an explanation."

"I'm not challenging that."

"What are you challenging?"

"Nothing. I just want to put a few questions to rest." The gray eyes gripped hers. "What happened to you in the Red Garnet?"

Her breath caught, and she started to frown, but she stopped herself. Ali and the others were this man's shipmates and subordinates. They would have described the whole incident in detail for him even if they had kept quiet about that part of it in front of the Patrol-Colonel. "I panicked."

"Aye. Why?"

Her eyes wavered. "I felt . . . something in there. What, I don't know, though believe that I've tried to figure it out. Maybe it was the rats' collective hunger, maybe some afterglow of the victims' horror and pain. Maybe it was something filthier, the eagerness of the subbiotics who could run an operation like that. They probably saw every stranger who walked into their lair as potential prey." She shuddered. "It was all over the place, choking and draining me. I— I had to get out of there!"

She regained command of herself. "I figured, too, as much as I could reason, that the others'd follow if I ran. Of course, a fight almost erupted instead . . ."

Her lips tightened into a hard line. "I've got no excuse. I blew it badly, and you'd have been within your rights to boot me off the ship."

"None of my lads asked for that," he responded quietly.

Her eyes, which had been fixed on her clasped hands, lifted. "Would . . . would you have done it?"

"No. I'd have upheld your contract. Your term of service is almost out, and you're not going back into space with us."

She just nodded. Jellico watched her for a moment. If he was ever going to hear the rest, it would have to be now, while she was thoroughly demoralized. "How can you function as a Medic?" he asked bluntly. Her answer to that could break her story, and it could give him some of the insight into her that he ever more strongly wanted to have.

"I don't have a problem with that," the woman responded without hesitation.

Her brows came together as she sought words to convey her meaning. "I'm definitely not what is usually thought of as an empath. I don't experience another's pain or emotions, but I do feel—uneasy when someone nearby is ill or injured. It is not a pleasant feeling. It's horrible, in point of fact, but it's not debilitating."

For a moment, anger drove back her pallor. "That's how I found the poor apprentice on the *Mermaid*. I knew something was wrong and hunted until I discovered him. If I hadn't, he'd probably have died where he lay. Slate certainly wouldn't have bothered looking for him even if he were missed in time. The bastard never even came to see him when he was dying." Her voice cracked. "Oh damn . . ." she muttered as she was forced to fall silent.

Míceál's fingers brushed hers. "It's all right to care, you know," he told her gently. "Space, you're a Medic. You're supposed to care."

Cofort withdrew her hand. "The effect isn't cumulative," she went on, her tone steady and impersonal once more. "I was afraid it might prove so when I started my emergency room rotation, but I had no difficulty. I was able to set the discomfort aside the same as if I were dealing with a single patient and get on with my work."

"Your gift has no real effect, then?" he asked thoughtfully.

"It might in a sense. I proved remarkably able at triage, and I could single out the most serious cases present, the heart attacks as opposed to the bad sprains."

"What about during the plague?"

She shook her head. "I wasn't conscious of anything particular then except for the constant fear and grief, but I was only a child, and we were all scared. I may have been picking something up, and I suppose I might have developed some inborn ability for handling the pressure, but I can't recall anything of the sort. I know the rest, such as it is, developed as I grew. It was a major factor in my choosing medicine as my specialty."

Rael seemed to slip into her own thoughts and said nothing more for several seconds. She roused herself abruptly and faced him. "What now, Captain?"

"We head back to the *Queen.*" His hands rested on the controls, but he did not activate them immediately. "I don't know what life is like in the Cofort organization, but the *Solar Queen* welcomes whatever talents her crew has. That extends to passengers and temporary hands. Bear that in mind if yours start working on you again."

Míceál brought the machine to a halt again just before they reached the outskirts of Canuche Town's suburbs.

Rael was surprised, but when she looked to the Captain for clarification, she found him staring straight ahead, his gaze apparently fixed on some point in the far distance. "Is something wrong?" she inquired anxiously.

"Wrong, no, but the *Queen* will be lifting tomorrow."

"Aye. By midafternoon if nothing delays delivery of the last Caledonia shipment."

"Are you going to accept Macgregory's offer?"

"No."

"Think carefully, Rael. He meant every word of it. You're not likely to run into a chance like this again."

"Do you want me to accept it?" she asked carefully.

"What I want's irrelevant. It's your life, and this is a major decision."

The woman shook her head. "No, I'm not going to accept. I don't like Canuche of Halio. She's Adroo Macgregory's homeworld, and he naturally loves her. I'm not going to tell him how I feel about her, but of all the Federation's habitable planets on which I might eventually choose to settle, this one's pretty near the bottom of the list. Besides, I don't want to leave the starlanes. That's where I was born, and that's where I belong."

Jellico's eyes dropped. He realized he had been gripping the controls so tightly that his knuckles glistened white under the stretched skin and hastily eased his hold. "I think that's the wiser choice, though maybe not the most financially sound one," he told her.

She studied him gravely. "I answered your question. Now answer mine. Did you wish me to accept Mr. Macgregory's offer?"

"No. No, I did not. It would've been a disaster. Macgregory's every inch an autocrat—benevolent maybe, but a despot all the same. A Free Trader's too independent to stay under the thumb of someone like that long-term."

"You'd have let me go ahead despite that?"

"I had no right to stop you, Rael, though I would've raised the question for your consideration and stressed it pretty strongly had you given me a different answer."

His eyes were somber. "That'll leave you at loose ends once we lift. Do you have anything particular in mind?"

Cofort nodded. "I was planning to approach Deke Tatarcoff. I've never known him not to be shorthanded, and I've given him good reason to respect my abilities. If that doesn't work out, I'll just hang around for a while. This port's busy enough that I'm bound to pick up a berth in fairly short order, even if it's just another single-voyage hop to some backwater hole."

She saw him start to frown and shrugged delicately. "If it looks like there's going to be a delay, I have no objection to taking on-world work for a time to keep body, soul, and store of credits together. Some of the hospitals in Canuche Town can probably use a part-time Medic, and should worse come to worse, I might even try to wrangle a temporary job out of Adroo Macgregory."

"It sounds reasonable," he said without looking at her. "I have to confess that I had some reservations about just leaving you here."

"I'm not one who's ever likely to let herself starve."

"No."

Her voice softened. "Thank you, Míceál Jellico," she said. She sat a little straighter. "Let's go back and develop those tri-dees. I'm dying to see what we gained for our efforts."

21

Jellico shivered. Even this far from the shore, the sea breeze was sharp and cold and would remain so for a while yet, until Halio had warmed the land sufficiently to reverse the thermal currents and bathe the city in dry, hot, inland currents.

That alteration in the flow of the breeze, quite independent of the predominant prevailing winds, which moved parallel to the land, was a real blessing to the inhabitants of the city during the blistering months of the summer. A heat haze might shimmer over Canuche Town's streets by day, but at night, people slept well beneath light blankets.

Rael joined Jellico at the hatch, and they descended together. Both had business in the city. The Captain intended to get the flier back to the rental agency before he had to pay a second day's charges for it, and she had asked to accompany him since he would be passing close to the Caledonia plant. She wanted to give Macgregory her answer face-to-face or at least deliver a personal letter to his office if he should not be there this early rather than merely calling in her refusal over the *Queen*'s transceiver as they prepared her for space. He deserved the courtesy of the greater effort on her part.

She smiled as she took her place in the passenger seat. The vehicle had done them good service the previous evening ferrying them all to the restaurant the crew had chosen for their last-night dinner. It had been a fine affair all around. If their eatery had not been another Twenty-Two, the food had been good, and they had enjoyed it and themselves, Ali Kamil as thoroughly as any of his comrades. He had seemed more at ease than she had hitherto seen him, certainly more so than he had been since they had planeted on Canuche of Halio. The confirmation of the industrial planet's apparently dark history and the reality of the peril still hanging over her had affirmed and the reality of his gift. That was a relief in itself, and it was a relief that they would soon be leaving the dangerous world behind.

"We'll cut around by the Cup," Míceál told her as they started out. "It's a bit longer that way, but I want to get a good look at the ships."

"You're the skipper. Besides, I'd like to see them close up myself." She stifled a yawn. "After crawling out of my bunk so soon in order to see Mr. Macgregory, I hope he is an early riser."

"That one? You can put credits down on it. He won't squander valuable daylight hours in bed."

"You needn't squander any time, either," she told him, "at least not waiting for me. Once you drop me off, just turn the flier in and go on back to the *Queen*. I'll find my way home."

"Not a chance. Van'd be asking what happened to my wits if I failed to make so obvious a courtesy call on our illustrious client."

They soon came within sight of the ocean. Only two large vessels were at dock in the Cup, the low, squat *Regina Maris* and another slightly larger craft with the name *Sally Sue* displayed on her prow and sides. A number of small boats attended to the freighters' needs or to their own.

Both of the big ships were the center of considerable activity. Míceál slowed the flier down to hover to better observe the scene. "Look at that, Rael," he said softly. "It's like a moment frozen in time. A few centuries back, that's what we'd have been doing."

She nodded. If that was all there was, they would be part of it. Trade was in their souls, and neither of them would have been content with the role of sedentary shopkeeper.

She frowned somewhat disapprovingly as she continued to study the on-worlders working around the *Regina Maris*. A bit of concentrated study stripped some of the perfection from the picture for one who was familiar with the management of bulk cargo. "They go in for a lot of fuss, don't they?" she remarked. There was not half this ado when a starship was being loaded.

Jellico started to agree, but then he frowned. Commotion was one thing; idleness was another. There were a lot of dock laborers just standing about, leaving the cargo lying where it was. Those people were paid by the hour. Whether he traversed a single planet's seas or the starlanes, no ship's master would tolerate a pack of idlers leeching away his always tight port expense funds. "She's in trouble," he announced sharply even as he sent the flier surging forward.

In another moment, they came to a stop beside a group of longshoremen. "What's the problem?" he asked.

"What's it to you, space hound?" one countered. There was no real hostility in the question, just a petty enjoyment in momentary superiority over the off-worlder with his supposedly more interesting lifeway.

"Most Captains sympathize with a ship in trouble," he responded more mildly than he would have done with one of his own kind.

"A bit of a fire on the *Maris,*" the speaker told him. Míceál's expression registered his concern, and the longshoreman continued quickly. "It's not the same thing as you chaps have to face in space," he assured them, "at least not here in port where the crew can get off quickly. This is nothing, anyway. They'll probably have it out in a few minutes."

"Maybe," interjected the older man standing beside him.

Jellico eyed him curiously. "You have your doubts?"

"I was the one who smelled the smoke and alerted her Captain. To my mind, he should forget about saving the cargo and really pour in water and foam. Masters have lost ships before by playing around with steam for too long."

"Steam?" Rael asked.

He nodded. "Live steam. It replaces the oxygen in the air, smothering a blaze while being reasonably kind to the goods stored around it. It's most useful in the early stages of a tightly confined fire, though. Give the flames any chance to spread, to escape into the hull between the holds, and you've got big trouble."

"You think that's happened here?"

"Well, it's not for me to say, but a fire large enough for me to sniff out just by walking near an open hatch is a deal more than a spark, and I'm willing to put down a few credits that they haven't gotten it licked even yet."

"How long have they been at it?"

"Full blast? Only about ten minutes. — Uh-oh, there goes the alarm. They want the Fire Department. That means they're kissing the cargo good-bye. — See, the crew're being sent ashore."

"There shouldn't be all that much to be damaged, should there?" the Medic asked, trying to recall what Macgregory had told them about the kinds of goods the *Regina Maris* was taking on. "Just the rope. Her insurance should cover that."

"Sure, and the rest, too, but exporters don't like to ship with vessels that sacrifice their cargoes too willingly. Also, the season's rush on nitrate'll be over soon . . ."

Rael Cofort's face went white. "What?"

"Ammonium nitrate. A fertilizer. My lads loaded fourteen hundred tons of it in her number two hold and another eight hundred and twenty tons in number four yesterday evening. The fire's between them in number three where the rope's stowed. Both're likely to be drenched and ruined . . ."

"Spirit of Space . . . ," she whispered.

"It's a common substance," he told her in surprise.

"Until you bring a flame or too much heat near it," Jellico said tersely. "Then it's a bomb."

"Bomb! What in . . ."

"Recently we saw an experiment to illustrate that. If that ship goes up, it'll be like a low-grade planetbuster. You people would be smart to take off, pick up your families, and keep going until this is all over."

"Right," one of the women standing near them cut in. "We'd find something left out of our paychecks if we tried that."

"Better lose a few hours' pay to panic than not be able to collect it at all because you're dead."

"I'll take responsibility," their chief informant declared, confirming the spacers' impression that he was the group's foreman. "I've got a kid up the slope in the Cup school. I'm taking him, my wife, and her mother and heading for the hardpan. The rest of you do the same."

He glanced at the pair in the flier. "What about you two?"

"We like living," the Captain replied.

The Canucheans wasted no time in clearing after that. Rael did not watch them go. Her eyes were fixed on Jellico. "Míceál, we can't . . ."

He gave an impatient shake of his head. "These eateries should all have public surplanetary transceivers, and they'll be empty with everyone out watching the fire. I'll warn the *Queen* and spaceport. You tell Macgregory and the Stellar Patrol."

As Jellico predicted, they found available booths in the first eating place they entered and both hastened to sound the alarm before the dreaded explosion rendered it worthless.

Tang Ya was on duty at the *Solar Queen*'s transceiver. He, like the rest of the crew, had heard his comrades' report of the Caledonia experiment and required no detailed explanation. "We're ready to go now," he told him. "All the rest of us are on board, praise the Spirit of Space. How long do we give you?" He hated to ask that, but for the sake of the ship and the bulk of her company, there had to be a limit on the time they could afford to wait.

"Lift at once and make for the hardpan outside the city. Set down again a mile or so to the south of it to get you out of direct line with any residual blast effects, and wait there until I tell you the fire's out here or until the commotion stops. If the *Maris* does go up, they'll be needing help at that point. Rael and I'll either make our way out to you or be tied up with the rescue effort ourselves."

Most likely, they would either be in need of saving or beyond it, but his Captain was as aware of that as he was. "Will do. We'll pass the word to the others here as well."

"Thanks, Tang."

Míceál's head bowed as he stepped from the booth. He loved the *Solar Queen* and had always imagined he would meet his death aboard her or striving in some manner for her.

The spacer squared his shoulders and looked up. Death

on Canuche of Halio might be a distinct possibility, but it
was by no means a certainty for either of them. There was
no reason to blindly assume that he and Rael Cofort would
not be returning to the starship and to the cold, dark
reaches of interstellar space that was her domain.

He had to wait a few minutes for his companion, but she
nodded gravely when she finally joined him. "I got to them
both," she told him. "Mr. Macgregory's starting a full evacuation immediately. He'll also contact the Fire Department
to let them know what we're facing and warn the hospitals
to move as much of their gear as they can, especially their
emergency facilities, out onto the hardpan so they'll be
ready to start taking on cases at once if need be. Colonel
Cohn's putting in calls for aid to the other towns all along
the coast. — What about our own people?"

"They'll do what they must."

They found the battle against the ship fire raging in full
fury when they went outside again, with fireboats and fliers
pouring streams of foam and seawater into the *Regina
Maris*'s hold, augmented by the closer attention of the
small firetransports crowding the dock and the men and
women carrying the fight to the deck itself.

As the efforts to contain the fire became ever more spectacular, so the crowd gathered to watch it increased in
proportion. Laborers delayed upon leaving their shifts or
before going to their tasks; office workers left their desks to
congregate outside their buildings or stood by windows
offering grandstand views; messengers and passersby with
more time to spare shouldered their way through to the

dock itself to secure as unobstructed as possible an observation post. Rael judged that there had to be in excess of four thousand people in and around the Cup's seafront alone and easily that many again scattered farther away along the banks and on the opposite shore. A number of small merchant and pleasure craft had also drawn near, keeping just far enough away as not to interfere with the work of the fireboats.

"The smoke's coming up white now," her companion observed. "It looks like they've just about got it licked."

"I sincerely hope so. I won't object one bit if I come out looking like a total vacuum-brain in all of this." Her mouth hardened. It was not over yet, not quite. "If anything does happen, most and probably all of these people are going to be killed."

Before Jellico realized what she was doing, she had started pushing through the onlookers, showing consummate skill in weaseling her way with the deft aid of elbow and foot into minute spaces that had not seemed to exist a moment before. He was hard pressed to keep up with her.

The Medic did not stop until she had reached the fire-transport that was her target. Its crew, engrossed as both were in managing the big fire gun, did not notice her until she had leapt aboard.

"This thing's got a public address system?" she demanded before either could recover enough from his surprise to order her off.

"Of course . . ."

"Switch it on!"

He complied, moved by her earnestness and air of authority. Besides, the fire was well under control, and he was curious.

"You people," the woman called into the mike he handed her, "the show's almost over, but the danger isn't. Until the last spark and hot spot has been extinguished, there's the chance of a serious explosion. You're exposed to the full force of it out here."

Míceál mentally nodded his approval. Even now, with the fire on the *Regina Maris* almost out, knowledge of the full peril she represented too suddenly imparted to all these people could provoke a panic that would almost certainly claim a large number of the lives they were striving to preserve.

A siren sounded farther up the shore. Rael glanced in the direction of the noise, then raised the mike again. "I spoke with Adroo Macgregory of Caledonia, Inc., before coming here. See, he has already evacuated his plant and ordered his people out of the city."

Someone near her laughed. "That kindergarten! Are they walking two by two with their fingers on their lips?"

She glared frigidly in the direction of the speaker, whom she could not actually identify. "This is a real evacuation, not a drill for which he planned well in advance. What in all the hells do you think it's doing to his business operations? People like Mr. Macgregory don't throw that volume of credits away unless they believe there's a damn good reason for doing so. — He called it right on target the last time he gave a similar order if I heard the story correctly."

Her audience greeted that with silence. Many looked uncomfortably over their shoulders. The storm to which she referred was recent enough history to still be sharp in the memories of all of them.

Míceál's eyes glittered coldly. Most of the watchers were inclined to move, but it would require some effort to push their way back, to reverse the general pressure of the crowd, and they were not sufficiently concerned to make the start.

Suddenly, he caught hold of the fire gun and whipped it around, depressing the nozzle as he did so. The powerful stream hit the pavement at the feet of the spectators with the force of a sledge, and those nearest it leapt back, cursing, as splintered pieces flew up in every direction.

"Get moving, now, or by all the Federation's gods, I'll give you a blast of this across the shins. If you're going to stay here and die, you might as well have a good excuse for doing it. I'm prepared to accommodate you and supply it."

The nearer fireman started to shove him aside, but the other, who had just closed their transceiver, intervened. "Let him be. They're right." His voice dropped. "Except if the *Maris* blows, it won't be a small, contained blast affecting only the ship and this dock. It'll take out just about the whole Cup and maybe a great deal more besides."

His voice rose again as he took the mike from Rael. "All right, folks, move along. Leave the Cup area entirely. We've just been informed that there is still some danger of a detonation. If one occurs, we'll have to be able to get medical help in quickly for any of our people who're hurt. — Get going, now. You're blocking ground traffic and making it hard to bring in anything by air."

The onlookers muttered but slowly began to disperse. By now, most of them were upset enough by the talk of explosions to be grateful for the excuse to leave the threatened area without having to appear panicked themselves.

"Quick thinking," the fireman told the two spacers. He shuddered. "It's almost over, but I wouldn't have been very happy working here all this time had I known what was actually shadowing us." He eyed the retreating civilians. "You two had best join them," he added sternly.

"That's our intention," the Captain assured him as he slipped over the side of the vehicle and lightly dropped to the ground. He gave his hand to steady Cofort while she followed suit.

With much of the pressure of the throng easing up around them, they experienced little difficulty in working their way back to their machine.

Rael opened the door but paused beside it. Her eyes were dark, troubled. "If something goes wrong, they'll be needing Medics."

"Only live ones. — Move!"

She wasted no more time but sprang into the flier even as Jellico himself did.

The vehicle rose until it was a couple of feet above the heads of the pedestrians and started toward one of the narrow side streets leading into the open dock area.

"Wouldn't we make better time higher up?" the Medic asked.

"We'd also fall a heck of a lot farther if we got thrown down by a blast concussion."

Rael made no comment. She fixed her attention on the street along which they were traveling.

All the structures lining it appeared to be old. They had been constructed of Canuchean stone rather than the metals and synthetics of a later stage, more prosperous colony, and all of them obviously had been put up at the same time from a single set of plans. One was the image of all the others.

Each of the buildings had an underground story, or maybe several, perhaps devoted to storage or deliveries. At least, the entrance was invariably a broad, steeply sloping ramp leading into an attractively arched, covered loading dock.

To Cofort's surprise, Míceál did not turn onto the avenue when they reached it. "Why are we sticking to the back roads?" she asked curiously, knowing there was probably an excellent reason for taking the slower, more irregular route.

"Maybe for no purpose," he responded grimly. "I hope we won't have to find out." His mouth compressed into a hard line. "I should be sent to the Lunar mines for criminal neglect. As soon as we reach the *Queen,* give your friend Colonel Cohn another call and have her order the *Regina Maris* towed out to sea for the final cleanup. There would be no danger to the city now if I'd thought of it sooner."

The woman frowned. "Neither did I. Power down, will you. We couldn't work out everything. We're just Free Traders, not a pair of professional disaster planners."

She glanced up at him, mischief suddenly lighting her eyes as she laughed softly. "You'd make one fine tyrant, Captain Jellico," she told him. "That was a masterful stroke with the fire gun."

"One needs a variety of abilities in Trade . . ."

Whatever else he might have said was silenced as light

suddenly erupted behind them. A clap of sound followed in the same breath, well nigh in the same instant, a wrenching, high roar of such volume and intensity that it might have accompanied the disintegration of a world.

22

Dane's eyes swept the bleak horizon, as if he could will himself to penetrate the miles and see what was happening within the Canuchean city.

The *Solar Queen* had left the spaceport as soon as she had given the alarm to her fellow starships, and the rest had been quick to follow suit despite the annoyance of the traffic controllers. Those in Trade might compete sharply for charters and goods, but for the most part, with certain savage exceptions, they trusted in one another above surplanetary authorities. As for the others on-world for different purposes, they were of the same or similar breed. They, too, would follow the advice and lead of their own. Now they were assembled on the hardpan, not too near so as to avoid the chance of chain-reaction disaster but still close enough to offer a comforting sense of community. Most of their crews were also assembled beside their vessels, staring intently eastward.

"I could try to talk those port guys into bringing a flier out to us," Rip ventured. "They're probably not so mad that they wouldn't do it for a share of the news. I could fly over the city . . ."

"You'll keep your scrambled-circuited fins planeted where they are!"

Shannon was not the only one to stare at Ali. The Engineer-apprentice gripped himself. He resumed his normal casual manner, but the deadly serious note did not leave his voice. "You'd be looking for a quick ride on Sanford Jones's comet, my boy. I saw fighters, big ones, blown out of the sky by the concussion of a major blast, never mind one of those little civilian bubbles. I wouldn't want to be in the air in one of them even this far out, much less hovering over Canuche Town, if that accursed ship blows."

"Is the *Queen* safe?" Jasper asked in concern. "And these others who followed us?"

"Out here, aye." It was Johan Stotz who answered for his apprentice. He and the Cargo-Master had just come out of the ship to join them. "Van and I've been running a series of possibility scenarios on the computer. We're well away from triple the blast we could expect even if two or more freighters went up, and shrapnel definitely won't reach us, which was our biggest danger at the spaceport."

"That's over four miles from the coast, closer to five, in fact!" exclaimed Weeks.

"Not an impossible distance for a big explosion," Kamil

said tensely. "It wouldn't take much. All you'd need is for a single piece of red-hot metal to pierce the liquid fuel reservoirs and none of us would have anything more to worry about, provided we'd led virtuous lives." He turned to his chief. "A fire storm could travel this far. So could gas."

"That's why Jellico insisted that we go south as well as inland. We're not in easy line with the city, and the winds're blowing toward it, not us. They're also augmented by the thermal breeze as long as the daylight and heat hold."

Thorson looked eastward again, then back to his shipmates as an idea came to him. "Could we try to focus the near-space viewer on the town?"

"Probably!" Tang agreed eagerly. "Devices designed for use in space don't work perfectly in an atmosphere, and we'll have to play with the magnification, but we should be able to get something. It'll be better than nothing, at any rate."

The *Solar Queen*'s bridge was even smaller than her mess, but none of them grumbled about the lack of space as they gathered around the big screen while their Com-Tech adjusted one after the other of the controls directing its operation.

Gradually, the image of Canuche Town appeared before them, at first hazy to the point of uselessness, then as clear as if they were spying on it through impossibly powerful but otherwise standard distance lenses. Deftly, Ya depressed the focus until it rested right on the eastern horizon.

"We can't see the docks," Karl Kosti said, voicing the disappointment of all.

"Hardly," Tang told him. "The whole seaport area is on a significantly lower level than the rest of the city. The viewer can't penetrate solid rock or bend around it. We'll know it if that ship explodes, but we won't be able to observe the blast itself or its effects on its immediate environs. — Sands of Mars! Look at all those people! There are thousands of them, and they all seem to be heading this way."

"Macgregory's staff and their families probably," Van Rycke deduced. "He's ordered evacuations before. The Captain or Rael will have warned him, too."

"I could check, see if there's something coming over the civilian waves or if the Patrol's broadcasting anything on the public channels . . ."

Ya shook his head even as he finished speaking. It would not be well to have any auditory equipment actively receiving if a major explosion occurred. As an added precaution, he increased light and radiation screening on the visual receptors.

For a few minutes, he kept the lines of moving people on the screen, confirming that they were indeed making for the hardpan, then switched back to scanning the serene infinity of roof-fringed sky on the horizon.

More minutes went by. The tranquility of the unchanging scene began to draw some of the tension out of the spacers.

A burst of light ruptured the field of blue. A vast sound followed it, loud and sharp even at this remove.

As the first great flash of brilliance faded, a column of brown smoke clawed its way some six hundred feet into the air. Several dark specks seemed to balance for a moment on it, then fell back into it and plummeted to the concealed ground.

"Her hatches," Dane heard someone, Shannon maybe, say.

Soon, in nearly the same instant, more debris shot into view, some of it dark, a lot glowing red. Much of what they saw was clearly discernible, stark proof of the sizes involved. Thorson gaped at it. That stuff was not just big. It was enormous, great pieces of what had moments before been the *Regina Maris.*

One sight, rather pretty in itself, puzzled him, as it did most of his comrades. Burning spheres accompanied by equally brilliant sparks and streamers filled one portion of the sky, held there a fraction second, and dispersed as would a burst of demoniac fireworks.

The Cargo-Master again supplied the explanation. "Rope. The *Maris* was shipping a load of it. The balls are aflame and are casting off fragments as they burn. — The Spirit of Space help the places where they land. They'll be more than hot enough to torch anything flammable that they touch."

Van Rycke's grim prediction was not long in finding fulfillment as explosion after explosion followed that first mighty detonation. They did not have to actually see the stricken area to know what was happening, not with computer-generated possibility and probability scenarios to augment their own knowledge and imagination.

Many buildings collapsing under the awesome force of the blast wave took fire directly from the explosion's heat as particularly volatile contents ignited or detonated. Others began to burn when flaming or blazing-hot shrapnel slammed into the rubble that was all that remained of many or through roof, walls, or splintered windows of those still partly standing, starting smaller fires that soon reached vulnerable materials. The exposed fuel tanks were almost immediate casualties, breaking and falling at once when the blast's fist slammed into them or crumbling and exploding when struck by flying material that made them out as accurately as would missiles shot by a sentient foe. Escaping chemicals, alone or in bastard combinations, released deadly gases. Others created corrosive pools or added still more fuel to the hellish caldron the seaport area had become.

The topography of the region magnified the effects of the already awesome disaster. In dooming its own, however, it to a great extent shielded the rest of Canuche Town as the high, sharp slopes deflected much of the force of the explosion back down on the already shattered communities below and caught the bulk of the debris it had set in deadly flight.

Pieces thrown high enough did get through, bringing fire, destruction, and terror wherever they came to ground.

Jan, who was senior officer in Jellico's absence, at last turned his back to the screen, unconsciously straightening his powerful shoulders as he did so. "There may be some new fires or an odd blast or two, but I'd say the worst's over. Those people need all the help they can get and need it fast if a lot more aren't going to die who should make it. — Steen, Johan, Tang, stay with the *Queen*. Keep her ready to lift fast again if you must, though I doubt that'll be necessary now, and hold the transceiver open. The rest of us'll see if we can't make ourselves useful."

The Canuchean refugees had set up their camp, a small city in itself, a good half mile north of the starship's emergency berth.

The spacers found little confusion there, and Dane Thorson had not been long within its bounds before he felt a fierce pride in these people.

He was seeing the spirit that had carried Terra's offspring to the stars and won them their place there, on planet after planet where survival itself should have been inconceivable. The refugees had a headstart in that everything was well ordered thanks to Adroo Macgregory's preparations, the training he had insisted upon giving his people, who, with their households, made up the vast majority of those currently assembled here. Those who had actually endured the blast itself had not yet begun to arrive in number. There was grief and fear, but the Canucheans were responding with the determination to fight, not permitting themselves to sink into despair. The very young and those otherwise unable to give aid were gathered together in the keeping of appointed caregivers. The rest were already heading back to their stricken city and seaport.

The Stellar Patrol was visibly active. Rael's warning had

reached them in time. They, too, along with the city's police and emergency services whom they, in turn, had alerted, had evacuated and gotten far enough out that they now had personnel and gear to send back in.

The *Queen*'s crew found Ursula Cohn at a makeshift command post seemingly surrounded by communications equipment and an ever-changing sea of grim-faced men and women, civilians and members of the various services alike, all either bringing reports to her or awaiting her orders.

Her strained eyes swept those around her. They stopped when they came to rest on Van Rycke and Thorson. "You people probably gave this town its life. You've certainly cut down on the amount of dying. Help's already on the way from communities all up and down the coast. By nightfall, we'll have mostly everything we'll need in terms of supplies, equipment, and manpower."

"By nightfall, a lot of people alive right now are going to be dead if they're left where they are that long," the Cargo-Master stated flatly. "We're here to lend a hand. The rest of the spacers'll probably be following pretty close on our heels."

"We can use you." Her expression clouded. "Any word from your Captain or Doctor Cofort?"

"No."

"We've commandeered every functional flier and transport we can find. I'm giving you and your crew priority status behind my people and medical personnel. I can't send you all back into the town on one vehicle, but every one of you'll be at work within half an hour."

"That's all we want."

"That transport over there is refueling for another trip in. You and Mr. Thorson can go with it."

"We appreciate that, Colonel. Thanks."

The two Free Traders hastened to claim their promised places, squeezing in so that as many others as possible would be able to board.

Dane kept his eyes lowered, not wanting to meet those of his chief. Van Rycke and Jellico went far back as a team, and they were a close one . . .

Suddenly, another thought pierced him. Poor Queex! Only two people in all the ultrasystem had loved him, and he had lost them both in one black instant of destruction.

23

Mícéal turned his flier perpendicular to its former course, threw it into hover, and flipped it onto its side so that its undercarriage faced the sea and the blow that was to come.

Even as the invisible fist of energy slammed into the machine, he leapt from it, yanking Cofort after him as he sprang.

The vehicle gave one jerk, as if it had truly been struck by a massive solid object, but the man was only dimly aware of that or of the way in which it was hurled against the building beside them. The flier had given them a fraction-second of shelter, and by launching themselves into motion, traveling with the blast wave instead of meeting it with their bodies in the full grip of inertia, they had won a measure of freedom of action. It would not last long, but if they moved fast and luck was with them, they might improve their chances of surviving reasonably intact—if his reasoning was in any way correct.

Jellico stumbled as he struck the pavement but managed to keep his feet. Shoving the woman before him, he dove into the nearest of the dark, refuse-littered entrances to the buildings' subterranean levels and slammed her to the ground.

Rael gave a sharp cry as she landed hard against a broken stone block and went limp.

The Captain knew she was hurt but could not pause to attend to her. They were too far in, and their time was almost gone despite his having moved almost instantaneously in response to the explosion's assault. Desperately, he jerked her inert body out toward the light, positioning them directly beneath the arch, close to but not actually leaning against the seaward wall.

Only a superhuman effort of will enabled him to do that much. The world around them was chaos, an insane whirl of sound, flying, crushing debris, and fire. The Trader Captain felt as if he were being pummeled by a crew of Malkites specifically trained to reduce a human body to dismembered pulp.

He set himself to endure. They were nearly three long blocks from the site of the explosion, far enough to blunt some of its initial force, and their hastily claimed hiding place provided some shelter. This much they could survive if fortune did not go back on them.

The same could not be said for the structures around them, utterly exposed and inflexible as they were. With the precision of a planned mechanical demonstration, one after another collapsed under the seemingly irresistible impact of the blast wave striking them head-on.

Jellico's stomach twisted in pure terror as a deep, crushing rumble told the fate of the building in whose entrance they cowered. Spirit of Space! Had they escaped being crisped or torn asunder or shredded by shrapnel and flying glass only to meet their ends in this rat's hole?

He hunched over Rael, striving to shield her, to give her whatever protection his body could provide . . .

It had begun in an instant; it was over in seconds. The physical torment ended abruptly, and the infernal din subsided, lessened by distance. Even the shouts and cries of the injured survivors outside became less immediate.

There had been no move or sound from his companion since he had flung her into this place, and Míceál hastily turned to her. Immediately, all his fear returned, closing his throat, very nearly stopping his breath. She was lying perfectly still, her eyes closed, the thick lashes looking ominously dark against the uncommonly pale skin. Was she dead? Could such beauty remain in dying, or was it merely that death had not yet had time to lay its full mark on her?

He reached out to touch her neck in search of a pulse, but in that moment, Rael moaned softly, and her eyes opened.

It was comforting to find the Captain bending over her, alive and apparently unscathed.

The open, albeit rapidly fading, dread on his face scattered that nascent sense of well-being even as it formed.

She hastened to sit up but fell back again with a sharp cry of pain she was not quick enough to quell.

Jellico's arm was under her shoulders in a moment. "What's wrong, Rael?" he demanded tensely. "How badly are you hit?" Just because he had managed to weather the blast wave's hammering without taking significant harm was no guarantee his comrade had been so fortunate. Internal injuries could take a while to kill . . .

"This business of having one's life saved has its disadvantages," she grumbled. "I think I must be one prize-winning bruise. I'll probably scare the starlight out of myself every time I go under the steam jets for a while. — Give me a pull up, will you? I should be mobile on my own after that."

He complied. The woman winced as she gained her feet but then straightened. "I'll live," she assured him after taking several quick, experimental breaths.

She eyed him curiously. "What made you dump us in here?" she asked.

"I remembered that the arch is one of architecture's strongest structures, and these ones were all solidly built out of good natural materials. Each of them also extended enough beyond the main part of the buildings that they might not necessarily be dragged down as well if the big structure went, especially if the brunt of the shock wave passed above them, as was possible since all of the arches are low to the ground. I just hoped I was reading it right and that it would be enough."

Jellico was hard pressed not to shudder openly. Any turn of chance, any frown of fortune at all, and they could both have been dead or worse. "What about the rest?" Rael

Cofort asked suddenly, sharply, "the other poor folk fleeing with us?"

As she spoke, she was already whirling toward the entrance, bracing herself as she did so. She did not anticipate seeing the gross primary injuries that would be encountered closer to the dock, those caused by the sudden, violent change in air and tissue pressure. The shock wave itself and the even more vicious blast wind had weakened and dispersed enough at this distance from their point of origin to spare them that—they could not otherwise have come through its assault so well themselves—but the area could not hope to have escaped the rest. Secondary injuries would abound, wounds resulting from flying shrapnel and glass and from falling masonry. Much tertiary damage had probably occurred as well. Their flier had been caught and tossed. Human beings had doubtless been thrown as well, and flesh and bone shattered when slammed into solid metal or stone at high velocity. When she left this place, she would be walking into pure horror.

As the Medic tried to fortify herself, she stepped out onto the narrow street.

Former street. It was now but a depression in a sea of high-mounded debris. The buildings on both sides had been flung down. Only a few of the arches remained standing, still marking the entrances to the now rubble-filled understories.

Precious few even of those had survived, she saw with an inner shiver. She and Jellico had been fortunate indeed in his choice of shelter.

The air was foul. She was aware of the stink of it even through all the numbing horror of the scene spread out before her. The odor of burning was everywhere, burning wood and synthetics, cloth and chemicals, the stench of burning flesh. A lot of people had been working in the shattered buildings that had become their tombs, and a great many of the ruins were afire.

Corpses lay everywhere, not in the windrows she had feared to see—the warning had been given soon enough to prevent that—but still with terrifying prominence. Most of those that she saw appeared to have been felled either by debris from the explosion itself or by material from the falling buildings.

Rael quickly ascertained which bodies she passed were no more than shells and paid them no further attention; there were still some of the living here as well, not many of them, and they desperately needed help.

She was bitterly aware of the pitifully little care she could provide. In living and dead alike, most of the injuries she saw were ghastly—eyes gouged out, noses sliced off, people with their entire faces gone. Here were amputated or shredded limbs, bodies torn open or pinned to the solid pavement in grim testimony to the power of the force driving the missiles that had struck them down. One poor devil had been bisected by a huge, thin spear of metal, apparently one of the drilling stems stowed aboard the *Regina Maris*.

Nearly all the living who had been hit in the head, face, or arms bore other grave wounds as well. Those even marginally capable of walking alone or with the help of friends or strangers had already staggered or been assisted out of the area in search of aid in other, hopefully less devastated districts of the stricken city.

The Captain, drawing upon his own considerable knowledge of first aid, was similarly occupied. He knelt beside the body of a woman. Flying glass had gotten her, and she had not died instantly.

Sighing, he came to his feet again. "I've seen wars, everything from primitive through interstellar, but I don't think I've ever run into anything as bad as this." They were not looking at the worst, either. Those caught much closer to the seat of the explosion would have sustained even heavier injuries, and this was, at least, a commercial area. The victims, though pitiful and tragic, were all adults. From the little he could see above the mountains of rubble, the destruction appeared to be equally horrendous on the primarily residential slope above. There were, or had been, children there, a lot of them.

The two spacers worked together more or less in silence. There was so little that they could do. They were survivors themselves, without supplies or gear of any sort. All they were able to offer was first aid, utilizing the victims' own clothing for bandages and whatever other materials they were able to glean from the wreckage around them. In each case, they did what they could and then moved the sufferer into the middle of the street, as far as possible from the threat of fire from the collapsed buildings on either side. After that, they had to leave him with the poor comfort of their assurance, which they both prayed would prove accurate, that rescue teams would soon be penetrating the shattered area and would collect the injured then.

The final case they handled was a big man deeply comatose as a result of a massive head injury. Jellico and Cofort lifted and carried him to the center of the street and placed him with the other living victims, although neither of them believed he would survive very much longer.

Rael slipped on the rubble as they were settling him. She fell heavily, barking both her knees, but she was scarcely aware of doing so as waves of agony ripped through her side and chest.

Despite herself, she cried out, and it was several long seconds before she could make the attempt to stand.

Míceál steadied her. His eyes were dark with concern as they searched her face. "That was the last one," he said gruffly. "Let's get the hell out of here. You need a doctor yourself, and I'll be more effective with some equipment . . ."

The woman pulled away from him. She turned on him in fury. "I'm a Medic, and I'm on my feet. You can help me, or you can go back to the ship, but damn it, don't try to interfere with my work!"

Jellico started to protest but stopped himself. "I'm with you," he said quietly.

She eyed him for a moment, as if not trusting him, then nodded. "Thank you, Míceál."

"Where to, Doctor? You're the Medic. This is your line. You call it."

"To the docks," she responded without hesitation. "The worst cases will be closest to that, and they may have to wait the longest before any real help can reach them."

"Most there will have been killed outright," he pointed out.

Rael nodded. "We'll work our way back inland again until we start finding a few we can try to aid." Or comfort a little if nothing else.

"All right. It's as good a plan as any."

Neither of them looked at the crumpled remains of their flier as they moved away from it. By the grace of whatever gods ruled this accursed planet, it had apparently not killed or seriously injured anyone, but neither of them could take credit for that fact. Not that they could have done anything had they stayed with the machine, apart from very probably dying in it.

The off-worlders worked their way down the street until they came to the place where it intersected with what had been the avenue.

Because the place was that much closer to the blast site and more open besides, the proportion of the dead to those still alive was greater than they had encountered near their shelter. A larger number of people had been caught here, however, and those who survived tended to be even more severely injured than their earlier patients, and the pair found themselves hard-pressed on every side by victims desperately in need of aid.

They had no choice but to triage those they discovered still alive, treating first the ones whose chances for survival were the greatest, leaving the most hopeless cases for last.

The choosing fell to Rael Cofort. It was a bitter task, especially so when one of those she ordered set aside was still conscious, but more lives would be saved in the end by ordering their efforts in this manner, and so she grimly held to the policy need had dictated that they adopt. Her strength was such that it kept Jellico firm in his determination to abide by her decisions, that and the seemingly unerring correctness of them.

Cofort had told him that she had proven capable at triage work when she had done her emergency room practical training, but he quickly realized that she was more than merely good. It was as if she were somehow reading her patients' bodies and selecting those in whom the spark of life was burning the strongest.

Her skills, too, were superb. With all the limitations under which they had to operate, that was still apparent even to a layman like himself. Rael Cofort was practicing actual medicine with the first aid they had to offer.

The Medic's side hurt abominably, but she strove not to visibly favor it as they clambered along the rubble-strewn remnant of the street. She would have been ashamed to do so even had she not been determined to conceal as much as possible of her continuing pain from Jellico. What right had she to study herself for so little in the face of the massive agony all around her?

She had little opportunity to dwell on her own difficulties. Conditions worsened with every step closer to the water that they took. Survivors were few, and they were not always easy to locate among the mountains of rubble and the mangled corpses of their fellows. Rael leaned on her talent, used the sickening unease that told her someone nearby was in trouble to locate those still able to receive help. It was difficult to pinpoint a particular source of suffering with the collective misery of the district pouring into her, but she forced herself to concentrate as she had aboard the *Mermaid*. Usually, it worked. Usually, but not in every case.

Sometimes, they located the victim but could not reach him. Sometimes, they could help a little but could not free their patient and had to leave him pinned or partly buried with only a cairn of debris raised nearby to alert properly equipped rescuers to his presence, markers whose meaning they would have to communicate to the appropriate authorities as soon as the opportunity presented itself.

Jellico's hands balled into tight fists by his side. He felt sick with frustration and the seeming hopelessness of their efforts. He could do little for the people they found accessible in the streets and nothing for the handful of buried victims. He could not even be of much help to Rael Cofort as she faced and made decision after wrenching decision. All he could do was stick with her, that and offer no protest in face or stance, do or say nothing to add to the weight she already carried.

They had traveled more than a third of the ruined street when suddenly both Free Traders stopped walking. They listened intently, their heads turning toward one of the remaining arches, the only one still standing on this block.

They spotted him quickly, a man sitting braced against its farther, seaward side, sobbing aloud. It was that sound which had caught their attention.

The pair hastened toward him. Rael's eyes closed momentarily as they drew nearer. He was clutching a human leg to his breast. It had been severed at midthigh, and the material still clinging to it matched the blood-stained trousers he was wearing.

"I'm a Medic," she said by way of introduction as she knelt beside him. "What happened?"

He stared at her blankly for a moment but then answered coherently enough. "I was walking along kind of fast when the explosion came. It knocked me down, but I got up again and started running. Then something, that metal thing over there, hit my leg. It was a red-hot . . . It hurt . . ." He squeezed the limb still tighter. "I fell, but I didn't see for a minute . . ."

While he had been speaking, the woman was examining both parts of the wound. "You were lucky," she declared, making herself speak matter-of-factly, as if she were discussing the result of a minor stumble. "The cut is straight and clean, and the missile was so hot that it cauterized as it sliced through."

"Lucky . . ."

"Hold on to that leg. They'll want to put it back."

"It's too late!" For the first time, emotion, anguish, broke through the numbness that had seemed to envelop him. "It'll be too late! There're too many hurt. They'll all need first-time treatment just to live before anyone'll be able to do a fix-up job like this. The leg'll be dead . . ."

"Nonsense," she responded briskly. "Ultrahyperbaric restoration can reawaken life in tissue detached for a full two weeks and probably longer."

Rael finished her examination. "You didn't lose much blood. That's standing you in good stead, but we're going to help you to the center of the street where you'll be easier to spot by the rescue teams. I want you to lie back and set your mind on getting well. It shouldn't be all that much longer now before you're under full, proper care."

"**S**pace," Jellico muttered as they moved away from the Canuchean. "I hope we don't run into too many more like that one."

"At least he'll survive and regain all or most of his mobility," she replied grimly.

It had been hard leaving the man, but he was not in dire peril. There was not a whole lot they could have done for him by remaining with him unless they had rigged up a stretcher from some of the debris and tried to carry him out, which they were not prepared to attempt at this point. There were simply too many others for whom prompt first aid could mean the difference between survival and death.

They could not have evacuated him in any event. Given her own injuries, she could not have held up her end of a stretcher, not for any distance. Whatever her will to the contrary, broken ribs demanded and would force a certain degree of consideration.

The Medic sighed. "I doubt we'll be able to do much of anything for very many of those that we'll encounter from here on in."

24

The off-worlders' hearts pounded fast and painfully as they continued to make their way along the short stretch that still separated them from the sea and the site of the great explosion itself. If things were so bad here, what combination of the Federation's hells would they find when they reached the source of all this chaos? Would they find anything, living or dead, whole or shattered, there at all?

Rael's gloomy words proved accurate, and they encountered only the dead on the little length that remained of the ruined street.

They reached its end at last. Both paused, steeling themselves to face the horrors they knew lay beyond, then they passed between the final segments of the great mounds of rubble that confined them on each side.

There, they froze. Before them lay the Straight and the remains of what had been Canuche Town's bustling docks. Now little among these splinters indicated what had once stood here.

The *Regina Maris* and the pier at which she had been loading were simply gone. Debris-littered water occupied the place where they had been. Of those who had been battling the fire, there was no sign, nor would there ever be for most of them. They had been atomized under the double impact of blast wave and blast wind, whose force at the point of their sudden creation could well have reached 2,400 miles per hour or more.

Bodies in plenty lay farther back, between their vantage point and the place where the *Maris* had been. All were grossly damaged by the forces generated by the explosion itself, by fire, or from having been thrown at high velocity and great force against ruthlessly unyielding surfaces. They had died, all of them, before flying debris or collapsing structures could pose any threat to them. They would have to be examined all the same, but that was merely an exercise in humanity with no hope of reward.

Rael shuddered. The loss of life would have been immeasurably worse had they not succeeded in driving most of the spectators off the pier when they had, but what they found here was still purely the stuff of nightmare.

She wrenched her eyes away from the slaughter at her feet. The havoc that had rent the land had not spared the sea. Water and shoreline were dotted with the wrecks of boats that had gathered too near in their interest in the fire. Most had been ripped apart, but a few had only been blown ashore or now silently rode the wavelets, crewless but otherwise apparently unhurt. The *Sally Sue,* the only big vessel berthed close to the *Maris,* had, like those smaller ghost ships, survived surprisingly well. A transport-sized hole had been blown in her prow, and she herself had been more than half beached, but she remained a recognizable entity that could be repaired and put back to work again.

For the first time, the spacers got a good look at the slopes, both above them and on the opposite side of the harbor. Neither shore had been spared, though the nearer, of course, had taken infinitely harder punishment.

As with the seaport and commercial areas, no building remained erect, only part of a wall standing here and there, and smoke seemed to be rising from a thousand different sources. For all the visible portion of Canuche Town, the catastrophe was total.

Of greater significance at the moment than the magnitude of the disaster was the sight of figures moving about amidst the wreckage, some carefully, some rapidly and erratically. Death was not quite as universal up there as it was closer to the sea. Distance had given the residents that much grace.

Even more heartening to see were the masses of people crossing the crest and heading down, a steady, organized flood of them. The remainder of the city had survived, then, and the rescue effort was under way.

"It'll be a while before they make it as far as here," Rael remarked, quelling the hope rising in her heart. There would be more deaths yet before this was finally over and part of history.

She frowned as she looked once more at the scene of carnage around them. "It should be worse," she said tightly. "The detonation had to have thrown out more fire."

"Everything's wet. I'd say there was a pretty big splash, luckily straight into the air and back into the bay again instead of a slosh and surge over the shore, or we'd have been drowned in our rat hole. The water must have kept the heat off the victims." The ones they could see here. Those on the ship herself and on the dock nearest her would have ceased to have physical form before they could be incinerated.

All around them was the irrefutable physical evidence of the explosion's power. Not forty yards to Jellico's left, a 150-foot motorized floating dock had been dropped after having been blown a good 200 feet out of the water below. He tried not to think about what probably lay beneath it, or of what he could see on top of it, either. There lay the incredibly crushed remnants of three firetransports. A fourth vehicle, less heavily damaged, had been brought to a stop against its side. That one bore the black and silver colors of the Stellar Patrol.

Rael saw the direction of his gaze and started for the displaced dock. Her own injuries made her grateful for her companion's help in scaling the monstrous thing, but she refused to give in further to them. If Míceál came to suspect the extent of the damage she had taken, he would pull her out of this hopeless fight, force her to return at once for aid. That she was not prepared to do, not while she herself was in no immediate danger and others decidedly were.

She glanced at the nearest of the Fire Department vehicles, then involuntarily up at Míceál.

The Captain shook his head. "Forget it, Rael," he told her

gently. "None of them survived. It's impossible that they should."

Still, they looked at each transport, confirming that there was no life in any of them. They held no dead, either. The blast had carried off the lighter bodies of their crews. Only one corpse was to be seen on the dock, a man's, naked except for one sock of a type adopted by seamen and others engaged in heavy physical outdoor labor the ultrasystem over. Jellico thought he might have been a sailor blown from a nearby vessel or else a dockworker. From the angle at which he was lying, they judged that his back had been broken in several places.

"There's nothing we can do up here," the Medic said. The gnawing unease was flogging her again, demanding action despite her weariness and pain. "Someone around here is hurt. Let's check out that Patrol flier first and then hunt around the base of this thing. — Damn it, I wish some of those Canucheans would light their burners and get down here! To judge by what we've seen thus far, anyone we come across is going to be in a pretty bad way."

"You're not in such a good way yourself," he said sharply after seeing her wince as she lowered herself to the dock in preparation to scramble over its side.

"I don't pretend to be as tough as you, Míceál Jellico," she told him irritably. "These muscles are going to be singing me a sad story for some time to come. — You could give me a hand down if you'd like to be helpful."

"Down here! Help!"

Both froze.

Jellico went to his knees beside his companion. The cry seemed to have come from the wrecked flier.

They could see two people. One was lying across the rear seat, one in the front, the latter almost concealed by the great, jagged metal shard that had felled him. Had they not been studying the machine so closely, they would have missed seeing him.

The spacers made no delay in climbing down. Rael hastened first to the victim in the back, that one being the more readily accessible.

After a few moments, she drew back, her mouth twisting. First aid had been attempted, but injuries of this magnitude rendered any such effort worthless. The woman had been eviscerated, and the damage done to her lungs, while not visible, must have been greater still. How the poor creature had survived long enough to receive any treatment at all . . .

"Rael! Over here! He's alive!"

She hurriedly backed out of the flier and ran to its opposite side, where Míceál was already beside the vehicle's second occupant.

The woman caught her breath in horror. "Keil!"

The Patrol-Yeoman did not look like the same man. He appeared years older, his face marred by pain, fear, blood, and plain dirt, but there was no doubting the accuracy of her identification. As if to confirm it, he turned his head at the sound of her voice. It was about the only part of his body, certainly the only visible part, with a full range of free movement. "Doctor Cofort?"

"That's right, my friend."

"Gayle? Yeoman Argile? She's dead?" There was more statement than question in that.

She nodded. "Aye. That was inevitable anyway. Most of her lungs had to have been ruptured."

His eyes closed in the infinite weariness of defeat. "I know. I had to try to get her out, though. — I was farther away and only got flattened, and the flier somehow wasn't damaged at all, so I took it and went back to the dock. Where it used to be. Gayle was near there, still alive. No one else was."

He paused, then went on. "I did what I could for her and tried to make a run for it. That's when this thing hit me and made an end of me, too. I think it's part of the supports of one of the fuel tanks . . ."

"Nothing's made an end of you, not yet!" She squeezed down beside him to try for a pulse count and to peer into his eyes. The pupils were even, at least . . . "Let me push in there so I can get a better look at you."

"I'm finished," the Yeoman stated flatly, his manner calm and quite certain but with an urgency underlying it. "So are you two if you hang around here any longer. Maybe you are no matter how far you can run now."

"What do you mean?" Jellico demanded sharply. Whatever one felt about the agents of the Stellar Patrol, they were not given to displays of hysterics even under gross provocation.

"See that ship over there?" he asked, pointing toward the *Sally Sue* with a toss of his head. "She's got several holds full of that damned ammonium nitrate, too, nine thousand nine hundred tons of it, plus a couple of thousand tons of sulphur and I don't know how many barrels of benzol on deck and below. She's on fire right now, or if

Andre Norton & P.M. Griffin

she isn't, the pier right next to her certainly is in several places. One blaze or another will get to her soon enough, and she'll go up with a bang that'll make the *Maris* explosion seem like a harmless little puff of a dry run."

262

25

Doctor Tau was wedged in between Jasper Weeks and Karl Kosti, sharing with four Canuchean laborers a transport somewhat too small to carry so many.

He was only vaguely aware of the discomfort of the journey. The people around them were taking almost the whole of his attention. Most of them were moving away from Canuche Town, lines of dazed, frightened refugees. A horribly high percentage of their number were obvious physical as well as emotional casualties of the disaster, struggling on with the assistance of their fellows to reach medical care at one of the temporary hospitals set up in the camp on the hardpan until the grave danger of fire subsided sufficiently for the facilities to return to the city itself.

He did not see any of the more severe cases, of course. They were being brought in by flier and transport, but what he did observe was sufficient to reveal the scope of the catastrophe that had stricken this community. His trained eyes appraised each group, and he silently shook his head. In saner times, many of these so-called walking wounded would rightly be labeled gravely injured themselves.

Just about all of Canuche Town's windows had shattered, and jagged shards of glass had flown everywhere, causing the greatest part of the injuries sustained in the outermost parts of the city. Others, and he realized there would be many more of them as people from farther within Canuche Town began reaching this point, had been struck by falling materials or were burn or gas cases. A few stumbled along, blood flowing from their ears and noses, victims of the blast concussion.

Once more, he shook his head. Already, it was a nightmare, and it would only grow worse as they neared the place where the explosion had occurred. He acknowledged the bonds laid on him by the ancient oath he had taken, but that notwithstanding, he was not looking forward to the work that lay in front of them all.

The spaceport, when they reached it, was alive with activity. It was to there that the relief convoys were coming, and several had arrived already.

Relatively little visible damage had been sustained at the facility. It was located far enough from the coast that only a minute amount of debris had reached it, and most of the power driving that had been spent. He had learned from Colonel Cohn, however, that two people had been killed when a piece of sheet metal had skimmed over their transport and decapitated them. The potential for grave disaster had unquestionably been here, and the starships had done well to lift when they had.

Once they passed through the port, their transport was not long in reaching Canuche Town itself and then the place where it was to pick up its load of badly wounded for the return trip.

Tau walked over to the waiting stretchers to see what he and his comrades might expect to encounter.

What he found there was no worse than he had anticipated, but seeing the actual victims drove the enormity of the horror more sharply home, and he returned to the others even more sobered.

Their instructions were simple—to start searching the thickly populated slope above the harbor. Whenever they found a group engaged in a rescue that called on them for aid or discovered someone who was trapped, they were to provide whatever help they could.

Since the *Solar Queen* trio had come bearing digging equipment and first aid supplies, they had no need to wait for gear to be issued to them. They separated from the Canuchean laborers who had traveled with them and started out at a brisk pace.

When they crested the rise above the slope, all three stopped as if on command.

The sight meeting their eyes was almost beyond credulity. Here and there, part of a wall rose up out of the ruin, windowless, roofless, more pathetic than the unidentifiable jumble around them. Nothing else remained. Even the bay was wreckage and desolation only.

Total as the destruction obviously was, Canuche Town

was already crying its defiance. Fire and smoke were everywhere to be seen, but so, too, were those assembled to quell them. Fire brigades stationed in less dreadfully visited districts, bringing their equipment and foam in by flier and on their backs, had poured into the port region and had already begun to isolate and beat down a number of the individual blazes.

That their efforts had begun to show effect so soon, that they were able to have an effect at all, lay in large part with the thoroughness of Macgregory's evacuation operation. The Caledonia plant itself was gone, a victim of the volatile materials already present within its walls, but with all the feeder and fuel lines shut down along their whole length, no new materials arrived to support the voracious fire that had consumed the installation itself. Had that not been done, given the key location of the place and the vast volume of the chemicals pouring into it, there would have been little hope of quelling the flames in this part of the seaport for a long time to come and no hope whatsoever for any living victims pinned in the rubble around it.

The spacers were spared the horror of having to watch bloodstained adults and children frantically seeking one another amidst the ruins. The first people into the district had shepherded wounded into the hands of medical personnel and then to the refugee camp, where efforts to reunite families had already begun.

That part of the tragedy should have been worse than it was, too, and once again, thanks was due to Adroo Macgregory that it was not. The Caledonia, Inc., workers and their people had formed a large percentage of the population of the heaviest-stricken areas, and no few of their neighbors, remembering the storm that had sparked such an evacuation before, had taken warning and fled with them. Those who remained, alive or dead, who had not already been discovered lay buried beneath the ruins of their homes and workplaces.

The Free Traders passed several groups striving to free the trapped. Because they had to start someplace, the rescuers had begun their efforts at the crest of the slope. These first parties had their particular situations on the perimeter in hand by then. Much as they would have welcomed more help, they were willing to forgo it, realizing how desperately laborers were needed farther downslope.

At last, they came upon a party more frantically engaged than any they had thus far encountered. The forewoman was alternately wielding her ax with no little skill and driving her navies on with a vocabulary that would have reduced any proverbial Navy Master Sergeant to a state of silent awe.

She spotted the three and summoned them in one instant. "Stop gawking, space hounds, and get to work! There's a damn big job on here."

They hastened to obey. "What's the specific problem?" Tau asked the grim-faced Canuchean when he reached her side.

She pointed down, and his breath caught in sick horror. There, far below them, was a small child, a toddler. She was held in place, but apparently only by her clothing, for she was squirming around and was shrieking her discomfort and terror. They could have reached her and drawn her out with no more difficulty than that of hard, careful labor had they enjoyed the luxury of unlimited time, but that last

Andre Norton & P.M.Griffin

they did not have. A slow fire was inexorably eating its way
toward her, and it was patent even from one hurried glance
that it would reach her long before they could hope to do
so.

"We won't get within twenty feet of her in time," he said.
"If that near. It's not far from her now."

"Would you suggest that we stop working and just watch
the show?" the woman snarled.

"No!" Anger and anguish mixed equally in Karl's bel-
low.

Jasper Weeks said nothing. He stood where he was,
watching the tot and the fire. "This is like a chimney," he
said quietly, as if to himself. "She probably fell or was
blown down there, and she's certainly not badly stuck."

"Very observant," the Canuchean snapped. "Now start
chopping, you son—"

"No, listen! You've got plenty of rope. Someone small
enough could be let down and try to get her."

Her breath caught. She eyed him carefully, then the
others. "It's got to be you or me. No one else'd have an
iceberg's chance."

"My idea. Besides, you're in charge here. You're needed
more." There was no point in pretending to be oblivious to
the danger a would-be savior faced of getting stuck himself
and joining the child in her fate instead of rescuing her
from it.

The other nodded. "Have at it, space hound."

With time in such short store, the work crew squandered
none of it. Even while their chief and the spacer were
discussing which of them should make the effort, they
fetched and began to ready the rope.

The harness they rigged was no more than a large loop held by a fixed knot that would neither release nor tighten in such a fashion as to squeeze in upon him. A smaller piece was fastened to it at chest height so that he would be able to tie himself and the little girl to it for additional support—if he could get to her in time.

Jasper stripped off his belt lest it catch on any of the jagged debris but left his clothing on. The uniform was close-fitting, and he would need the protection it would afford.

Kosti, by far the biggest man there, drew a length of the line about himself. He would belay while a monstrous stone block served as anchor.

Weeks pulled the rope over his shoulders and lowered it until he was sitting in the loop, then gingerly let himself over the edge.

It was at once apparent that he had set himself no easy task. What he had described as a chimney was in fact no more than a relatively clear space in the sea of rubble, open more in the visual than the physical sense. He was not at all certain he would be able to get by all the obstructions extending into it. Also, the fire seemed much closer from this angle than it had from above.

It was a drop of less than fifty feet, but there could be no hurrying the descent if he did not want a broken leg or to find himself inextricably wedged. Every few inches, he had to wriggle and twist to escape collision with one shard or another, and there was no point in beginning to count the number of times he struck something despite all his care. Assuming he lived to leave this miserable hole, he would have some interesting bruises to show for his work.

Weeks swallowed hard. He was down about twenty-five feet now, and it was not his fear that was making him sweat like this. It was getting hot, and smoke was fouling the air.

Worse, the space seemed even tighter, and a new dread entered his mind. If it got much narrower than this, he would not be able to come back up with the girl in his arms, if he could reach her at all. He would have to send her up first, and he very much doubted the line could be lowered to him again, which would have to be done slowly for fear of its catching and tangling before . . .

It seemed that he was dropping by bare inches instead of feet, but in the end, he came within reach of the child, just barely ahead of the lead tongues of the fire.

Jasper tried to keep himself between the flames and the tot. They had not yet reached the point of actually touching her, but the heat was already blistering.

He could not quite come even with her, and she was not of an age that he could expect to get any help or information from her. He leaned over at a precarious angle until he could see how she was held and gave an audible sigh of relief. A piece of pipe had torn through the skirt of her frock, which had then become twisted about it. He could get to it readily and slice through it with his knife without hurting her.

The spacer grabbed hold of the little Canuchean with his left hand and held her tightly despite her yowl of protest and fear. He could not risk freeing her only to have her fall farther down.

It was done, but they were out of time. The material covering his thigh was smoldering.

"Karl, pull! I've got her!"

Bad as the journey down had been, the ascent was worse. Twice, he was seriously afraid they would not be able to pass at all, and several other times, they had to maneuver through places very nearly as tight. It required careful work to get through, and that took time, a constraint not binding the fire licking hungrily below. Ever in his mind and in the minds of those above was the knowledge that if the blaze suddenly leapt up toward the greater supply of air on the surface, they would both be cooked as they hung there. Only the fact that the ruins in this place were porous and also quite poor in flammable material had saved them thus far, a tenuous leash indeed to be holding so fearful a force.

They passed the worst stretch. A little more speed was possible after that, the small increase that could be permitted without threatening to snag the line or batter the pair too greatly.

There was no escaping some hammering. Weeks wrapped himself as a living shield around his tiny charge, but in so doing, he thereby vastly reduced the efforts he could make on his own behalf. Time and again, his body struck hard against solid projections, on several occasions sharply enough that he was scarcely able to retain his hold on rope and child.

Suddenly, unbelievably, there was only clear air above them. Hands reached out, drew him onto solid ground.

Jasper was conscious of broadly smiling faces and unrestrained cheering. He was smiling himself as he handed the little girl over to Craig Tau, then the world seemed suddenly to tilt sideways, and a not unwelcome darkness settled over it.

26

Van Rycke paused at the crest. "It doesn't take much for us to do a proper job on ourselves, does it?"

"How could everyone have forgotten how dangerous ammonium nitrate can be?" Dane half asked, half demanded. So much misery, and most of it could have been averted had the salt been handled with the deference its nature demanded.

"Because no one else has used it on a large scale for a very long time, so it hasn't had a chance to cause trouble. A lot of other things have and, thus, replaced it in our collective memory." He grimaced. "Who expects death and destruction to come from a common, old-time fertilizer?"

Thorson did not try to suppress the shudder passing

through him. All those poor people . . . "Where do we start first, sir?" The disaster was so vast, they would be of use no matter where they went.

"Down at the water. Nobody seems to have gotten that far, so the need'll be greatest there, once we get far enough away from the explosion site that people could live through it. Of course, we'll stop if we encounter anyone in dire trouble higher up."

The younger man nodded his agreement but made no verbal answer. Their unvoiced hope was a slim and forlorn one. Their comrades had been very close to the *Regina Maris,* maybe on the vanished dock itself. There was precious small chance that either of them had survived.

The Cargo-Master moved rapidly despite the rubble-littered streets, so quickly that Dane had to push himself to keep pace.

At first, there was little to be seen apart from the ruins of homes and businesses, but as they descended, corpses became an ever more frequent sight. While people remained still trapped or in need of care, little attention could be spared for the dead, and bodies were left lying where they had fallen or had been dropped after having been pulled from the rubble.

The apprentice tried to avert his eyes, but he found himself staring at the grim remains. The horror was such that it generated its own fascination, one he was powerless to resist completely.

He looked into the frozen face of one dead girl and stopped in mid stride. "Mr. Van Rycke!"

His chief turned around. He glanced sharply at the woman and then started to move away once more. "She's dead. Has been almost from the start." It depressed him to look at her. She was, or had been, younger than Thorson when he had first joined the *Queen.*

"But she's been shot!"

Jan faced the corpse again. She lay where the force of the killing blow had thrown her, the once luminous eyes wide and starting, still showing the surprise of an instantaneous, utterly unexpected death. A large, round hole with burn damage at its edges marred the exact center of her forehead.

Van Rycke searched the ground around her for several minutes. At last, he picked up a small, partly flattened blob of metal and held it up for Dane's examination. "There's your pellet, or one like it. That it struck like this so far upslope was a vile turn of chance, but the load of screws, nails, and other small items the *Maris* was carrying will have created real havoc below. We'll be seeing more samples of its work if we get that far down."

Frank Mura, Shannon, and Kamil pushed their way right through the residential section down into the commercial district. Only a few groups had penetrated this far as yet, and they had decided among themselves that they might be able to accomplish more good there than on the better-organized heights.

All three were quiet. Apart from the heavier nature of the materials comprising these ruins, there was little to differentiate them from those above. The destruction was such that there was no means of telling upon a casual glance whether a specific site had once held a home, office, or factory building.

There were more dead as well, and the corpses were more visible. The closer proximity of the explosion assured that, as did the fact that no one had yet been through this area to remove or stack them.

They encountered living victims as well. Many, they were able to help. For others, there was little they or anyone else could hope to do. In every case, the Free Traders did as they had been instructed and moved the injured into the center of the street for easy sighting and pickup by the fliers that would soon be coming over this part of the district.

A cry, a wail for help, halted them. Even with the three of them searching and the shouting continuing, it took several minutes to locate its source, a crevice roughly half a foot square in the mound of rubble beside them. Inside, they could just see the face of a man.

Working with infinite care lest they dislodge more debris and turn that narrow place into a tomb, they slowly enlarged the hole until they were able to draw the victim out.

Incredibly, the Canuchean was whole apart from the most minor scrapes and bruises. He appeared dazed, but that was the shock of what had happened to him. There was no sign of head or other major injury.

He went of his own accord to the middle of the street and sat down, fixing his eyes on the slope above, which was fairly clearly visible from that place. "I was kind of lucky, I guess," he said more or less to his rescuers. "I was at my computer when I heard a loud bang and instinctively dived under the desk. I didn't even have time to turn around when the ceiling came down. It couldn't have been much more than that, or the desk couldn't have protected me.

"Anyway, when everything got quiet, I crawled out and just kept going until I got stopped here. I didn't want to go back into the dark, so I waited. Somebody had to come sometime."

He gave a great sigh. "That was my house up there, right next to where the grade school used to be."

"A lot of people got out," Rip Shannon told him gently, "and a lot of others have been rescued by now. It wasn't quite as bad higher on the slope even if it looks from here like it was."

Ali's voice was sharper. "You said only the ceiling seemed to have come down on you. Could anyone else be alive in there?"

"I— don't know. It was dark as an unlit mine, and I didn't hear anyone. There were six of us on the computer staff, though, and ten in the clerical pool next door . . ."

Rip started to swear, but Mura's raised hand silenced him. He gripped his temper. It was not the Canuchean's fault. The man was stunned, and his mind could not yet grasp anything much beyond himself and his own situation. He had given them their lead. The rest was up to them. Hopefully, help would reach them before too many more hours had passed.

The spacers quickly traced the Canuchean's escape route to its source. All of them were slender, agile men armed with good head lamps, and they were not long in discovering that his report was accurate. By some presently unaccountable quirk of chance, the moderately large room in which they found themselves had taken relatively light damage, and they located its five other occupants without difficulty. One was dead, his neck broken, and another was fairly severely injured, but the remaining three were little worse off than the initial survivor.

These last, they led out first and then carried their more critically hurt co-worker, leaving the dead man for a future trip.

Before going back inside a second time, Mura gave a hasty report of what they had discovered over his portable transceiver. Conditions that had shielded one floor or room might have been repeated elsewhere, perhaps many times over. That could be the salvation of a lot of lives if it were known, and he dared not assume that they would be able to deliver the information in person. They would have to venture again and again into the ruins, where any shift of the freshly piled, unsettled rubble or any other mischance could bury them forever.

Frank drew his sleeve across his face to wipe off the sweat, smearing the coating of grime, soot, and blood into an even tighter clinging paste.

The second office, which housed the clerical workers, was not so well preserved, and the one beyond it was infinitely worse. After that third chamber, they had been compelled to quit the ruins altogether lest they just bring the whole thing down on the poor wretches still trapped there. Only when a backup company armed with major emergency equipment arrived in response to Mura's report were they able to resume the massive effort.

It seemed to be about over now, he judged. They appeared to have discovered all the survivors at this site. At least, all that had come out in the last several trips were bodies and parts of bodies.

His eyes shut with infinite weariness. Had Japan suffered like this, he wondered, before volcano and giant wave had combined to throw her islands, population, and ancient culture beneath the cloaking surface of Terra's ocean? It had taken two days and the night between them. Had desperate rescue teams struggled on even as they were doing here in the face of ever-mounting calamity throughout all that first day and night and maybe part of the second day until an implacably furious nature had left none alive to save or be saved?

The Steward shook his head and looked with concern at the party just pulling itself out of the ruin. That was not his own history. It was not the history of his parents or grandparents. For Ali Kamil, this was his boyhood returned. Apart from the fact that the cause had been cruel accident rather than human savagery, he had seen all this, lived it, and he had survived. Would he be able to do so a second time?

Frank watched the Engineer-apprentice haul himself erect and claim the luxury of stretching cramped, exhausted muscles. His face was blank, a mask, but his dark eyes were alive and afire, blazing like a pair of young stars pulled out of the depths of space.

Kamil had been tireless in his efforts. More than that. They all had worked and were working, but Ali had proven to be worth any three of the rest of them. He seemed to have no fear of the treacherous rubble and ventured time and again into it without hesitation or apparent qualm, and once inside, he rarely failed to accomplish his mission. He had an almost uncanny feel for it, for locating hidden, otherwise lost survivors, for figuring with a minimum of lost time how best to shove or pry or lift away the material confining them. When this day was over, it would be the darkly handsome space hound that the greater part of the people brought alive out of this place would have to thank for their deliverance.

27

Jellico twisted around. The *Sally Sue* was clearly visible from the shattered Patrol flier, and so, too, were the clouds of smoke and the sullen glow of flames rising from the broken dock beside her. He could not tell whether the freighter herself was already ablaze.

He came to his feet. "The ship's my business," he told Cofort and the injured yeoman. "A Medic's what's needed here at the moment, and that we've got."

Rael looked up at him. "Míceál . . ."

The Captain shook his head. "You're hurt," he said quietly, "and Keil's hurt worse." His voice dropped. "He's also been alone through too much of this already."

It was a command, however softly voiced. The woman's

head lowered, as much to conceal the weight of grief and loss she feared she would not otherwise be able to mask as to give her assent.

Jellico said nothing more to either of them. He turned from the pair and ran for the threatened freighter. Maybe there was no chance, probably there was none, but he was not going to surrender to the Grim Commandant without the best damn fight of his life. He would not quietly give over Rael or that wounded Yeoman or the rest of his crew, most of whom would by now be working in the ruins above, oblivious to the peril once again overshadowing them all.

His lips tightened. If only the Patrol agent's transceiver had not been shattered in the crash he would at least have been able to sound the alarm, but one quick look had been sufficient to tell him he would send no warning out by that route, and there would be no point at all in trying to do so on foot. With the possibility of flight blocked, the fires would have to be kept away from the *Sally Sue*'s cargo if a second, even more violent explosion was not to rip them all to shreds.

For one instant, he knew a stab of regret as hard and sharp as a physical blow. Perhaps he should not have refused Rael Cofort's help, he thought. If nothing else, they might then at least have met their deaths together.

Angrily, he put that from his mind. The Medic had her own work to do, and with one or more cracked ribs, she would have been hard pressed to carry the strenuous activity that probably lay ahead of him if he was given the time to half begin. Fate had assigned each of them his own task in this one. They had no alternative, either of them, but to accept that fact and get on with it.

The need for speed lay on him like the lash of a force whip, with only minutes or maybe mere seconds standing between them all and oblivion, but the course he had to run was neither smooth nor straight. Rubble of every conceivable size and nature lay strewn in his path. Some of it he could sidestep or jump. Some large pieces forced him to detour altogether.

Each time he had to try a new way, his heart beat faster in fear. If he miscalculated, failed to follow the route he had so hastily planned out for himself, and wound up in a morass of big stuff or blocked by a wall of rubbish that would require real climbing, he might as well just sit back and wait for death . . .

The *Sally Sue* was in front of him. To his relief, he saw that she was as yet untouched. Only the dock beside her was aflame. It was not a massive conflagration, either, praise the Spirit ruling space, but rather several small fires, two of them already perilously near the freighter, burning independently of one another.

Luck was with him. Access to the dock had not been blocked, and the freighter's deck was reasonably close to its surface. The Free Trader raced for her, dodging the flames and those places where the surface was splintered and either raised or altogether absent.

Only when he reached the *Sally Sue* did he at last come to a stop. Her rail was near but still far enough to make the gaining of it a challenge in itself.

It was a leap, he thought, even for a fully fresh man, but

to judge by those fires, he had no option but to succeed and to do it in his first couple of tries.

Jellico steeled himself, tested his balance, and sprang.

His hands closed over the sturdy curve of the railing even as his feet slammed against the side. With that for a brace, he leapt again, this time vaulting over the rail onto the deck of the imperiled vessel.

Míceál did not pause. He had always liked watercraft and had indulged that liking by learning as much as he could about them, seeking practical experience as well as theoretical knowledge when he got the chance. That should stand by him here. Canuche of Halio was a typical industrial mechanized colony, and her people were not particularly innovative. They had no need to be with respect to the forms of transportation they adopted. The information he had picked up elsewhere should apply well enough here to allow him to accomplish what he had to do.

The freighter's hatches were open, blown off by the force of the explosion. He ran for the sternmost one and half climbed, half dropped below. To his relief, the seacocks were where he expected to find them, and he threw them open, letting the cold ocean water into as many of the holds as were low enough to receive it.

That done, the spacer returned to the deck and darted once more to the prow.

He had come up none too soon. One of the fires was already licking the *Sally Sue*'s side.

Jellico's tongue ran across dry lips. The metal plates would not burn, but her deck would once the flames came so far.

That was irrelevant. As far as he knew, the ammonium

nitrate inside did not require the actual touch of fire to go up. A significant rise in temperature would probably accomplish that just as effectively.

The fire guns, too, were stored where reason and his knowledge of similar vessels said they should be. He freed the one closest to the charging fires. Now, if only it still functioned. Equipment like this was built to keep on working under emergency conditions, but an explosion of such magnitude at such proximity . . .

The foam came. Míceál played it on the nearest fire, driving it back, away from the ship, then sprayed a longer stream on the second blaze that was making fast inroads toward her.

For the first time, he felt a touch of relief. As long as the press of battle remained close to this level, he should be able to hold the ship, provided the gun kicked over to seawater when the supply of foam was exhausted. There were others, of course, but none quite so well situated, and there was no guarantee any of them would work if this one did not.

Twenty minutes went by. A third fire was challenging the *Sally Sue,* bigger and hotter than the others and stronger by a large measure in its advance.

Great black clouds of hot smoke formed its van. The stuff stank, and he wondered precisely what was feeding it. His throat and chest felt as if they were burning in their turn with every breath of it that he was compelled to draw.

The stream of foam sputtered suddenly and was gone. For an eternal instant, he was left with a limp feeder hose in his left hand, then it stiffened once more, and a strong, cold, silver river shot from the gun.

It looked lovely in that moment, but the man's eyes followed it somberly. The supply might be unlimited, but water was not as efficient as foam, and all the fires on the dock were rapidly gaining in strength, threatening to merge into one overwhelming conflagration.

They were definitely attacking along a wider front. It was a rare moment now when he was not faced with a serious assault, usually with more than one, and not a moment at all when the ultimate hopelessness of his stand was not starkly apparent to him.

Míceál acknowledged his doom when he finally noticed the barrels. There were about twenty of them lying in a jumble on the farther side of the dock, where the flames and smoke had combined to screen them from his sight and awareness. A sudden, brief clearing of the air revealed them, tall, sturdy metal cylinders with the word *benzol* emblazoned across them. He did not know how much heat that stuff could take, but he imagined there was a point, probably not terribly high, at which it would go up. When that happened, the *Sally Sue* would follow, and they would all die, Rael, himself, everyone in Canuche Town and what remained of Canuche Town itself. She was carrying so much more ammonium nitrate than the *Maris* that total obliteration was a certainty.

28

Rael Cofort's head remained bowed. She should be with the *Queen*'s Captain, fighting this battle beside him, if need be, dying beside him.

Her hands balled. He had been right to order her to stay where she was. She had her own business here, a patient in deep need of help, and she was patently unfit for heavy work. Her efforts to examine Keil's injuries had so aggravated her own that it was taking all her will not to surrender, not to sit back and give herself over to the pain rending her side.

That could not even be considered. She was a Medic, and she would function as one while the need was there and life remained in her, whatever her own discomfort and whether she was fated to die before her work was completed or not.

Keil Roberts was severely wounded. If he did not get into surgery, he would die of those injuries eventually, but she could patch him up well enough to hold him until he could be flown out.

The missile transfixing him could not be removed. She would have been afraid to try that alone even if she were physically equal to the task. There was too much danger that she would not be able to stanch the ensuing hemorrhage rapidly enough. He had lost too much blood already, and any further significant drain would severely compromise him.

She would need bandages. Rael went to the rear seat of the flier and drew her knife from her belt. Working swiftly, she cut what was left of the tunic off the dead woman and ripped it into large strips, then returned to her patient.

Luckily, the full weight of the huge missile had not come directly down on him. His right leg had been caught and viciously torn, but the massive thing pressed on him in such a way as to greatly retard the flow of blood. He was still alive because of that, but the respite was only temporary. The slow, steady drain had already badly weakened him, and unless it was brought to a stop soon, it would kill him.

The woman crawled and squirmed along the floor of the transport until she was beside Roberts and able to work on his injuries. It was a cramped, punishing position, but she could function. That was all she could allow to matter. She fixed her concentration on what she had to do, ignoring the agony that was her body. Fortunately, Keil could not see her face and was probably too absorbed in his own pain to be aware of any discomfort she was not strong enough to conceal.

It was slow work, but at last she was able to wriggle back out and creep to the door of the transport, where she could sit upright and rest for a few moments supported by the seat and metal frame. Her eyes closed, and she struggled to breathe evenly, fearing that any deep or ragged movement of her chest would sharpen the agony in her side to the point that it would overpower her. It would not take much more at all to do that.

The worst stabbing soon lessened with the easing of her position. The Medic straightened and carefully studied her patient.

She was satisfied. He was deathly pale, of course, and in pain, but he seemed to have weathered her treatment well enough. There was no more she could do for him now except offer support and encouragement until help arrived. If they or anyone else were around much longer to give or receive it.

For the first time, Rael permitted herself to look in the direction of the *Sally Sue.* Her heart gave a great leap. It was a terrible sight, and it was magnificent. Flames were clearly visible now. The several small fires had grown fewer and larger as one had merged into another, presenting a far more formidable and threatening aspect. At present, three of them actively imperiled the freighter, and those Jellico was struggling to hold at bay.

Pride swelled in her even as tears blurred her eyes. Courage was necessary to a starship Captain, but to her mind it was one thing to face the dangers, known and unknown, of interstellar travel, even the blasters and lasers of a pirate wolf pack, and another to stand alone against the awesome, mindless primal power of fire.

Her hands clenched and whitened by her sides. It was a foredoomed effort! The dock provided too much fuel for the flames. They would swell and grow until no individual could hope to oppose their advance . . .

"He needs help," Keil observed quietly.

She glanced at him, then nodded and came to her feet, stifling the gasp the movement drew from her. Her work here was finished, and she was needed on the deck of the *Sally Sue.*

"Rael!"

She turned quickly. Van Rycke and Dane Thorson! "Míceál!" she shouted, pointing to the ship. "The Captain! He's trying to save that freighter. She's loaded with ammonium nitrate!"

29

Dane took one look at the war his commander was waging and broke into a run.

His young body was hard and unwearied by the fast but relatively untrying advance he and Van Rycke had made to the coast. The rugged way ahead of him did little to slow him even when he had to jump or detour around some major obstacle, and he reached the pier in rather less time than Jellico had taken.

Once there, he did stop. He frowned. Why was the Captain turning his gun on the back of the dock, just about at the limit of its useful range? There was fire enough far closer to claim his attention . . .

He saw the barrels, probably the remnants of a larger

consignment, the most of which must have been flung into the water during the explosion and its aftermath. The better part of these had been knocked over as well but had stayed fairly near to one another. The flames were licking at the closest of them.

His eyes darkened. He recognized as well as Jellico had before him the danger they represented. The containers were obviously well insulated, but they were designed to guard against mischance, not long-term, direct contact with open fire. The contents must be getting perilously close to the explosion point.

If even one of them went, that would be the end. The rest would rupture and go up in almost the same moment and the freighter a breath's space later. Even if by some miracle she did not, she would have taken fire many times over, multiple fires that would set her off in a matter of minutes. The end result would be the same.

The Cargo-apprentice dove through the tall, narrow band of flame assaulting them, moving so quickly that he gave the fire no time to bite on him. He flung himself at the nearest barrel, seizing it in his arms and shoving it back toward the edge of the dock.

He released it again in the next moment with a sharp cry. The metal was hot, not quite glowing but not terribly far from it. His flesh felt as if it were searing beneath his clothing.

Steeling himself, he grasped the cylinder again. Tears welled in his eyes. His gloves were giving his hands some protection, but the lighter tunic provided little defense for his chest or arms. They were burning.

Cursing, he manhandled his burden to the end of the pier, flung it over.

He did not pause to listen for the hiss of hot metal striking cold seawater or to see the answering rise of steam or splash. The other barrels were in equal danger, presented an equal threat. Each would have to be served in the same manner.

The next one was on its side. It would roll easily, but he would have to use his knees as well as his hands.

It was no less hot than its predecessor. As he had anticipated, his trousers gave no greater protection than the tunic had, and this time the pain in his hands equaled anything he felt elsewhere. They were already damaged, and the gloves were only meant to guard against the hazards of rough manual labor, not to meet the challenge of fire and extreme heat. He could not have expected them to shield him forever.

The burning increased with every moment he remained in contact with the metal. The apprentice wondered how he would be able to endure that level of punishment long enough to dispose of this barrel, and his heart and courage sank at the thought of the eighteen more remaining after it. All of them had to be removed, or his efforts would be valueless.

It would not be that bad, he told himself savagely, not all of it. The third barrel, aye, he would suffer with that one, but the others were farther back, out of direct contact with the flames and at least a little distant from their heat. They should not be so brutally hot.

He staggered toward his next target only to be driven back from it. Jellico had seen him and had been trying to give him as much cover as possible, but another of the fires had pushed too close to the ship, and the Captain had been compelled to switch his attention to that, leaving this front free to continue its assault.

Thorson pushed right into its shimmering shadow. What difference whether he seared himself like a steak against the container or was turned into a human torch, he thought bitterly. He would die equally painfully either way.

For one instant, he thought he would take fire, but though his exposed skin blistered, he managed to push the barrel over and out of the flames' direct reach. It was not quite as hot as the others, he judged as he rolled it toward the edge. It had not been on the front line as long as the other two. Hope stirred in his heart. If that held true for the rest, and the effect was magnified by distance, then he might win this impossible race. Even with the hungry fire advancing unchecked and himself already fairly severely burned, he should be able to shift reasonably cool barrels quickly enough to put them once and for all out of danger. They were not all that heavy in themselves, and he was nothing if not experienced in moving cargo by this time. What would happen to him after that was another matter, but it was not his immediate concern, and he refused to allow himself to dwell on it. The task before him demanded his full attention.

Míceál started at the sight of a movement, a man, opposite him on the dock. At first, he thought it was an illusion, delirium even, the product of smoke and flame and his own imagination, augmented by the increasingly pungent fumes he was compelled to breathe, sickening and weakening him beyond any weariness. He recognized Thorson then, but before he could try to shout instructions to him, the young man realized their peril and moved of his own accord to dispose of the barrels.

The Captain cringed at the thought of how hot that metal had to be, but there was no help for it. They had to be dumped.

Was that still possible? The apprentice had proven his courage and determination often enough, but he had never been challenged like this. The cost of every contact with those containers and the ever-present, ever-increasing horror of the fire itself would have been sufficient to break an older, more experienced man, whatever his knowledge of the stakes riding on him. Jellico could not say how much of it he himself could have taken.

There was almost nothing he could do to help. Those barrels were located right at the limit of the fire gun's range. Its stream reached barely far enough to discourage the fire from sweeping over Dane, and even that pitiful defense would have to be terminated long before the job was done. The *Sally Sue* was under too heavy an assault herself . . .

Míceál whipped the fire gun down, training its muzzle on the dock just before him. An arm of fire had worked its way along the pier and was licking right at the ship's side almost at his feet.

It was a small advance, and he was not long in driving it back, but the three major fires had now become one. Jellico's heart was heavy. Thorson's suffering and sacrifice were for nothing. He would not be able to keep up his own part. He would be able to hold out a few minutes more, five or perhaps ten, but the deadly little fires had become a conflagration that would soon sweep over him and the ship he was battling to save. He would go down still fighting, but that would be small comfort to those he had failed to save. It had just been too big a task for only one man . . .

A thud sounded beside him as someone sprang onto the deck.

His head turned sharply. Jan Van Rycke!

The Cargo-Master grinned but said nothing as he raced for the nearest fire gun, seized and activated it.

It functioned, praise the Spirit ruling Space, and a powerful stream of foam belted a gap in that part of the fire wall nearest them.

Three minutes later, another stream joined it from a point near the freighter's middle. Rael!

Míceál's spirit sang. This equipment was designed to handle major trouble—witness the stand he had been able to make alone guarding so broad a front. With the three of them manning the guns, they had a chance—not a certainty—but for the first time a true chance of defeating the primal force before them.

30

They had won. They had seen the fire fall back, great patches of it dying under cold water and smothering foam, well before the air above them had suddenly filled with Fire Department fliers, all spilling what had seemed like half an ocean of foam.

Jellico smiled at the memory as he wearily leaned back against his pillow. The four spacers had just about drowned along with the flames, but he did not recall hearing any protests. He himself certainly had not been inclined to object.

A knock brought him back to his present surroundings. It had been soft and rather timid and was not immediately repeated. Rael Cofort.

He sat up quickly and began refastening the collar snaps on his tunic. "Come in," he called as he pressed the last into place.

The woman obeyed instantly. She had Queex with her, draped over her arm, but almost without thinking, she set him on Jellico's desk. Her eyes fixed on the Captain's face, studying him intently. His voice had sounded hoarse, but that was nothing, merely the result of the abuse his throat and lungs had taken. It would clear up of its own accord soon enough.

"Mr. Wilcox said you'd knocked out," she said.

"Mr. Wilcox should keep his mouth shut," he grumbled.

"Not with me pestering him. — You're all right, Míceál?"

"Aye. I just started running out of fuel. Since there's no need to play ultraman at the moment, I decided to call it an evening."

"Smart move. It's no fun having one's lungs scrubbed." She moved closer to him and touched her fingertips to his forehead. "There doesn't seem to be any fever."

"I told you I was all right," he responded irritably.

"I know, but I am a Medic. Habit's hard to break."

She turned to the desk. "I guess we should leave and let you get some rest."

"No. Stay a bit."

Jellico's cabin was full size, unlike hers, and was outfitted with a permanent desk and a chair.

She released the seat from its fastenings and drew it next to the wide bunk.

Míceál saw her grimace as she sat down, and now it was

his turn to examine her closely. "Eight broken ribs. I knew you were hurt, but I didn't think it was that bad."

"It wasn't until the end, or at least it didn't hurt so much. I completed the job on myself when I was working on Keil. It took a lot of maneuvering to get in to him."

"Well, I started it. I was the one who threw you onto that block."

"Considering the shape those who'd been near us were in, I don't think I've got much call for complaining," she told him dryly.

"All the same, I am sorry."

Rael smiled, but her eyes were somber. "Thanks for not telling me to leave Keil back there and run."

"I did think of it," he admitted, "but I knew there was too much titanone in your spine for you to listen, so I spared you the insult."

She gave him an incredulous look and laughed. "I was terrified, my friend. In fact, I terrify easily. It's just that . . ."

The Captain smiled. "Precisely, Rael Cofort."

He shifted into a more comfortable position. "I more or less lost contact with the universe back there just after the fliers pulled us out. What happened? I know you assured me everything and everyone were clear, but Medics have a bad habit of softening down the story for the supposed wounded."

"You were pretty sick," she told him gravely. "That was straight poison you were breathing. A little greater concentration and . . ."

"Well, I'm fine now. — You called the Fire Department?"

She nodded. "With Mr. Van Rycke's transceiver, and Keil kept on calling after I went to join the battle. — He's going to be fine, by the way," she added triumphantly, "though he wouldn't have lasted much longer without us."

"Without you."

She shrugged. "Dane's about the worst hurt. Doctor Tau has him bundled up in burn cream and bandages at the moment, and he won't be shoving cargo around for the next few weeks, but he didn't take permanent damage, praise the Spirit of Space. We got the cream on him fast enough that there won't even be any scarring." She smiled. "Sinbad's with him now, offering feline company and comfort.

"Jasper took some very bad bruises and minor singes. He'll be stiff and damn sore for a while, but otherwise he's all right."

"How's Ali?" he asked quietly.

"Sound out. Both Doctor Tau and I are sure of that. Whatever memories this aroused, he's faced them and filed them where they belong. — He's a strong man, Míceál, stronger than I would've thought just meeting him."

"People tend to underrate him." He swung into a sitting position. "What's going to happen to Canuche Town itself? And there's the little matter of our charter. Now that the blasted life-and-death business is over, I'd like to know how that stands."

The Medic smiled. "You'll live! — Mr. Macgregory's terribly busy, naturally, but he did talk to Mr. Van Rycke for a few minutes. The waterfront is to be restored and the rest of the damage repaired as soon as possible. The Caledonia plant will not only be rebuilt but will be enlarged. Needless to say," she added grimly, "ammonium nitrate will be handled with proper respect everywhere on-world from here on in.

"As for the *Queen's* business, she's to lift with her cargo as soon as she can. By the time she gets back, another shipment will have been brought in from some of the nearer factories and will be waiting for loading at the port. Adroo Macgregory has no intention of losing out on a good business opportunity merely because he's suffered a setback here. — His phrasing."

Jellico laughed. "A man after my own heart! — We'll lift as fast as we can fuel up." He frowned slightly. "Assuming we can get any fuel. Everything'll be in short supply around here for a while."

"Friend, there is nothing the *Solar Queen* wants or needs that she won't get on Canuche of Halio. The other ships're in pretty solid, too," she added. "Their crews followed ours with manpower and supplies when they were needed most, and they'll get precedence after the *Queen* on any charters going on this planet in the foreseeable future. This is one place where the Companies won't even have a chance, not for a very, very long time to come."

"It's worked out well enough, then," the Captain said slowly. "For us. The Canucheans lost a deal more than buildings and goods."

Rael nodded slowly. "I wish we all could've moved sooner."

She shifted in her seat. Míceál was beginning to look tired, and she was feeling weary herself.

She picked up the hoobat, who had been watching silently from his perch on the desk. "Shall I leave Queex? He's been worried about you."

Jellico winced at the Taboran's answering screech. "Doctor Cofort, you'll never make a xenobiologist if you insist on anthropomorphizing an X-Tee creature's reactions . . ."

"Queex is a shipmate, and I know him well enough by now to recognize when he's upset, which he has been since we all limped back on board," she informed him haughtily.

"I stand corrected, Doctor. — Hand him over here."

Queex scurried up the man's arm, then dropped to the bunk and settled himself in the still-warm spot its proper occupant had vacated with a great, rasping whistle of contentment.

"I hope he doesn't object to being shifted," Jellico commented. "That's my place, and I'm not about to surrender it to a hoobat."

"I'll fetch his cage," the woman promised. "He'll probably be happier in there anyway."

"Praise the Spirit of Space for small favors," he muttered.

He ran his finger down the surprisingly soft feathers. "He's all right where he is for the time being. One of the others can get the cage later on. — You're not going to be lifting anything heavier than flatware and a cup until those ribs heal."

"Aye, Captain," she responded meekly to the command in his tone.

The feeling of contentment suddenly deserted Jellico. He glanced uneasily at the Medic, recalling some of the things she had said—and not said—during this visit. She had mentioned Thorson's being unable to work but not that she would take over the lighter portions of the job for him, and she had spoken of the *Solar Queen*'s lifting with her cargo; she had not used the words *we* or *our.*

He lowered his eyes and pretended to concentrate on Queex, whose head he carefully rubbed. "Are you still planning to leave the *Queen?*"

"Captain or not, you just try to put me off, Míceál Jellico!"

He smiled broadly, partly from relief, partly to conceal it. "That borders pretty closely upon insubordination," he observed.

Fear gripped Rael, however, and she did not answer him as he expected. The *Solar Queen* had encountered a small galaxy of trouble since she had joined the ship's company. Superstition had a powerful hold on some space hounds, even among the best, the bravest, the most intelligent of their breed. If Jellico had come to believe she was, in fact, a jinx . . .

Her eyes fell. Initially, she had intended using her association with the *Solar Queen* as a means of gaining control of the funds currently tied up with the *Roving Star* and then, as soon as she had acquired the experience and reputation she required to bolster her credentials, to cut loose again and return to her brother's organization on her own terms. Slowly, without her even realizing it, that purpose had altered, and for all her Trader's discipline, she was hard-pressed to face this man without betraying the misery the possibility of his rejection, the possibility that he might fear her, aroused in her. "Seriously, Míceál," she said in the low tone that was all she could trust herself to use steadily, "you are the skipper. If— you don't think I fit in with the best interests of the ship for some reason, I'll take my earnings to date and pull out, no questions asked."

"No!"

She looked up and smiled. There was no mistaking the decision in that roar. "After all this, I wasn't sure I'd be wanted . . ."

"I want you, damn it!" Míceál gripped himself. He was annoyed by the sharpness of his own response. He made himself go on quickly, as if without hesitation, in a quieter tone. "Doctor, life's been interesting since you've come aboard, right enough, but what you don't seem to realize is that life's been interesting aboard the *Solar Queen* since the day she was launched. That's not likely to change, and I'm not about to quit the starlanes or my ship as a result, especially since things seem to get just as lively in the supposed safety of a planet's surface."

Rael smiled once more, somewhat shyly this time. His vehemence had taken her a little aback, but it was surprisingly pleasing. "Maybe we'll have a bit more peace and quiet from now on," she ventured hopefully. "We've surely earned it."

"Maybe," Jellico agreed. He, for one, doubted it, but whatever fortune was to bring, he found himself looking forward to facing it. The *Queen* had seen her share of trials in the past and had claimed a reasonable quota of profit, and right now, her future and his own seemed to shine bright with promise.